An
Exceptionally
Simple
Theory

(of Absolutely Everything)

A novel by

Mark Winkler

Kwela Books

All characters appearing in this work are fictitious.
Any resemblance to real persons is purely coincidental.

Kwela Books,
an imprint of NB Publishers, a division of Media24 Boeke (Pty) Ltd
40 Heerengracht, Cape Town, South Africa
PO Box 6525, Roggebaai, 8012, South Africa
www.kwela.com

Cover design by Michiel Botha
Typography by Nazli Jacobs
Set in Berkeley
Printed and bound by Interpak Books,
Pietermaritzburg, South Africa

First edition, first impression 2013

ISBN: 978-0-7957-0450-5
ISBN: 978-0-7957-0451-2 (epub)
ISBN: 978-0-7957-0608-0 (mobi)

For Erwin and Liz,
who made it all make sense

If a system is consistent, it cannot be complete.

KURT FRIEDRICH GÖDEL, 1906–1978:
The Incompleteness Theorem (Vienna, 1931)

Chris and Tracy

A scratching, a scraping wakes me into the warm summer dawn. I look over at Tracy. She's asleep, snoring softly, a dried dribble of blood stretching the corner of her mouth into a clown's smile.

I want to wake her to ask how she's feeling, but that wouldn't make sense.

The scratching continues. It couldn't be Gabriel, not at this time of the day, so I swing my leg off the bed, grab my crutches, hobble across the wooden floor. The rubber toes of the crutches squeak with each swing. Squeak, thunk, squeak, thunk, I go. I look back at Tracy; I haven't woken her. She's used to me squeak-thunking around the house at all hours, has been for the past fifteen years.

There's a spare bedroom next to ours which Tracy uses as a second dressing room; her accoutrements are simply too numerous to fit into the one we share. Jimmy Choos, Christian Louboutins sit patiently waiting for her, two pairs deep at floor level around the room; some I know have never been worn. Hangers dripping with designer wear, price-tags indirectly proportional to the amount of fabric, are suspended above the shoes. Drawers contain unknown treasures of lingerie. In a corner, her fitness gear, untidily piled, incongruous in the pristine personal boutique. A phone lies on a low set of drawers in the middle of the room. It's discharged itself overnight – these days it has only about an hour's battery life. I should replace it but never do, the memory of the chore always crowded out by everything else in my head.

The sound, a threatening, getting-in sound, is louder in Tracy's dressing room. It's coming from the sloped ceiling next to the dormer window. I look outside where the sun is spraying its first drops of light onto the green of the plane trees that protect the house, and I see that a family of squirrels has taken up residence in the eaves. They've chewed a six-inch hole through a section of facia board, and are now sharpening their teeth on the roof beams. I bang on the sloped ceiling beside the dormer window, but although they're usually skittish enough to flinch at a falling leaf, they ignore the sound: one simply pokes its little Disney nose out of the hole and smirks at me before withdrawing back into my house. I bang again, harder, longer. The gnawing ceases for all of five seconds, and then starts up again. They'll give us rabies, those squirrels. They'll chew up the beams, and while we're sleeping the roof will come crashing down on our heads. They'll chew through the wiring and set fire to the place. They'll have babies, and their babies will have babies, and within weeks the collective weight of squirrel generations will bring down the ceiling and the house will be a disaster of dust, ceiling boards, toxic glass fibre, squirrel shit, and flocks – herds? swarms? nibbles? – of rodents will run around chewing holes in the furniture, devouring shoes, skittering up and down the curtains, boring through mattresses in mere seconds and –

"M-*mmm*!" A noise issues from the bedroom. My banging has woken Tracy. She's sitting up, holding her swollen face, fresh blood dribbling into the tissue she holds to her mouth.

"Wha' – wha'at?" she asks.

"Squirrels," I say.

She digs a tea bag out of her mouth. It's soggy with saliva, red with blood from a hole that, just yesterday, had housed a molar. The dentist hadn't so much extracted it, she told me, as chipped it out with a hammer and chisel. Poor Tracy.

"Squirrels can't make a noise like that."

"The banging was me. The other noise is squirrels eating up our house. They've chewed a hole the size of a garage door in the facia and have moved in, lock stock. I was banging to chase them away, but they just laughed at me."

Tracy lies down again. "Don't exaggerate," she says, "you always exaggerate. It's tedious."

Today I have squirrels; today I don't feel like fighting.

"How are you feeling?" I ask instead.

Tracy shrugs, tries to wrinkle her nose but the Botox resists. "Terrible," she says.

You're exaggerating, I want to say, but don't.

I bought this squirrel-ridden house almost three years ago, just before my thirty-seventh birthday. It's in Tracy's name, a protection from creditors should my business land in trouble. She saw it as an early Christmas present to herself; I saw it as a belated birthday present to me. It was a rambling old place, neglected and syphilitically filthy, but the unbroken view of the mountain and the treetops in the distance and the trees in the garden told me it was mine and I fell in love with it in the way teenagers fall for their first – fundamentally, unshakeably, and oblivious to faults or incompatibilities or consequences. Instead of tearing the thing down, my love dictated that we retain what we could of the original structure. Romantic, but stupid.

In hindsight, a flash of which hits me every morning as I hop down the precarious steps – risers that rise too high, wooden treads that were created for nine-year-old feet – in hindsight, a double-storey house was probably not the best purchase for someone permanently on crutches. And me an architect; who would have thought.

I'm halfway down when Tracy calls for me to take the phone downstairs and place it on the charger. I ignore her and open the front door for Schultz, who is whining to be let inside in his old broken-voiced way. He tries to jump up on me, as he does every morning, as he used to do when he was younger, but now his front paws only lift a few inches off the floor. The brown dots of his eyebrows are raised expectantly, and he bounces until I give his head a good rub and a hard pat. Wags his curved tail and heads off to lie farting under my desk. To be so measurably, consistently happy to see the same person every day for eleven years, well.

I squeak-thunk my way to the kitchen where, as usual, the kettle is empty. Hop to the sink, hop back, kettle on, hop to the fridge for milk, hop past the cooker to get two mugs from the cupboard. The instant coffee and sugar are in a separate cupboard across the kitchen, require more hopping to retrieve. Somehow, in three years we've never contrived to arrange fridge, kettle, mugs, coffee, sugar within reaching distance of each other. Hopping complete, I pick up a crutch that's slid to the floor from its resting place against the counter, and then I stare at the shiny silver kettle as it makes its warming-up noises. The kettle stares back with its own version of my face, bloated and distorted, cheeks distended and drooping, hairline pushed back as though the hair has been violently knotted behind the head. Suddenly-thyroid eyes, each buttressed by a bag. I raise my eyebrows and the hair-line retreats further. I lower my head, and the face grows an enormous forehead as the chin shortens, forcing the lips into an imploded little slit.

An unkissable mouth in an unlovable face.

Is this how I will look when I am old – older? My hands rest on the counter; my forearms are powerful from all the crutching about, but the skin has developed a web of tiny wrinkles punctuated with deepening pores. There's a mole I've never noticed – or is it a liver spot? – between the first and second knuckle of my left hand. I turn my hands over. The years of crutching about have calloused my palms: they're as thick as soles. The kettle shakes as it comes to the boil, and so does the face in it. I think of those pop statistics that people trot out without checking the maths: if you live to be seventy, you will have spent twenty-three years sleeping, seven driving, three shaving, seven having a dump, and so on and so forth. I am thirty-nine and a quarter; how much time have I spent waiting for kettles to boil? How much time do I have left to wait for kettles to boil? Because I always wait. I've learnt that if I wander off I'll find something to do in the meantime, become distracted and only remember much later that I'd been trying to make coffee. By then, the kettle will be cold, and the milk in the mug gone strange, and I'll have to start all over again.

I've learnt other useful things as well over the years.

That instant coffee tastes better if you put the milk in before the water. That the slow lane moves quicker than the fast in morning traffic to town. That if you crimp your fingers inwards when chopping a carrot – just like so – you won't slice off their tips by mistake.

I take my coffee to my study – well, I squeak-thunk there, deposit a crutch, squeak-hop back to the kitchen, drink off the spillable portion, squeak-hop to my desk. Where I Google and write down the numbers of pest-control people who might want to come and make the squirrels go away. I learn two more useful things doing this. Firstly, that squirrels are a protected species, and as they may not be poisoned most pest controllers want nothing to do with them; and secondly, that because today is New Year's Eve, it takes twelve calls before one guy answers his phone – then tells me he's driving up the coast, won't be back for three weeks.

Between the Googling and the documenting of squirrel people, after checking the news sites and my share prices, I find myself with nothing really to do. I suppose the word is "bored", but. I've been bored for a while, I realise – or imagine – but it's more than that. There's a tugging in me, but I don't know what's doing the tugging or where it's trying to tug me to. It's attached to my abdomen, to the lower region of my stomach, my navel perhaps, and it feels like that moment when you've just woken up to a recollection of something awful and for a minute or so you're not awake enough to identify it. But now there's no revelation, no resurgence of memory to decode the feeling, and it remains, not quite gut-ache, not quite nausea, just a quiet nagging.

So I poke around Google, sipping coffee that's cooling and beginning to grow a grey scum over itself. There are apparently a billion web pages out there; something, surely, must be worth its pixels.

But no.

Perhaps the holidays have gone on too long. I can only watch Tracy paint her toenails so many times before I know it's time to get back to the office. I'm not sure what to Google so I type in "what's tugging at me" and get 12,600,000 results in an instant. They contain links to religious tracts, solipsistic blogs, New Age waffle, porn sites. I guess you could type anything into Google, say, "Indonesian macroeconomics in the nineteenth century", and it'll turn up at least three porn sites. But none of the results – or at least none of the dozens I look at – can answer my question. So I Google myself and find that it turns up 15,300,000 results. After twelve pages, not one of them is me. I suppose I'm not the only Chris Hayes on the wired planet.

I hear a noise, a thumping on wood, too big for a squirrel, followed by a muttered curse. Schultz twitches in his sleep: it has to be Gabriel, sixteen and six foot tall, all arms and legs and size eleven feet, the everything of him connected by bones and skin and not much else. He has been over-whelmed by teenaged clumsiness and yet insists on going up and down our ridiculous stairs in his socks. The noise tells me that he didn't clear the last three on the way down.

"Gabriel, don't say 'fuck' please," I call.

"I'm fine thanks, Dad," he says. "And I didn't say 'fuck'. I said 'that sucks'."

Gabriel's dyslexia is so bad that half the time he probably can't tell whether the steps are going up or down. He's struggled ever since the other kids in the class were reading "cat" and "hat". Often, people think he's stupid, which he isn't, and I've told him to allow his intelligence to be his secret weapon, but he hasn't got the hang of that either.

I can hear him starting to make coffee – should sixteen-year-olds drink coffee? I don't know; I'll Google it some time. I find myself waiting for the crash of a dropped mug, but it doesn't happen.

I'm on page thirteen of the Google results for Chris Hayes and still none of them are about me. Besides the Waspy locations where you'd expect to find people with the same name as mine, there are Chris Hayeses living in Shanghai, in Nairobi, in Lima. Some are property developers, others musicians or teachers or freelance chauffeurs. One, like me but not me, is a partner in an architectural firm. He's based in Dubai; but what if Dubai was code for a parallel universe – would expat Chris Hayes have a teen-aged son too, a wife who becomes blonder and skinnier as time goes by? Would he also have a missing leg, and if so would it be the right one and not the left, because surely a parallel universe would be a mirror of this one? I imagine a snapshot of him and his family with the Burj al Arab or the Yacht Club or the streets of Jumeirah in the background; his Hayes family's faces on backwards and his Tracy's beauty spot on her right cheek instead of her left. Even the Arabic writing behind them would only make sense if read from the left, and that only if you could read Arabic.

This non-finding of myself is becoming tedious, so on a whim I decide to Google Kathy Whatshername. I haven't thought of her for years: we copulated frantically, manically, during the summer holidays when I was twenty-one and she was twenty-six. Once I start doing the maths it all seems to be a very long time ago, so I stop. It takes a while to remember her surname and when I do remember, Google turns up 4,880,000 results, but the first ten pages aren't her. For a while Tracy tried to get me onto Facebook, and maybe I should, but then she'll have to be my friend and she'll see the weird people I might dig up out of the past, which is all Facebook seems to be good for, and then I'll have to explain myself. Not that there would be a lot to explain. I only Google Kathy because of an impulse that hits me like a small stroke, unwanted and unexpected. I don't want to hook up with her or even speak to her. I just want to see if she looks like the face in the kettle yet.

Gabriel sticks his head into my study.

"Morning, Dad," he says over my shoulder. Sometimes he greets me, sometimes he doesn't.

"Hi, Gabe," I say.

"Who is Kathy Simons?" he asks. I really need to turn my desk around. I've been meaning to ever since we moved in: I can't stand my back to a room, mostly because of what Gabriel's just done.

"New employee, and none of your business," I say, hiding the browser window, which makes me look guilty – of what I don't know, but guilty anyway.

I turn around to look at the ironing board that is my son. Streaks of coffee decorate the outside of his mug.

"How are you, Gabe?" I ask.

"Fine."

Everything's fine with him. How's school? Fine. How was your test? Fine.

How's the weather, your new shoes? Fine, fine. How do you like being ravaged by hormones and confusion, what's it like falling down the stairs twice a day, how do you feel about the fact that you may die a long and painful death from a dread disease one day? Fine, fine, fine. What's not fine is the sorry kid's face with its furious pizza-textured rash that nature has inflicted on him precisely when he is least equipped to deal with it. It makes him look at once older and younger than he is. Becoming a teen-ager has made him not only spotty but moody and unpredictable, and to deal with it I have had to remind myself repeatedly that at this point in his life, Gabe himself doesn't know whether he's coming or going. Although it's probably more of the former, judging by the wads of used Kleenex Tracy finds in his waste-paper bin every day – a snippet of information that made me shiver at the time: there are some things you don't need to know about your child. Yet there are many things I know but have never needed to, things that take up precious bytes of my brain, an organ which un-accountably does not come with a delete button.

"What are we doing tonight, Dad?" he asks, cheerful in a brittle kind of way. I know that something is coming, can't quite spot what it might be.

"Going to the Joneses."

"Aw, Da-ad."

"It'll be fun. Barry says that Peter is dying to see you."

"He's such a p–, a dork, I mean."

"You were going to say pussy, weren't you?"

"No, actually, I was going to say prick, but thanks for the suggestion. But hey, listen Dad, can't I, like, um, go to the beach instead?"

There it is, then. "Let me think about that a moment . . . Like, um, no."

"But all my friends will be there."

This is when it's hard to be a parent.

I read somewhere that the bits of the brain that understand the concept of consequence finally knit together only in the early twenties. I don't doubt this at all. So while I want to discourage him by listing the dangers of New Year's on the beach, the examples I have, each of which demonstrates a likelihood of being killed, maimed or at least mortally embarrassed, will simply sound like fun amplified, like placing an iPod into a powerful docking station. Consider a few snapshots of New Year's Eve, 1989, twenty-two precious and vanished years ago:

Here's Warren Greathead getting stoned on something a surfer gave him to smoke, and then losing his car keys in the sand while the surfer's girl-friend gives him a blowjob;

There's Kevin Thingummy, doing loud wheelies up and down the road and then forgetting to put his foot down when he stops and ending up with the bike pinning him to the ground. We are too paralytic with laughter to help him up, so he lies there being bottle-fed more Carling by his adoring fans until one or two of us recover sufficiently to pull the bike off him;

Jason Whatshisname generating third-degree burns when he tries to re-arrange the logs on the bonfire with his bare hands because he doesn't like the shape they made;

The unobtainably beautiful Sonya Oelschig – some names you never forget – swallowing most of my tequila only to throw it all up down my back as I hug her a happy New Year, and then crying like a baby that I don't love her because I won't take her home with me;

Kirsten Something and her well-endowed friends skinny-dipping while everyone in the parking lot turns on their headlights – onto *their* head-lights, so to speak;

Et cetera, et cetera, and so on and so forth.

I know it's different now. We drank whatever we could get our hands on, back then, and some of us smoked grass, and while that was pretty much it, we still managed to wreak havoc. Endangered our lives, even though there was no crack or heroin or coke or crystal to be had, no Rohypnol or Ritalin to fall victim to. Today, you're not allowed to drink on the beach, let alone make bonfires, so you'd have to end up doing other things, things that are far more clandestine, far worse. There are so many more things, stupid things, for kids to get up to on New Year's Eve with no sense of consequence, because when you're a kid you're nothing short of immortal.

Back then.

I sound like an old person.

"Not all your friends will be there. Peter Jones will be with us."

"He's not my friend, Dad. He's just a kid the same age, that's all, like a dork the same age actually. Please can I not, like, go to the Joneses and go to the beach instead?"

"Er, like, let me think about it for a moment –"

"Stop doing that." He is beginning to shout; his red-splotched face is tending towards purple.

"Okay. No, you can't go."

"Why not?"

Good question, but completely expected.

Because you will meet people who are just the same as I used to be, or worse, as most of my friends were, and those people will be worse still. Because I won't be there to make sure you're okay. Because when I was your age, being sixteen meant doing your homework or suffering your father's headmasterly clothes-brush and drinking Horlicks every night and being in bed by nine and sipping half a glass of wine at Christmas lunch. Because like every other sixteen-year-old you have the discernment, discrimination and decision-making ability of an oyster: viz. none. Because you are living under my roof. Because thou shalt do what I say, not what I do – did. And because I was eighteen before *I* got to spend my first New Year's on the beach.

"Because you're sixteen years old." I know I have only two or so years left of that argument, but at least it means I have two or so years to concoct a new one. "And I am not hauling you around the Peninsula on New Year's Eve. It's not safe."

"What's not safe, giving me a lift or me being, like, on the beach?"

"Both, actually. Because I'm not planning to drink Coke all night to play taxi driver. Because even if I do, there will be hundreds of other drivers full of New Year's cheer. And for God's sake, please stop saying 'like'."

"Well, give me taxi money then," he says. Dyslexic maybe, but not thick, my Gabriel. He's missing the point, though.

"Gabe, look into my eyes – look at me. It's not the sober taxi driver, it's the drunken other guy. So, no. Not going to happen. Understand?"

Gabe changes tack. He lets his shoulders droop, a coat hanger holding up an over-washed shirt. He hangs his head, takes a deep breath.

I wait for the whine.

"Ah, please Dad!" he whines.

"Gabriel, look at me." He slowly looks up. His old-young eyes are pleading but he has forgotten to rearrange his mouth and the bits around his nose; they come together to snarl at me in a nasty, lupine kind of way.

"No," I say.

He lets out a roar, or what would have been a roar if his voice was properly broken, and he stamps his foot and turns and runs up the stairs. I hear him trip on the second step from the top.

"And don't slam the door," I shout over his stumble.

He slams the door.

I turn back to my laptop. Select Google's "Images" option for my Kathy Simons search. And there she is, just the third image along, pretty, still, in her round-faced way. I click on the picture; it takes me to a page with a larger image. I'm horrified to see the dry tributaries at the corners of her eyes, the eyelids that droop and yet have somehow swollen, the rings that encircle her neck, each separated by a centimetre or two. The thickening of her nose, the deep furrow cutting upwards from the inside of her left eyebrow. The hair gone mousey, unsprung, no longer glossy, flicked up. The scrotummy texture of her cheeks shameless on the slick screen of my Mac; not even middle-aged, grandmotherly rather.

The ravages. And so un-long ago.

And then my eyes play tricks: my memory of her superimposes itself onto the screen and I see the younger Kathy emerging, her eyes growing brighter and her skin smoothed out; I manage to hold the illusion only for a moment before the younger woman recedes and the elder returns, weathered and thickened and aged. And with it, the thought that this is exactly how people must see me. When I don't feel like that at all, when I feel so much like the memory of me.

"Wha' you doing?" Tracy asks me later. I look up and see that she's still dabbing blood from her mouth. The red of it matches her lipstick, her nails.

What I'm doing is kneeling on the floor outside Gabe's room with my weight on my good knee, keeping my balance with the painful end of my stump, attacking the hinges of Gabe's door with an electric screwdriver.

"I'm taking his door off."

"Why?"

"Because I told him that if he slams his door one more time, I'm going to take it off."

Tracy lifts a Botoxed lip, shakes her head, minces off on her Louboutins, descends the stairs like a cautious antelope. Gabe is lying on his unmade bed with his arms crossed, glaring at the ceiling, iPod pummelling those so-fragile, once-perfect membranes in his ears. If you look at the maths of it, $3(½) \neq$ us. Somewhere, there's more, has to be more than the pieces of ourselves which we present to each other.

There was a time when Gabriel was young and malleable, virgin clay in my hands, a soft ball of possibility. It may not have been for a very long time, but while it lasted we'd sit on the carpet in front of the roaring winter fire and I'd teach him how to draw. Proportion: how the parts of the human body relate to each other; dimension: how to bring out shape from the flatness of things; perspective: horizon lines, vanishing points, foreshortenings, all the two-dimensional tricks of three-dimensional depth discovered by the Renaissance masters, perfected by Hergé. So why has he chosen to forget everything I taught him? On his walls are scratchy, insecure little works that crouch on lined paper in unashamed medieval distortion. I'm not so much concerned with the content – demons and monsters, reptiles with claws, maidens with the odd tit hanging out, a woman being poured out of a Coke can, a man carrying himself in a wicker basket, a levitating heart squirting cartoon drops of blood – as I am worried about how badly they are drawn, how his drawing style is deteriorating as he grows older. I'm concerned about the derivativeness: long flat horizons, stretched shadows, stolen directly from the Dali posters and postcards stuck on the opposite wall. I accept that it's no longer cool to sit and draw with me, but why has the boy not taken on any of my expertise and experience; indeed, why has he thrown off what he once knew? You try to teach your kids two things: how to do some things better, and how not to do other things worse. You don't expect them to go backwards from there.

We go to the Joneses, laden with beer and wine and chips and a twelve-year-old bottle of Chivas that's now eighteen years older than it was at the time of bottling. Barry was a New Year's baby, and every year I give him the same bottle of Chivas that he gives back to me on my birthday in September. The label on the bottle is fraying at the edges and the cap is scratched and slightly dented. It was funny for the first two or three years; now it's just habit, this endless swapping of a scruffy bottle of whisky that neither of us can bring ourselves to drink.

Barry and Lynn live a block away. In a normal suburb, getting there would have meant a short walk, but here among the oaks and the plane trees, here where financial accrual is declared loudly on plots with tennis courts and twenty-metre swimming pools, a walk is out of the question: here, we drive. Besides, Gabriel reasons, what if we were mugged and stabbed on the way home in the middle of the night? Which, I concede, is a valid point. So we pile into the Range Rover once we've loaded our share of the refreshments, drive for forty-three seconds. I ring the buzzer, wait for the wrought-iron gates to swing open, park behind a string of other four-by-fours in Barry's second-gear driveway, unload ourselves and the pointless stuff we've brought. Hooked over my wrists in bags that bang against my crutches are three bottles of wine, the Chivas and a two-litre bottle of Coke; a sulky Gabriel is carrying two six-packs in a plastic super-market bag. Tracy's high heels force unnatural, bird-like little steps – or perhaps it's the tightness of her jeans that's preventing her legs from swing-ing from her hips. She's carrying the heavy stuff – two bags of prawn-cocktail chips and a packet of pretzels – elbows in, wrists out, the packets pinched between thumbs and forefingers like dead mice. Gabriel, at sixteen, is hormonally incapable of walking beside his parents. It's either fifteen steps behind, or rarely, as now, five steps ahead. In the yellow of Barry's driveway lights I see him swinging the bag of beer at the end of his arm. I open my mouth to warn him of the likely outcome, but before I can form any words the bottom of the bag rips and the two six-packs crash onto the fake cobblestones.

"Oh my God," says Tracy. "Are you all right, Gabe?"

I'm amazed.

The beer has landed miles from the boy; how could he possibly be hurt? My beers, on the other hand, are lying on the cobbles, hissing and foaming. Three of the bottles are broken; another is terminal, its contents squirting out from under the cap.

"Jesus, Gabriel," I say.

"Don't say 'Jesus'," Tracy says. Put your tits away, I want to reply, but I don't.

I feel a Gabriel lecture coming on about the importance of considering the possible results of one's actions, but he pre-empts me. "Sorry, Dad, but I'm not, like, clairvoyant or something."

I hold my bags out to Gabriel. He looks at me, at the bags, baffled.

"Take them, Gabe," I tell him. Then I get down on a knee and a stump, scrape the broken glass into the remnants of the broken bag. I open the screw-cap of a leaking beer, run my finger over the neck to check for splinters, and take a drink. It tastes flat and warm and strangely sour, so I empty it onto Barry's driveway and add the bottle to the contents of the broken bag. Tracy looks on, a curl on her upper lip. I take the bag with the Chivas back from Gabriel, add the remaining beers, hook the bag over a wrist, stand up, make for the house.

Why we do this thing of carting stuff to each other's homes, dragging these coals to Newcastle when we know that the hosts are unlikely to run out of beer, wine, soft drinks, chips – not tonight, not ever? I don't know.

Petitely plump Lynn opens the door, gives us each a hug. I'm surprised, as always, at how well her body fits into mine. Her dark hair hangs loose,

24

smells fresh. If she's wearing make-up, I can't see it. She takes the dripping bag from me, looks up with raised eyebrows.

"Don't ask," I say.

The La Vitas are already here, along with two other couples we don't know. The Unknowns. Tony La Vita, third-generation Italian, second-level friend, now an A-list pizza chain king, together with his beautiful, terminally sad-faced wife, Julie. Barry takes the bags of alcohol from Gabriel, deposits their contents into the fridge and hands me a beer. I can feel the Unknown couples' eyes on me. I know their expressions without looking at them: they're slightly doe-eyed with sympathy, eyebrows and corners of mouths turned down. I know that each of them is burning to know how the leg was lost. I know they're dying to make empathetic noises; they're hungry for the details, hungry to mourn its loss vicariously, craving the story of the gore and the pain that wasn't theirs, hoping that it never will be.

There are kids, of course, small ones and middle-sized ones, some in the pool, others watching the Disney Channel, the smallest tearing about, sensing an extraordinary night and testing to see what they can get away with. One of the boys hurtles around a corner and sets an expensive-looking vase rocking on its base. An Unknown mother shoots out an arm, sun-browned, gold-bangled, to stabilise it.

"Daniel! Grow up!" she hisses at the boy.

Be careful what you wish for, I want to warn her, but I don't.

Shortly after Gabriel was born he contracted some kind of rotavirus, as young kids do, and I'd bitched about the lack of sleep to my parents. "Just remember. Small children, small problems. Big children, big problems," my father responded. My epigram-laden, pipe-smoking father.

I glance at the growing problem that is my son. Peter hasn't appeared yet, and Gabriel is leaning on the kitchen counter scowling into a glass of

Coke. He looks like he is trying to compress his long frame into a small one, stands hunched, slouching, his shoulders rounded and his head hanging forward off his neck like a blotchy and too-heavy fruit. He looks on the verge of losing all control of his bones and his joints, and for a moment I wonder if this infrastructure might give way altogether, collapsing into a handful of pick-up-sticks that rattle to the floor. I want to berate him because a son should be someone who makes his father proud, is supposed to be a being who holds his head high and confronts the world face-on and is thrilled at the young blood that flows through his veins and the growing strength of his four intact limbs and his untarnished lungs and unscarred liver that process the clean air and the good food and the pure juices (Coke aside) that find their way into his body. I want him to be shaking a dry, firm hand with the adults. Want to watch him introduce himself with a smile and a strong voice and then stand around and join the banter with the confidence and wit that should be his. But Gabriel has nothing to give them, nothing to gain from them; to hide his thoughts in the sibilant bubbles of Coke is at worst a brief distraction, at best a temporary tactic for invisibility.

Meanwhile, Tracy has intercepted the aw-shame looks that the Unknown couples have been casting my way. She's very good at this, distracts them with her oft-proven techniques, which include looking the women up and down sniffily and shoving her cleavage under the noses of the men. Barry drags us all away to the deck that looks out onto the galaxy of lights that define the Flats below, the lights of the little people, stretching to the black void of the ocean beyond. He has made a fire in a large steel contraption at the end of the deck. When its flames have calmed to coal, Barry will throw on steaks and chops. He may have a Maserati and a Cayenne in the garage these days, but Barry's culinary tastes never really left home. He knows me well enough not to offer me a chair, but one of the Unknown husbands doesn't and drags one up while exhorting me to sit as though I was a sick person, which leaves me with the choice of accepting the seat or cracking him across the shins with a crutch.

I sit.

In my wardrobe at home, standing in a corner, is half a leg. It has titanium bones and a skin of high-tech rubber that feels almost real but doesn't, like the skin you feel and don't feel when you do the old dead-man's finger trick. I wore it for a while, or tried to, but I could never get used to the pain of my weight bearing down on the stump stuffed into the thing. Besides, my limp drew other kinds of stares, pretty much as a toupee might – does he have a leg or doesn't he? Isn't he too young to have had polio? Hobbling about on crutches with my trouser leg neatly folded up was, I reasoned, an honest way to declare to the world that yes, I am an amputee – I am not wearing new shoes, have not twisted my ankle, have not had a toilet accident – I have simply lost half a leg.

"You're lucky," the surgeon said to me when I came around after the operation. "We've managed to amputate at the knee, which is the best result for wearing a prosthesis in the future." That was the first time I heard that I'd lost my leg; I didn't feel lucky at all.

Barry pulls up more chairs so that everyone can sit. He's that kind of guy – says nothing, just does something about the mutual discomfort of me sitting and everyone else standing. Unasked, he brings me a beer, a trendy boutique beer. It's colder and crisper than the beers I brought. I try to relax and make a few comments that aren't that funny but get the Unknowns laughing more than they should. One of the husbands asks what I do and I tell him that I'm an architect, and I can feel everyone weighing my profession against the fact of my missing leg, and then I feel their surprise that there's no logical contradiction between the two. Everyone relaxes a little more. It's not a seismic shift – the men don't kick off their shoes and the women keep their tops on; it's a miniscule exhale, a barely perceptible dropping of the shoulders, but I'm sure that greater things – peace agreements, multinational mergers – have rested on even smaller changes in the prevailing mood.

There's a brief hiccup when more Unknowns – three, including the couple's daughter, down from Johannesburg for the holidays – arrive late, having lost themselves amid the foliage of the suburb. The new Unknowns smile, awkward. But the rest of us exude an aura or a cloud of pheromones that reassures the newcomers. Which is just as well, because this time I'm the one staring, firstly at the daughter, who is sixteen and flawless, wearing a tiny silver figure nailed to a tiny silver cross that hangs between breasts I suppose I should not have been looking at, so I look at the mother instead. She reminds me of some famous actress from years back whose beauty was amplified by eyes that were ever-so-slightly crossed; I can't help but notice a similar crucifix to her daughter's trying to fight its way out of her cleavage. And then I try to remember exactly when it was that I stopped looking at daughters and started looking at their mothers, but I can't.

Lynn leads the girl off by the hand to introduce her to Gabriel and Peter, who has by now emerged and is trying to interest Gabriel in some hand-held electronic device. Peter is shorter than Gabriel, much, and he's podgy and bespectacled. With his pasted-down and side-parted hair, he has the air of a little old man – a professor or an accountant – but when he looks up at the approaching girl his eyes widen and his jaw drops. I hope that Gabriel will draw himself up to his full height and smile broadly and shake the girl's hand, but instead he shrinks a little more, nods, pulls his fringe down further over his forehead.

We eat. We drink. We talk. The glances have now all stopped sliding towards the trouser-end that is folded over my stump. There's no history with the Unknowns, no past indiscretions to gloss over, no rusty hatchets to keep buried under carefully chosen words. Easy. One of the Unknown wives says the word "fuck" and we relax more. There are no prudes here, we know. We are adults. We can swear if we want to. We can tell rude jokes and relate off-colour stories as long as we rubberneck first to make sure that there are no kids in earshot. I look over towards the kitchen counter to see if Gabriel is bending his ear in our direction, but Peter is sitting alone, fiddling with the gizmo in his hand. I'm glad Gabe can't hear us, us old people telling boring anecdotes and swearing to try to impress – comfort? – one another.

We finish eating and fill the awkward time between eleven and midnight with more anecdotes, a few more drinks. I'm sure that Tracy has snuck open another button on her blouse, but I don't care. Her eyes are glassy; she shouldn't be drinking while on antibiotics, but. Then, midnight, more or less, because of course everyone's watches and cellphones are out of sync and nobody is sure when the moment actually arrives. An illegal barrage of nearby fireworks settles the debate, and we wish each other all the best for the coming year, dragging the kids into the adult circle for a moment. Hugs and good wishes, goodwill glowing with sentimentality and alcohol.

Why are they so important now, these embracings and blessings? Why not on 5 January or 19 March or 27 October? I don't know. It depresses me always, these happy, three-quarters-pissed New Year's people, smiling with all their teeth hanging out and sloshing their drinks around, wishing total strangers whatever their Hallmark vocabularies can dredge up, hugging those of the opposite sex just a little too tightly, just a little too long. Celebrating what is to come, when all that is certain about New Year's Eve is another stroke through the threescore-and-ten. It should be a mourning for the passing of time – just last week, just yesterday – when we were younger than we are now. And then Barry makes things worse and appears with an old six-string which he tries to tune as he walks towards us. I can see that the B-string is broken, hanging useless off the head of the guitar, but he's not deterred and launches into "Auld Lang Syne", appallingly, belting out the lyrics I've never understood. Tuneless, meaningless. I'm surprised that the neighbourhood dogs stay quiet, because Lynn, Tracy, the Unknowns all join in the discord. I can't, can't let go like that, though I envy their lack of inhibition, their willingness to howl along with Barry's jarring guitar. A glance at Gabe tells me he can't bring himself even to watch; like me, he's cringing and wishing that Barry would reach the end of the song.

When he does, we all clap and laugh.

"More!" one of the Unknown husbands shouts. "Encore!"

Barry smiles a "no" and leans the old guitar against the wall. "Always leave them hungry," he says. He sits down next to me. "Actually, it's the only fucken song I know," he mutters. Encore Boy gets up and walks over to the guitar. He isn't that steady, I hope he's not driving. He picks it up, holds it left-handed, strums, opens his mouth to sing, sees I'm the only one watching, puts the guitar down again, rejoins the circle around the dying fire. Lynn and the Unknown wives have begun clearing things up. Plates with chop bones that still have pink attached, boerewors ends, shreds of salad. I'm pleased to see that the clean-up has started; I'd like to go home. But Barry disappears into the house again and emerges with a bottle of tequila, making my heart sink. If the world accepted honesty, if we could just say what we were thinking, I'd stand up and announce that I've had enough, I'm heading for bed. But I can't, of course: any words of departure would be understood to mean that it's been a shit party and I can't wait to leave, now that the formality of twelve o'clock has come and gone. The devil is in the unsaid bits, in the gaps between the words and the spaces between the lines. So I resign myself to sitting around for another hour or so, to swallowing a shot or two of tequila, having another helping of dessert, talking more. Which everyone else seems to be doing very well. Some of the Unknowns are in stitches over a common recollection. Tracy is leaning in to an Unknown just a little too closely while he regales her with God-knows-what, making her laugh. She's easily amused by other people. Barry is handing around shot glasses. Beyond the glass doors, I see Gabriel and Peter and the pretty girl sitting on barstools at the kitchen counter. Peter is on the right, talking and gesticulating. I know that he knows that his physique allows him to be comfortable: he has nothing to gain with the girl, and therefore nothing to lose. She is sitting between the boys, her eyebrows raised and a hand over her mouth in amusement or shock – I can't quite decide – as she listens. Her back is turned to Gabriel, whose only visible means of support are the elbows he's tucked behind him on the counter, the bony wings of a sad pterodactyl. He is looking at his jiggling foot, watching it as he flips an untied shoelace from one side of his shoe to the other, outside to inside, inside to outside. My son, my teenage son. I want to take him by the shoulders and shake him and slap him on the back of the head and tell him that soon I'll no longer be able to hold him back from his friends and his beach parties. That the weight of a few more years will remove the zits and the clumsiness and will fill him out a bit and allow his brain to grow a little more so that he is better equipped to tell right from wrong. That he will then face a glorious, untainted future stretching like a blank canvas from his feet to the horizon – and I want to warn him that the canvas will be far less forgiving than his father ever was, because every mark he makes on it will govern the next mark, so he had better make every choice fucking count unless he wants to hit thirty-nine and a quarter looking over his shoulder, unless he wants to become the next generation's forensic archaeologist and sift through a sandpit of past

choices in the hope of finding the seminal potsherd, the traces in the cop-
rolite, the original artefact of misdirection to understand where, when, how
it all went wrong.

Tracy catches a heel between cobbles in the driveway, almost falls over.
"Oops," she giggles. Gabriel walks five paces behind me, scuffing his shoes.
I'm thinking about squirrels and teeth. I'm thinking about how teeth are
removed not from the heads of young people, but from the heads of old
people, and I am trying to reconcile this with the fact that, at thirty-seven,
my wife is hardly old. Or is she? In ancient times thirty-seven would have
been a fine lifespan. If you hadn't composed your first symphony by twelve
or conquered Asia Minor by twenty-three, chances were you wouldn't live
long enough to do it. And here, in a tooth, was empirical evidence that the
decay had begun – no, it began long ago and now was simply manifesting:
today a splintered piece of enamel and old fillings and infected nerve-
endings, tomorrow arthritis, frigidity, impotence, gallstones, strokes, incon-
tinence, cancer, dementia, and the sneering looks of the young who cannot
conceive how very soon it will all come to them. And squirrels; I have squirrels. Squirrels living in the roof, bent on destruction. Young people do not
have squirrels, and if they do it's somebody else's problem – the parents',
the landlord's.

Squirrels are an old person's problem.

Chris and Sylvia

I put Schultz out, though his brown eyes implore me not to. Schultz now tolerated rather than adored, all greying chops and gas and bad breath. I make sure the windows and doors are secured, switching off lights behind Tracy and Gabriel as I go, turning on the alarm before I squeak-thunk my way up the stairs. Gabriel has retired to his crepuscular, doorless lair without saying good night. Tracy is in our bathroom, naked, rubbing vitamin oil onto the scars that run like fine white cords under each breast. She's been doing this every evening for six months since the implants; I don't have the heart to tell her that if the scars haven't gone by now, they never will. I pee – one leg, one crutch, one dick – hoping that this simple act will purge my body of the evening's excesses of beer and tequila, yet knowing that it won't and that I'll remember them well enough in the throbbing light of day.

I get into bed, lie there with a forearm over my eyes. Tracy emerges from the bathroom. I start making gentle sleeping noises and shift my arm a fraction so that I can spy on her from beneath it. Tracy has white stuff on her face, a bare Pierrot clown halfway through its make-up session. Her body has hardened over the years and is now gym-stringy and ungenerous, if not actually undernourished. Ribs join the sternum like the bones of a skiff above the too-large breasts, asymmetrical abs appear and disappear across her midriff as she breathes. She has taken to Brazilians; the welcoming, fluffy nest that she once shared so generously is now mean and tight-lipped, prickly to the touch, its cropped exclamation mark of hair contradictorily and disturbingly pubescent. She walks over to the mirror, checks out the flatness of her stomach from the side, runs her forefingers along the blades of her hip bones, turns to look at herself over her shoulder, cups her bum-cheeks in her hands and lifts them up slightly. The cheeks each produce a folded overhang of skin – flaccid rather than fat – against the top of her thighs when she lets them go. It won't be long before she raises the subject of a bum-lift with me. But she won't be doing so tonight. She is frowning, turns the frown on me.

"You were weird this evening," she says.

"I'm sleeping, Trace," I lie.

"You were thinking of Dalia."

"Oh my fuck," I say, more surprised that I actually hadn't been thinking of Dalia at all than at the accusation.

"Of course you were. You always think of Dalia on New Year's Eve."

"Well, this year was different. She never entered my mind."

"You were weird, especially at first. You only chilled after a few beers."

I hear Gabriel's voice in my head: Don't say "chilled", Mom.

"You know how I am with new people."

"You're thirty-nine, Chris. You've been meeting new people since you were two."

"Well before that, actually. And I've always been exactly the same with all of them."

"Only on New Year's Eve."

I don't feel like an argument. The bed is sucking me in, wrapping me in its seduction, unconditionally promising me the sweetness of sleep. Tracy finds some skin-firming unguent or other and turns back to the mirror to rub the stuff onto her buttocks.

"Whatever," I say.

Gabe: Don't say "whatever", Dad.

"So you *were* thinking about her?"

I lift myself up on my elbows even though I don't want to. "Tracy, I was not thinking about her. I was chatting and laughing with the best of them. I had fun. And so did you, by the look of things."

Tracy snorts quietly, puts on an old T-shirt of mine, gets into bed, switches off the light, turns her back to me. I automatically put my hand on her hip. She shakes her butt like a wet dog and wriggles to the far edge of the bed, out of reach. This strange woman, my once-wife, this lodger who shares my bed, who won't share herself. I am furious with her, not because she is rejecting my advance – which in the first place wasn't an advance, and in the second is used to being rejected – but because I hadn't thought of Dalia until Tracy mentioned her name, and now I will probably be thinking about her all night.

"Thanks for doing that thing of yours," I say, to show her that I am a bigger person than she might suspect.

There's a silence. But then she can't help herself.

"What thing?"

"That thing you do to distract people from trying not to look at my leg."

"I didn't know I did a thing like that."

Sometimes an old person's problems become a young person's again.

New Year's Day for the last five years has brought with it the ritual of going to visit my mother. Not that I don't visit her during the year, which I do, as often as I can bear it, but the day used to carry with it the promise of new hope, and that's why I started doing it.

I suppose professionals with couches and notepads would call it denial, but originally my hope was that it wasn't Alzheimer's, that her dilliness, once so endearing, was temporarily magnified by my father's death, that everything would be okay again once she had mourned and accepted his passing.

And then, of course, there's the guilt.

My mother – or Sylvia, as I now think of her, because she is no longer the mother who raised me, and because to her I am now a sometime nurse, a sometime doctor, her husband, the ghost of her own father or brother – Sylvia lived with us for almost a year after my father died. Towards the end of that time, Tracy and I began referring to her as The Poltergeist: taps left running, the fridge standing open, laundry in the garbage, dentures in the cutlery drawer, the gas cooker turned up high to heat an invisible pot. Then, one evening, The Poltergeist was replaced by a demon at once sublimely innocent and chillingly dangerous.

Tracy and I, as we used to do back then, had gone out for an evening together, leaving Gabriel in the bath while Sylvia supervised. We re-turned from dinner and a movie to find the boy still in the tub, shivering, turning blue, scrubbed pink, crying hysterically. Sylvia had not allowed him to get out, because she was certain that he'd just got in; every time he tried to climb out of the tub she forced him back again, forced him to wash himself, and when after the sixth or seventh wash he refused to do it again, she took the soap and the facecloth and scrubbed him down herself, kept on scrubbing until we came home. From the foot of the stairs we heard her shouting – and Sylvia never shouted – shouting that the child, who was barely ten, had to wash himself before he'd be allowed out of the water. And Gabriel, almost hypothermic, red from scouring himself in trying to appease his grandmother, flayed almost to bleeding where she had taken over and continued the scrubbing, crying in gasping sobs at a nightmare that had gone on for four endless hours. Tracy pulling Gabriel from the bath, wrapping him in a towel, also crying by now, screaming at me as though I had been the perpetrator. Me leading Sylvia to her room by an elbow, hating the dotty half-smile on her face as much for what it signified as for what it didn't. Her words making the hair on my neck stand up as I ushered her into her bedroom: "Isn't it time for Gabriel's bath now?"

In the morning I feel as though I have cotton wool in my ears and cellophane over my eyes. A distant headache from the beer and Barry's tequila. Fuzzy, not in my skin. I invite Tracy and Gabriel to come to the care home where Sylvia now lives, not because they'll accept, but because I should. They are both still asleep: when I whisper in her ear, Tracy shakes her body beneath the duvet as though she is having a small fit, kicks her legs, moans, burrows deeper. Gabriel simply turns away from me, folds a pillow around his head, holds the sandwich together with his forearms.

It's early and the roads are New-Year's-morning quiet. One or two joggers are already up and at it, three cyclists swap slipstreams. Along De Waal Drive, the carcass of an abandoned car lies on its back in the grass that grows on the median. I slow the Audi. See skid marks, glass, stains of fluid on the road, yellow police tape. For auld lang syne.

The nurse behind the reception desk is short, plump, pink, her upturned nose a comical complement to her looks – the inadvertent humour of genetic splicing. Her breasts spill onto the counter as she works on some papers, and they stay there when she looks up to greet me.

"Hello, Mr Hayes. Happy New Year; so nice to see you after all this time."

The devil in the unsaid bits.

She walks me down corridors that smell of old people, urine, carbolic. Fusty, funky. The dust in the shafts of summer sun tastes of aspirin.

Withered people, husks from which the spiders of age have sucked the juices, leaving only thin skin with scabs that won't grow over and thoughts that won't connect. An outburst – anger, frustration? – from a tall man with a metal cane. Crumpled women in wheelchairs stare down the tunnels of time to worlds of porcelain dolls and tin soldiers, worlds before television or stereo FM broadcasts. The nurse warns me that Sylvia has deteriorated, and that the disease which broke her mind is now breaking her body. Lucid periods ever more infrequent, mere punctuations in full-blown dementia. She has forgotten how to walk, had done, a month ago. She has to be fed, diapered, cleaned. She fears many things, sees many others, most of which are not there. She rages at everything and nothing. And is raging, I see, as we walk into her room.

"Why don't you fuck off and get me breakfast?" Sylvia growls at the nurse and snaps her head around to glare at the window.

"I'm so sorry," I say to the nurse: an absurd apology, but Sylvia had never in her rational life spoken like that.

The nurse puts her hand on my arm. "Don't apologise. It's part of the whole thing, and believe me, we're used to it." She turns to Sylvia, goes down on her haunches beside the wheelchair. Knees turning from plump pink to anaemic white as the skin stretches over them. "You had breakfast not half an hour ago, darling. Remember – yoghurt, tea, some nice eggs?"

"Ali's wife always brought the freshest eggs," Sylvia says to the window, to the wind-polished sky beyond. "When she told me they were going to bulldoze District Six I told her to stop being silly, and then they did and I could do nothing to help." She turns to the nurse, looks her up and down, raises her eyebrows. "My nurses do not squat on the floor. They stand proud. And look at your uniform, girl, good heavens, you only have half of it on! Not even tights, just bare legs! You leave me no choice but to report you to the duty sister."

The nurse stands up, strokes Sylvia's shoulder, pats it.

"She used to be a nurse herself," I say. "A sister, actually. So." Again, an absurd apology.

"I know. She's always carrying on about our uniforms. I suppose they were kind of different in her day." She smoothes the blanket over Sylvia's knees, adjusts the curtain to shade the old woman's eyes from the morning sun.

"Just ring the bell if you need help," she says to me.

"Hi, Mom," I say once the nurse has left us alone. Sylvia turns towards me; perhaps it is the unexpected tone of a male voice that catches her attention.

"Doctor, these people never feed me and my hip hurts. Why all the hiking when my hip hurts? I lost my boots on Sunday."

"Sylvia – Mom, it's me, Chris."

"Chris, Chris . . . rhymes with piss."

"Chris, your son."

She grunts as though I am lying. "Never had a son. Borrowed one once. And when I lost the library card, well, you should have heard the . . ."

I turn her wheelchair towards the bed, sit on the floral cover, look into her faraway blue eyes and tell her my news. Gabriel – yes, your grandson – blossoming into a tall and handsome young man. So clever. Draws like Frank Lloyd Wright, like Raphael. Sends his love. So does Tracy – you remember Tracy, of course you do, she's fine, as pretty and sweet as ever. We have squirrels in the roof, can you believe that? Old houses and their maintenance – it's not the money, you know, Mom, it's the complications of it all, the effort, it's the knowledge that you'll just have to fix it all over again soon. Same for everything, all the stuff in the house, the cars, the business. You work so hard to get it, then you have to work twice as hard to keep it together, to keep it meaning something. As Dad used to say, it's like trying to put an octopus into a string bag. Keep fixing, doing, forgetting to *be*. Who wrote "the centre cannot hold"? I don't remember. Barry played his guitar at the New Year's party. It was awful, he really shouldn't have. Sorry, Ma. I shouldn't whine so much – it's small stuff, really. A big new contract for the firm, a mixed-use centre in the middle of town, exciting project, progressive client, great budget.

There's nothing there. She's staring at the sky through the window again, so I try a different tack.

You wouldn't believe how much Tracy's changed. Been going to gym so much she could probably do a full triathlon with a millstone around her neck. Like biltong now, though. And had her boobs done six months ago. Biltong with breasts, well. I never minded her real ones, but she insisted, said she wanted it for her, not for me. Now she's got tits like a porn star, which is ironic because we hardly have sex any more. Never, actually. Hardly talk, either, unless it's to bitch. She uses her new tits like an assault weapon, blam – or should that be blam-blam? – in your face. Even a gay guy couldn't help gaping.

Still nothing.

And to tell you the truth, Gabriel is so different, difficult, I don't know what to do with him. I'm struggling to keep up with the changes in him. The body and the brain and the emotions of him all growing at different rates, in different directions. It's not what he does, it's what he doesn't do. I'm scared for him – scared that he'll grow up into a non-person, because non-people get sucked into non-lives. He's sixteen now – how is he possibly going to live to seventy? He can barely cross the street on his own, can't hold a conversation unless it's to beg for something or whine. Yes, he has problems – but we all do, don't we? I mean, look at you. Look at me. Just look. Just look at the two of us.

Nothing. No thing. No. Thing.

Do you realise it's nineteen years since Dalia died? Nineteen years since she died pretty much in my arms. And you know what, I don't miss her. Haven't missed her for years, didn't even think about her last night, when. I feel bad about it, feel like I should still be pining, feel guilty that I'm not. Is it okay that the space has been filled by the days in between? Is it okay for her to be dead and for the hole she left to be filled with memories of everything that's happened since? Is it okay that I've filled the hole with good sense, money, family? Or should I have preserved the hole by stuffing it with cotton wool or beeswax? I don't know.

I look at the backs of my hands, the pores of them. Turn them over, feel the hardened heel of one with the thumb of the other. Breathe in the closeness of the room.

I have this tugging, Mom. This tugging right here, in the middle of me, as though something is trying to pull me down. Or up. Or along. Trying to pull me somewhere else. Or trying to pull something out of me. Maybe it's my stomach or spleen or something. I'll get it checked out at my next physical, so don't nag me about it. It's a tugging that's trying to pull me right, but I can't follow it until I know what I've done wrong. Or. Or maybe it's everything tugging in all different directions from the same anchor point – Tracy one way, Gabriel the next, the firm the other, the squirrels and the teeth and the endless slow decay of things another way yet. Gravity downwards, youth backwards, hope forwards, memory sideways, the future up, the past down, the present whichever way present circumstance dictates. Do you know what it could be, Mom, this pulling of me in all directions? Not, huh? I was hoping, but. I wonder if Dad would have known. He knew everything worth knowing – except maybe how to make money. Do you still miss him, Mom? I do. I miss you both, actually.

And then, the glaze clears and the eyes focus.

"Chris?"

"Yes, it's me, Mom." The sudden acid threat of tears at the corners of my eyes. Maybe a few minutes, please, just three minutes, two, one even, where the fog lifts.

But.

"Hmph. I never knew a Chris." The arms cross and the glaze returns, and with it a fascination with my stump. I try one last time. "*I'm* Chris," I say. "Your son."

"Michael?"

"No, Chris."

A shake of the head. "I never had a son. Borrowed one once until –"

And then her head snaps up and her eyes widen and fill with tears. Are they old tears, dammed up behind those blue eyes for years, decades, carrying dissolved within them the sorrows of a lifetime, or are they new ones, divined overnight or over breakfast to wash away new fears, fears yet unfaced?

"Get out of the bathroom!" she wails. "You *know* you may not come into the bathroom when the door is closed. Oh my, I can't believe you're sitting right here *staring* at me while I'm in the bathroom! For shame!" She puts her hands over her face and sobs with the horror of it and then the air in her room thickens with the instant rot of shit, its rough bass notes and bitter-sweet top notes saturating the stuffiness and, I fear, my clothes – I fear *me*, my hair, my skin, my bones – so I hold my breath, lean over to kiss her powder-soft, blue-marbled temple goodbye.

The sky has been torn open by the strong southeaster – if a smoker tossed a cigarette out of a car window right now, the entire mountain would be aflame. But only the runners are about; the smokers are all still in bed, nursing sore heads, regretting.

There are police cars and tow-trucks at the stranded vehicle now. Men are standing about, their jackets worried by the wind as they scratch their heads and wonder how to right the car.

Is that how they'd left my car all those years ago? Abandoned for the night after being eviscerated, its occupants split up and ferried in different directions, one to the hospital to be revived, the other to the morgue?

Nineteen years. Nineteen years since I lost my leg along with the part of me that lived in it, that fraction of my twenty-one gram soul, the part the surgeons never told me I had lost. A New Year's party, Dalia driving after her usual night of limes-and-soda, me pissed-but-not, making up nonsense couplets. Dalia laughing, pulling off when the light turned green, and then. Then.

Then.

Then I remember why I hate "Auld Lang Syne" so very much. I find myself hoping that the occupants of the upended car are either properly dead or properly alive, not in some ruined place in between.

I am struggling to go home, my car complicit with my mood, slowing to a crawl before I notice: after Sylvia, I cannot face the indolence of Tracy, Gabriel sleeping through his most vibrant hours. I turn off the highway after the University and take the steep little road up to Rhodes Memorial. Hop through the car park, feel surprised to find the coffee shop open. It's too windy to sit outside; a yawning waitress ushers me inside. There are Christian posters on the wall. The waitress brings me a menu and a badly designed pamphlet that poses the question, Does God Exist? and provides possible answers next to three tick-boxes: Yes, No, Maybe. When was I last in a church? I don't know – God in man's image and all that. I push pamphlet and menu aside and tell the waitress that just a coffee will do. She looks relieved. "Glad you didn't order tequila, I couldn't deal with the sight of it right now," she says and shivers. I'm tempted to change my order, to demand a tequila and to down it while she watches, but I don't.

I'm the only patron, but the coffee takes an age. When it arrives it is tepid, and I suspect that party-girl forgot about it and left it standing after it was poured. Or perhaps she was in the restroom, temporarily incapacitated by her night on the town. I mean to complain, or to rile her by asking what the Bible teaches about excess, but I can't be bothered. Instead, I watch the wind tearing at the stone pines while on the other side of the Flats it piles clouds onto the tops of blue mountains, like a great cosmic child trying to see how much ice-cream it can cram into a cone before it all falls out.

I don't have the experience or the practice that nurses have. It has to be easier when you're a nurse – your charges are the organs, the lives, of other people. It must be a simple matter – no, a necessary one – to let a carapace grow over your softer bits, to build dense layers of keratin, and to top it all off with Teflon so that the ornaments and the food and the words that are thrown at you cannot pierce.

I am unprepared for any of it, have no such protection. Unprepared most of all for the barb of denial, the sting and the burn of it. My defences are paper-thin, academic – she is ill, she is mad, and none of it is her fault. I know she is in control of neither her mind nor her mouth, but that doesn't stop me from wanting to go back to the home, to shake the old bitch, slap her, shout at her – for hours if need be – until something sinks in and there's some kind of acknowledgement.

But the truth can be told in different ways. The accepted truth, one I'd held to all my life, is that after Michael and Sylvia adopted me, I became their son; I suppose now she, or her disease, has simply rephrased it. Because she is factually correct, of course. She'd never had a son: there had never been conception, never been a birth, so no panting or pushing or blood or torn birth canal, no placenta, no cabbage-cradled breasts or cracked nipples. Sylvia had never *had* a son, she'd simply had one handed to her.

But still.

I go home because there is nothing else to do. Pick up the dog shit on the lawn – one leg, one crutch, one poop-scoop. Make lunch because the combination of antibiotics and alcohol is still hurting Tracy, and Gabriel would rather eat Coco Pops straight from the box, starve even, than make himself a sandwich. Afterwards I sketch out some ideas, not very good ones, for the new Murray development that I'll have to start on in earnest next week.

Google nothing. Read a book whose words don't hang together despite the writer's respect for syntax, grammar, story. Feed Schultz because nobody else will. Long for nightfall. Shower when it comes, go to bed. Lie there thinking about the son that Sylvia never *had*.

And then, at three in the morning, Gabe snoring, Tracy deceptively peaceful in sleep, even the squirrels quiet, the question: the endless, forever question, poking always just beneath the fabric of me, perfectly defined, but like a malevolent spirit never spoken of. The question now stabbing, at last, through the heavy cloth of sleep like a needle through skin –

Then who did?

Chris and Tracy

When you've been away from work for a while, it's something of a shock to realise that nothing has changed. The pencil I'd left on the layout pad, at an angle just so, the few papers I'd put in order and crisply stacked, the message note I'd crumpled and dropped into the empty dustbin late that last working day, all just as I'd left them, a small shrine to last year; each component a strand in a thread of continuity that you'd somehow hoped had been broken.

Ivan pokes his head in, today's yarmulke a bright Mondrian.

"Hi, Boss," he says – coloured with the usual sarcasm, not enough to offend, just enough to make its edge felt. He raises his coffee mug as though it were a glass of Veuve. "Happy New Year, here's to putting the naughties even further behind us, and to untold wealth and success in the teens."

Don't say "naughties", Ivan. Don't say "teens".

I wish him a healthy and a happy one in return, which he brushes off by reminding me that Rosh Hashanah was last September, that I really should make an effort to come this year so that I can wish him a proper New Year, thanks me nevertheless. And then steps into my office, shuts the door, sits down without asking.

"We need to discuss Ndlovu, Chris," he says.

The first day of the working year, and already Ivan is picking at that old chestnut. Ndumiso Ndlovu – "NN" to his black-empowerment buddies – is scratching at the door for a slice of Hayes Inc. Can't draw a straight line, but he wants to own an architectural firm to complement his string of construction and plant-hire companies. Has a habit of smiling broadly across the table, is softly fat for his age – which is young, given his accoutrements and influence. Under his Zegna suit, I imagine layers of leopard skin and smeared buckfat, secret pockets of bones and stones combining to construct charms and spells; thorn-toughened feet wrapped in Crockett & Jones, prepared at any minute to kick the colonist back to where he came from.

Which is, well.

I sigh, sit back. "We've been through this before. I'm not selling, Ivan," I say.

Ivan sighs too. "It's not an outright sale. It's 25.1%. That's all we need to secure government and big business work. Just like that," and he snaps his fingers.

Onto the wheel so early in the year. The same argument, the same points raised in December, last August, at our annual shareholders' meeting in June, with nothing added that might spare the hamster.

At this point in the discussion I would usually remind Ivan about how much money we'd made over the past year, the past three, five: *our* money, made without BEE representation. Money that we've never had to share with anyone, least of all with a professional front man who in all likelihood would bring little, if anything, to Hayes Inc. And what I've never said, never will: you own a successful enterprise, and that grounds you. Its foundations are dug deep into the earth, and they root you, they embed you in this unwelcoming country.

But now I want to nudge Ivan's sterile line of debate off course, so I hold up my hand.

"I get it, I get it," I say. Ivan stops mid-sentence, mouth open.

"You do?"

"Yes, I believe I do. You need the cash, so you want to sell your shares to Ndlovu. Not so?"

"My God, Chris."

"If that's the case, then let me know and I'll buy you out. Buy back your shares. I don't need a spare wheel on this if that's how it is."

Perhaps I've cut too deep. Ivan seems offended, hurt even. But I hope he gets it now, gets that I didn't start this practice simply to sell out at the first opportunity. He stands up, shaking his head, stops at the door without turning back to face me.

"Do you need me in the Murray briefing?" he asks the door handle.

"I'm sure I'll be fine, thanks, Ive."

I know he likes "Ive" about as much as I like "Boss".

I shuffle through the concept sketches I'd done over the holidays. They're worse than I thought; they do nothing to place the development in its environment, the façade is hideous, the layout of the retail and pedestrian areas impractical. The initial brief was far from clear, but still I can't share these sketches with Murray, so I jot down a few notes, wheel out the old PowerPoint with its stock renderings of adventurous but impractical references. Have coffee. Wonder why I ever stopped smoking. Hobble off to the boardroom. And wait for the twenty-five minutes that Anton Murray is late. The kind of waiting where you can't start doing something else because you know you'll be interrupted as soon as you do; the kind of waiting that seems to add minutes to every passing second.

Murray arrives with a young woman in tow – Alison, Alice, Alicia. He is tall, fiftyish, greying. Designer haircut, Breitling, the ball of a paunch over the belt of his jeans. The girl is first-job smiley, has long blonde hair that's elegantly styled and not quite natural, green eyes, bone structure that would make Tracy dislike her instantly. She takes the lead, apologising for being late. Murray smiles – indulgent, condescending – lets her finish. He's fucking her, I think, and push down a feeling I don't want to feel, a feeling that makes little sense in the context of having met the girl only moments before.

Murray takes over. He wants things big, he wants them compact, he wants them universal, he wants them unique. He wants parking, shops, offices, residential units. He wants something to rival the Guggenheim in Bilbao or the retro-mod Pompidou or the Blue Building in Barcelona, he wants organic and warm; he wants geometric and he wants linear, he wants classic with a contemporary twist, Modernism but not Post.

He doesn't know what the fuck he wants.

What I want – need – if I am to help him, is clarity.

I see the girl looking down, silenced into taking notes, blathered into blushing. She holds her hair back with the side of her left hand as she stabs at her pad with a pen, drawing blocks around some words as she goes, underlining others, circling a few. "Girl": I am thinking like an old person. She may not yet be thirty, but there is little that is girly, girlish, about her.

"Maybe," I suggest to Murray, "you'd like me to do up some rough concepts?"

"Now that is brilliant. I like options. Choice, you know, instead of being clusterfucked into a corner."

My heart sinks: I should have kept my mouth shut. Options are the worst.

There's a knock on the boardroom door. Sam, the receptionist-cum-PA, opens it, shrugs with her eyebrows. Behind her is a waiter from the over-priced café downstairs, hang-headed, sheepish. He's holding two polysty-rene containers that reek of garlic, lemon, other things Mediterranean.

"Ah, lunch," Murray says. "Hope you don't mind, but I could eat a small child. Today's been a complete mare so we ordered on the way up." He stands up to take the food, hands one of the containers to his young woman. Does she enjoy this crassness, these lumps of slang that he tosses about so freely? Her blush is returning, blotchy on her cheeks. No, perhaps she doesn't. Murray opens the lid, which intensifies the odour. He scoops up a blob of hummus with a triangle of pita, bites into it. Leaves a teardrop of hummus on his chin, unwiped.

"So," he says while chewing, "I was thinking." His words are indistinct, muffled by the food in his mouth.

And so it goes. His focus switches to pinching strings of roast lamb between pieces of pita, on dipping chips into a rank dip. It's impossible to clarify budget, scope, timeframe, anything. I am irritated; now hungry myself, I pour a glass of water from a jug in which the ice has melted. The water tastes of fridge and the meeting has run fifteen minutes over and I know that I have something pressing to do although I cannot quite define it. It may simply have something to do with closing the meeting, escaping from the suffocating verbal foam that issues from Murray. I feel myself beginning to fidget and twitch like a smoker deprived of nicotine for too long.

The girl speaks up. She's nibbled at a few corners of pita and a chip or two. "I'd like to come back to you in a week with answers to your questions. Perhaps I can call you, or come and see you? Anton – you're pretty busy for the next while, aren't you?"

He inspects his Breitling's complex little dials. "Hectic, Al. Tell you what, let's thrash it out in the car and you get back to Craig whenever." He's only halfway through his meal, and it's clear that he intends to finish it.

"It's Chris, Anton. Not Craig."

Murray raises a semi-apologetic hand without looking up from the trough of his lunch.

"Thank you," I say to the woman. "Now if you don't mind, I'll leave you to your lunch. We're well over time and I'm a little late for my next engagement."

To leave, I have to stand, of course. Have to take up the crutches that have been leaning quietly against the chair next to me. I crutch around the table towards the door. Murray stares openly; as I crutch around to his side of the table I hear him suck air through his teeth. His eyes flick up and down, from the absence of the leg to my face, as though he is struggling to reconcile the one with the other. I stop, look at him, think of shaking his hand. But he turns away from my stump and back to the mess of lamb and hummus and pita in front of him. The girl doesn't look up, has closed her container and pushed her food away, is poking at her iPhone, angrily, I think, the mottle of her blush worse than before.

My "next engagement" is nothing, a fabrication. But I have more important things to do than watch a client with attention deficit disorder eat lunch, or most of it at least, as he drops the rest on my boardroom table. But the firm is quiet. The recession has bitten – architects are always the first to suffer – though not as deeply as it might have. Still, January is looking far slower than usual. I look at my notes and replay Murray's garble in the hope of finding the smallest crystal of sense, because sometimes a tiny crystal will be the seed of what the client is trying to express and if you nurture it, the crystal will grow, slowly at first, and then more quickly, and when it grows like that you know you're onto something: you know that you understand and that you can replay your understanding to your clients, and if you're any good they'll think it's all their idea and sign off the work and the costs, there and then.

But there's nothing in the notes, they're just a bag of candyfloss, a barrel of phlegm. No nuggets, no bones, no crystal – nothing solid, at all. Like the empty barking of Schultz, the hoarseness of his eleven years.

And then my BlackBerry.

It's Tracy. She's crying, gasping, barely coherent. I calm myself out of my Murray irritation, try to calm her. I realise that she's had an accident in the Range Rover, and the glass-boxed world of my office reels around me. Again, I think, scrotum tingling, tightening, my hand and the phone a ball of sweat: again. Her muscled body and impact-hardened bones offer scant protection from the flying glass, torn metal, splintering plastic – the mallet of impact crushing and shattering everything that's not already cut, lacerated. The spears and arrows of broken automotive components.

"I've broken my –"

"You're breaking up, Trace. Deep breath, say again slowly."

I hear her breathe once, twice; then her voice is marginally more controlled. "I think I've broken my wheel."

Tracy, my brain thinks without me: Tracy doesn't have a –

So, the short of it. Tracy has hit a kerb in the Range Rover, at quite an angle and an impressive speed, it seems; the left front wheel has sheared off its hub and come to rest at forty-five degrees beneath the vehicle. Her nose is bleeding from the impact of the airbag: she suspects black eyes tomorrow. Her shoulder hurts from the seatbelt tensioner, her high-heeled ankle has twisted against a pedal, and her left wrist is sprained because she didn't release the wheel in time.

She is in Durbanville, she says. But may as well be on Neptune.

Because Durbanville.

Durbanville lies past the flanks of Table Mountain – *our* mountain – beyond the flatland of industria where it laps against the hump of the distant Tygerberg. It's a tidemark of middle-class compromise, fine if you speak Afrikaans and like face brick and lapas and brandy with Diet Coke; otherwise, it's a cultural Atacama where people drive Hiluxes and own speedboats and quad bikes and consider a mixed grill and koeksisters the acme of fine cuisine.

"What are you doing in *Durbanville*?" I ask.

"Nothing. Visiting a friend." Which is it, I want to ask, but don't. "Do you need me to come and fetch you?" My tone must be irritated – hers certainly is.

"Don't bother. There are tow trucks here. Actually, they were here almost before I hit the fucking kerb. They can take the car away. I'll get a cab."

"You sure?"

"Yes. I'm fine. It's just Gabe."

"Just Gabe what?" For an instant I imagine that he's with her, know he can't be.

"You'll have to pick him up from school."

I breathe in. Out. "What were you doing when you crashed, Trace? Durban Road is three lanes wide."

"Nothing. On the phone. I was – I was trying to call someone."

"Who?"

"Lynn. Julie. Gabriel. Chantelle. My mother. What the fuck does it matter? I took my eyes off the road and had an accident. It's not like you've never had an accident."

An accident.

I swallow back my anger.

"Okay, Tracy, whatever. Call me if you need help."

I put the phone down. My white shirt has blossomed with sweat, grey blooms at the armpits. How did I come to be here, in this office with its precious finishes of glass and chrome and its studiously preserved brick-work? How did I come to have a partner who seems to resent the share-holding I handed to him; a beautiful un-wife whose attractiveness and affection decline in proportion to each visit to the gym, each slice of the scalpel; a dog I seldom pet; a son who won't speak to me unless it's to ask for something? I get up and hobble to the gents, not to pee, though – my bladder has shrivelled like an old gourd, my cock shrunken by half, as it does when I've had a scare; I need to wash the sweat of fright from my hands, regulate my breathing.

Sam the PA is yawning behind her PC as I crutch past her. Clicking and yawning, she is: Solitaire, I guess – that thief of time and brain cells, beloved of secretaries and receptionists, an unbudgeted expense to the employer. She looks up and smiles at me, looks down again. Sam is twenty-two or so. I wonder if she's ever played Solitaire with real cards in her life. Wonder what she'll eventually come to if she doesn't stop. I push open the door to the gents. Wash my shaking hands. Realise I do need to pee after all, do so at length, wash my hands again. And again.

When you were adopted in the seventies, your new parents were handed few artefacts relating to your origins. A fragment with unknown markings, a bent pin, a glass bead, little more. There were laws then that prevented children from seeking their biological parents, and prevented these parents from seeking their discarded offspring. Information was scanty, any effort to reconstruct the past mammoth and archaeological: it required knowledge, skill, effort, imagination to rebuild a past from two scraps and a crumb.

One scrap: I was born at Johannesburg General Hospital on 27 September 1972 and adopted from the Princess Mary Adoptive Home that October.

Another: in those days, before Madonna and Malawi, before Asian kids were welcomed by cool Caucasian parents, before AIDS orphans were coveted like designer labels, those in charge of things would try to match each child closely with its adoptive family. Features with features. Religion with religion. Biological backgrounds with adoptive backgrounds. So I assumed that my parents – or one of them at least – were immigrants, as my father was. So, were they English, like him? With his sad scruffy tweeds and pipe-smell and shepherd's pie and alien Yorkshire syntax that his pupils used to mock: "No rooning in the corridors"; "No joomping on the beds"; "If I was sat in your shoes"; and so on. Toes lost to diabetes, teeth long, hooked, yellow, black at the gums. Or were my parents from Italy or Greece or Armenia, come to take advantage of an exchange rate that supported entire clans back home in those years, bringing with them genes that would explain Roman noses and cleft chins and thick dark hair like mine?

The crumb: in the mid-nineties, the laws were changed. Biological parents and their offspring were all of a sudden permitted to search for each other, though any meeting had to be by mutual consent.

So while Sam yawns – wanting to win her game but hoping she won't so that she can savour victory later – I Google.

Princess Mary Adoptive Home: twelve results, six unequivocally stating that the home had closed its doors in the early eighties. Joburg General, a sprawling state hospital where *She* had gone to purge herself of me, like you'd flush away a goldfish that has outlived its novelty.

Where to start?

I change tack and ask Google for adoptive tracing agents. Two come up in Cape Town, one beyond the pale – in Durbanville, actually – and the other based at the Marie Stopes Clinic in Claremont, two minutes by car from my home, ten to walk if you have two legs, twenty if you have only one.

I try the Durbanville number. I'm testing, don't want this too close to home at first. The phone rings. And rings. And then there's a voice that tells me the number is not available.

I dial the Claremont number, but only halfway.

Because, then.

Then there is Sylvia. There is – was – Michael. How deep would the betrayal be if I punch in these last few digits, if I complete this so-ordinary process of making a phone call? My father (adoptive) is dead; my mother (adoptive) is demented. So: am I denying their sacrifice, their love, if I dial the last few numbers?

Then again: practicality. There are constant reminders in the shape of medical forms and insurance applications that pose sets of questions which should be easy enough to answer. Is there any family history of heart disease, cancer, diabetes, insanity? And then the white lie of ticking the "No" boxes, the dishonest truth of it. There's no history of these things because there *is* no history. What there is, though, is your child, a child whose genetic inheritance did not begin with you but reaches into the blindness of time before you. There is *his* right to know about diabetes, Crohn's disease, schizophrenia, hypertension – a right far more fundamental than the rights of insurance companies and medical schemes.

There is the certainty that you are not looking for love, not looking for money, not even looking to forgive or not forgive. Just the visceral sense that *you have to know*, even after all these years. Especially after all these years, before it's too late, because as time slides by, more and more of your links to the past are buried or cremated.

And with it, the danger of knowing. The danger of knowing something you can do nothing about, a knowing that may well negate the value of the knowledge gained. And the finality of it. The loss of a kind of innocence, because when you don't know, it doesn't matter. But what does matter is the years since you were born, the years of astonishment when you were a toddler, the years when your maths and English results were tops and pride shone in significant eyes, the years of encouragement when you most needed it; the years of your father sitting in the freezing rain in his fraying tweeds to watch you lock down in the scrums and jump at lineouts and never score a try, your mother at the school concert when you played in the punk band, smiling stiffly in her pink and frilly outfit, clutching tightly at the handbag on her lap, not understanding that the on-stage anger wasn't about the music at all, that it was about teenage rebellion which you never thought would hurt her but did.

And there's the tugging.

Perhaps it's a tugging towards discovery, or a tugging towards forgetting, towards simplicity, a tugging away from the web of complexity that wraps around you more tightly by the day. Perhaps it's tugging because even before I lost my leg I only had one foot on the ground anyway. A man dropped into his existence, landing like Mr Bean on a cobbled sidewalk in those old Atkinson skits, an unwanted alien beamed down. A white man dropped into Africa. A husband dropped into a marriage, dropped into fatherhood. Dropped into middle age. Talent dropped into ambition, ambition into business, business into capital, capital into boredom, and boredom converted into badges of success and the flotsam that takes even more capital to sustain. And all the foundations and the concrete and steel in your buildings amounting to nothing – one foot and the two square inches of rubber at the ends of your crutches your only true connections to the world beneath you, behind you.

While others grow from somewhere. From the roots of a nation and the seeds cast by a towering family tree; an act as simple as a backward glance over a shoulder an instant reassurance. What is rooted is mere rootlessness, the permanence of transience, manifested by the sense that this is not my country, that I am here by the grace of others, a long-term visitor with a cloudy future and no home to return to.

I've left it too long before completing the sequence of numbers; the phone is hooting in my ear, so I reset and dial again.

A woman answers. "Marie Stopes Clinic, how can I help you?"

"I'd like to speak to someone about the tracing of biological parents, please."

"That would be Marietjie van der Westhuizen. She's in a consultation, though – can she call you back?"

I give my cell number. Tempted at the last digit to make it a wrong one. Don't; give the correct one. Put the phone down. Crutch past Sam on my way to wash the sweat from my hands again. In the corridor Ivan is wrestling with a large rectangular object and the bubble wrap that sucks to it.

"And that?"

"Art, Boss. The next big thing." With a flourish he removes the wrap, revealing a predominantly white canvas with a central haemorrhoid of scratchy images smeared with reds, terracottas, burgundy. The images have been laboured onto the canvas substrate in pen: an anguished face, a doll-child, a donkey, second-hand political slogans, childish phrases of rebellion and self-assertion. A scrawl of words as naive and ponderous as the images. Maybe Gabriel is onto something.

"It's a Forest Blair. She's about to be really hot. Thirty grand now, projected value in five years, double, maybe more," says Ivan. "So, to thank you for the profit share, I'm loaning it to us for a while."

"Janice didn't like it, I guess?"

Ivan grins. "Not so much. Wanted it in the garage with all my signed sports art. But hey, it's great, don't you think? It's progressive. It works here, that's what we do, anyway. We progress, we *are* progress."

Later, a look at the finances with Shahid, our unimaginative but scrupulous accountant. I ask him again to go through the profit-share pay-outs. Thirty grand would have done rather more damage to Ivan's portion than to mine. And the Ivan I've known is smart with his money – and *our* money – he's not the kind to take a thirty-grand long shot on an unknown artist. Shahid knows my suspicions. I can almost hear his eyes roll when I ask him – again – to take me through the numbers.

"Chris, I would be the first to know if Ivan's doing anything dodgy, and you would be the second," Shahid says. "He makes a good income. I'm sure he has his own investments that help him to buy the odd painting."

A valid point. But.

But what if Ivan has indeed come up with some smart scheme that lets him dip into company coffers? Allows him to help himself when money is tight, when things are needed? A secretive siphoning, nothing dramatic enough to raise flags, while the slow dripping of cash grows his own personal stalagmite.

Shahid shows me regularly – and the auditors annually – that the books are clean, that Ivan cannot be doing what I can't help thinking he is doing. And again, disproving my suspicions, Shahid pulls out the records of the War Chest – cash on hand, investments of profits, values of smaller buildings we have bought, renovated, rented out as income has allowed. In terms of our partnership, mine and Ivan's, seventy-six per cent belongs to me, and while the dividends are less than last year's, thanks to the slow recovery from the antics of the world's bankers and their sub-prime circus, it's a whole lot of not too bad.

I am reassured – for now – that Ivan is behaving. But this look under the lid of the War Chest, well. What if, I begin to think, and then there are images of a small bungalow on a beach with a weather-beaten Land Rover under a palm tree, no phone, no widescreen TV, no project brief within a four-hour drive – the images begin to arrange themselves into a coherent slideshow, as compelling and clear as a good PowerPoint presentation. I force myself to stop the show, to turn it off.

And then home.

Tracy with blood-crust in her nostrils. She was right about the black eyes: lids swollen, purpled.

"Want to talk?" I ask. No words; the look says it all.

Gabriel in his doorless room. "Hi, Gabe," I say.

"Hi," he says, as though I am broccoli he's being forced to swallow.

My house, but not. The painters coming next week to do a new shade of pastel once the squirrels have been removed. The gutters full of plane-tree leaves. The cobbles, solid, heavy, elevated to toe-stubbing height in places by persistent grass. The Boonzaier sun-drenched, its rough oil paint cracking and peeling, a many-thousands restoration, a many-more-thousands sale, needing effort to move it to a shadier wall and even greater effort to sell. The Bose sound thing – nothing through two speakers, and then when you take it to the shop it works perfectly and the spotty boy behind the counter packs it up again, condescendingly. The Range Rover, pirated and held to ransom by some low-life with a tow truck. Tracy, caught between collapse and self-improvement, magnifying decay by fighting it. And Gabriel: well, Gabriel.

And then my phone at eight-thirty, number withheld. I imagine Murray and another half-hour of uselessness to suffer through, but it's a woman, thick Afrikaans accent. I don't know her, suspect telesales.

"It's Marietjie van der Westhuizen," she says, and I can't think what she wants because who on earth is Marietjie van der Westhuizen?

"Yes?"

"Apologies for calling so late, but you phoned earlier about adoption tracing," she says, the smallest hurt in her voice at my curtness.

"Sorry, yes I did." Mouth dry instantly; a need for secrecy, so I crutch my way outside with the phone between my ear and shoulder.

"It's five hundred rand."

"I'm fine with that."

"Payable up front. You can settle when we meet, please. Once you pay, we go."

"As I said, I'm fine with that."

Three days later, I leave work early to meet with Marietjie at the clinic. It's a dark old house that's grown carbuncles of ill-considered extensions, its windows crusty with time and the southeaster; inside, shiny enamel-yellow paint on the walls to shoulder-height. A receptionist clicking away with her mouse, her face underlit by the green of Solitaire.

Marietjie van der Westhuizen's desk is old, as big as a bed, chipped and scratched along the edges and on the corners, cheap laminated board showing through, with thick stacks of paper in yellow folders strewn across its surface. The branches of an old oak overhang the window, its wind-driven shadows waving imprecisely through the dirty glass, stealing the light.

Marietjie is older than she sounds on the phone, dumpy, her scalp pale through a corona of sparse red hair. Large black-rimmed glasses like Billie Jean King used to wear. A formless dress patterned with indeterminate flowers.

She interrogates my motives. Have I had a recent death in the family, have I recently married, or divorced, or had a child? None of the above, I tell her, and ask about the relevance of the questions.

"They're the most common triggers for requests like yours."

"My mother – adoptive mother, I suppose – has advanced Alzheimer's."

She nods, satisfied. "That would probably do it. And it's getting worse, isn't it?" She nods again in answer to her own question.

"Well, there's no going back."

Silence.

And then she explains that part of her responsibility is to prevent unpleasant situations where the adopted child seeks to extort money or love, to offload their own unwanted offspring, or in other ways to impose dependencies on the birth parents – but she must also prevent the inverse: birth parent imposing on the child. Blackmail, stalking, is verboten from both sides. Her eyes flick to the watch on my wrist, to the Lacoste crocodile on my shirt. She apologises, doesn't mean to offend, but has to tick the box.

"I have no intention of doing anything like that, I assure you."

"I assume you want me to concentrate on finding your mother, first and foremost?" she asks.

I'd never really thought about it. Mother. Father. The real, unreal, ones, the not-Sylvia, the not-Michael, without whom I would not be sitting in Marietjie's office. I'd never thought about it, not consciously, but there's a clear mother-shaped thing in my head; I look for a father-shaped equivalent: it's there somewhere, but foggy, indistinct.

"How did you know?"

Marietjie shrugs, smiles faintly. Sadly, perhaps. "Experience. For every ten men who speak to me, nine prioritise the birth mother. Women are different. About half of the girls want to find their dads."

She looks at me, looks at the tears that come from nowhere – tears distilled in a chamber of me I never knew I had – a ridiculous wave of emotion squeezing from my eyes.

Marietjie smiles again, the same smile, pushes a box of Kleenex towards me.

"Experience?" I say, taking one.

She gives another smile.

"The good news is that mothers are usually a little easier to trace. They were there at the birth, at least. The fathers, especially back then, usually did a runner if there was no shotgun wedding involved."

Back then.

I tell her in thirty seconds everything I know about my birth, my mother. She probes a little further, takes notes.

"Religion?"

I am tempted to answer "No, thank you". But I don't. "Brought up Anglican," I say.

"Do you have a birth certificate?"

The question amazes me. "I've never seen one. Never thought about it, actually."

"And you're certain it was Joburg Gen and Princess Mary?"

"As certain as I can be. I'm not going to get more clarity out of Sylvia these days. Any clarity, actually."

"Sylvia?"

"My mother. Adoptive mother," I add, not so much for Marietjie's sake, but because right now I'm not sure how to think of her. Marietjie warns me that it could take months, that there may be further expenses, that the costs may in fact double. I am uncomfortable, irritated by this preoccupation with the fee, with piddling amounts I would easily spend on a business lunch or on Tracy's weekly phone bill. I take out my cheque book, start filling it in. "I don't mean to be patronising, but five hundred rand seems very little for what you're offering to do."

Marietjie shrugs. She starts to sort papers, signalling that the interview is reaching its end. "That's what it costs. It's the same for everyone. Some of my clients struggle to pay even that."

I look at her, but she's sorting paper. I cancel the cheque, turn to a fresh one, begin again. This time I add an extra zero, hand her the cheque.

"A donation." She says it, doesn't ask it.

"Sort of. Well, part of it is my fee, of course. But if possible, I'd like the balance to be used for the next nine people who come in here and can't afford you."

"Thank you, that's very kind."

I am suddenly embarrassed. It would have been better to drop an anony-mous bundle of cash through the letterbox than to flaunt my ability to throw money around. And if it had to be a cheque, I should rather have presented it after the investigation: now, it's instantly tarnished as I hand it to her, carries with it a subtext of bribery, a desire for preferential treat-ment. It would have been better simply to pay the requisite fee.

"I'm sure these things take time," I say in case Marietjie is thinking what I fear she is thinking. "I'm not in a hurry, so."

"Thank you, Mr Hayes," she replies. Stands up, sees me out into the wind.

Tracy is unusually observant when I get home, despite the swelling and purpling around her eyes.

"You look like you've seen a ghost," she says.

"I'm fine. Taxi pulled out in front of me down the road, gave me a bit of a fright. You're not looking that great yourself – how are you feeling?"

"Shit. I'm going upstairs, getting into bed. My bones hurt."

Tracy always wants to be in a part of the house where I'm not.

"It's only just gone five-thirty."

"I know. I just want to lie down with the curtains closed, no light, no noise, no phones, nothing."

"Have you taken anything?"

"Thanks for reminding me." She backtracks to the kitchen, puts her BlackBerry down on the counter, opens a cupboard, rifles around, digs out a bottle of painkillers. Pours a glass of water, swallows a few pills, heads off towards the stairs with uneven steps.

"Good night," I say. She grimaces, says nothing, stops.

"Oh, there's an e-mail with a quote from the panelbeaters," she says.

"How much?"

"Just over thirty-five."

I am surprised. "Thirty-five hundred isn't too bad."

"Thousand, Chris. Thirty-five thousand."

"Jesus, Tracy." Even though it will be for the insurance company's account, I am angry.

"Sorry." She shrugs, carries on up to the bedroom.

I scratch around in the fridge and pile a plate with a few incompatible leftovers, dribble some Tabasco over it in the hope of improvement. Consider a beer, consider a glass of wine, settle on a glass of water. Don't like drinking when I'm irritated. See that Tracy has, as usual, left dirty dishes in the sink for Martha to take care of in the morning. Sit down at the counter. Tracy's phone is next to my plate. I take a bite of my food, pick up the phone, turn it over in my hand, check out the chips in the silver trim, the scratches from keys and coins and hairbrushes in her handbag. Touch the red button as I fiddle with it, which wakes it up. Notice that the phone's wallpaper shows an arrangement of flowers – peonies, pansies, petunias, whatever. So unlike Tracy, that chocolate-box image. Notice also that there's a notification of an unread text message, so I open it. It's from Jono, and it's the most recent in an endless chain of messages from Jono.

This one reads: *Feeling better, babe?*

Who the fuck is Jono?

Why is he calling my wife "babe"? And why does he care about how she's feeling?

I skim through the chain of messages. I see words, phrases that don't connect, don't need to be connected to be clear – *love; hot; want you; see you later big boy; ok babe; see you soon big boy; can't you just come now babe send him on a long errand or sthing; can hardly WALK today, bb!; Lol; x bb; x u2; ur the best; 11am ok?*

And so on and so forth.

I put down the phone, reconsider the beer, the glass of wine. Hobble off to the drinks cabinet, pour a shaky whisky.

Go back, pick up Tracy's phone again. Exit the message folder, press the green button. Find her call to me after she hit the kerb, three days before, at 12:23. At 12:25, a call to Jono's cell number. I go to her address book. There are two numbers listed under his name, the cellphone and a landline. The prefix on the landline is 979, somewhere out north. Bellville, perhaps. Parow. Or Durbanville.

My wife is fucking some loser from Durbanville.

I go back to the text-message folder. There's a draft message to Jono, unfinished, at 12:21. *That was really* is all it says.

What had she left unsaid? Really what? Fantastic? Amazing? Earth-shattering? Really deceptive?

It was really irritating, that's what it was, because she was busy texting this Jono bastard at precisely the moment she drove my Range Rover into a kerb.

I put her phone down, don't need to see any more. Push my plate and its inedibles away. Hop off to pour another whisky. I'm not a big drinker, rarely drink on my own, never when I'm upset.

But.

Gabriel

The school year of 2011 dribbled into the summer holidays and Gabriel considered telling his father that they had probably bumped up his exam results again, which is precisely what the teaching staff had done after a long staff-room debate.

They'd considered his obvious intelligence, weighed it against his dyslexia, discussed whether his inability to express an idea with a pen would handicap him for life. But, they agreed, technology would probably help him get by without ever having to write a thing. He might become a successful architect like his father, perhaps, and the teachers – none of whom had ever been an architect – nodded sagely, because architecture had to do with drawing, not reading or writing. But please not an artist – not that any of them had ever been an artist – because underneath the frustrations and the disappointments of adolescence, Gabriel was a good kid, didn't deserve to starve in a garret. Finally, they concluded that it would be best to let him at least achieve his Grade 10, perhaps even his Grade 11, because once the boy reached Grade 12 the results would be out of the school's control and he would be out of their collective conscience.

The head of English was convinced that Gabriel's semi-literate scrawl concealed a certain complexity of thought, especially after seeing the rather disturbing drawings that had fallen out of Gabriel's exercise book. Sexual, violent, demonic even: blood, naked women, vampires, dismembered humans populating endlessly flat plains of the nightmarish landscapes. Mr Swanepoel had opened his mouth to say something to his colleagues, but instead placed his dead pipe between his teeth – no smoking in the staff room since 1998 – and bit down on it. Thought better of saying anything, having also read a sheet of poems that had fallen to the floor: brief, burped phrases a stunted Dickinson might have penned, the sketches perhaps a pictorial of what Gabriel couldn't say in words, like something an inarticulate Ezra Pound might have drawn – or a William Blake, who drew what he couldn't write, wrote what he couldn't draw.

Gabriel saw right through the exam results, as, he knew, his father did. His critical, demanding, disbelieving father who overlooked his genuine achievements – asked more than once where he'd copied a drawing from, hinted at a less-than-honest way of achieving a pass – yet usually believed Gabriel when he lied. Not that he lied often: he chose his opportunities carefully, learned the effectiveness of omission. Learned that telling the truth seldom cut it.

As he discovered again on New Year's Eve.

On New Year's Eve, Gabriel could simply have lied by saying he'd be spending the evening at a friend's house – George the Dog's, Somph's, Grumpy's – because look at what the truth had got him. A braai at Barry's. A bunch of old folk sitting about drinking and giggling like primary-school kids when they swore. Mom checking out the other women, flirting with the guys, Dad quiet as always, waiting for someone to ask him about his leg, relaxing only when they didn't, once they stopped glancing at it. Little Peter Jones and his fat face carrying on about his iPhone. Showing off all sorts of whizzy shit that was just plain boring.

And then Barbara arrived. Barbara with the face, the body, the legs. To look at her hurt, like looking into a welder's torch. You could see the sparks flying off – and as you focused on them they were gone – but you could never look at its white-hot core.

Peter's mouth dropped open at the sight of her, then shut. Then he opened it again and chatted as though she was his sister. He held her attention for three minutes with the iPhone and the things it could do. And then she stepped around Peter, slid up to Gabriel.

"Hey," she said.

"Hey," Gabriel replied, arranging his fringe to reduce the dazzle, the great void of nothing to say consuming him from the inside out.

Then Peter threw something away – the chance of a kiss, a snuggle, maybe more, maybe less, but something. "Gabriel is just the best artist ever, did you know that? He can draw like, like, like famous people," Peter piped. "Shy as a virgin, though – hey, Gabe, *are* you a virgin, or are you just pretending?"

Barbara lit up at the promise of talent and ignored Peter's cracks. She asked Gabe to draw something as she scratched around for a pen and a notepad in the fruit bowl. Riding on instinct, Gabriel drew Mickey Mouse: four deft circles, a snout. He filled in the black of the ears, the widow's-peak hairline, the nose. Stuck Mickey's tongue out. Handed it over, mock-proud. Barbara rolled her eyes. "Whoo-hoo," she said. Gabriel took back the pad, turned to a new page. Moved back a little from Barbara. Looked directly at the bright light of her, drew breath like a high jumper faced with a bar too high, slashed a few bold lines. To his own surprise, they worked. Strong, clear, calmer than his heart. He added a few more to give definition, hunching as he did so, looking at the girl less and less, beginning as he always did to tickle his work, to overdo it. But she couldn't wait any longer and snatched the pad away from him, catching the drawing before the artist had throttled it. Said, "Oh my God," and put a hand to the crucifix around her neck: she might have been looking into a mirror – a mirror that didn't reflect the subcutaneous rash of pimples, didn't show that bit of her nose she didn't like, the frizz that lifted from her hair when it rained. Showed instead the bare lines of the girl that she wanted to be.

"See?" said Peter. "Told you." He was still convinced that his strategy of smarts would win, not understanding that his words did nothing but swell Gabriel's prowess, that they only swung the balance of power away from him, his iPhone.

"You draw, like, like Dali," Barbara whispered at her portrait.

"You know Dali?" Gabriel said, pleased that this unlikely girl did, aggrieved to learn that his monopoly on the artist was not complete.

The girl snorted. Gabriel may as well have asked if she knew Lady Gaga or Kings of Leon.

"Do you know that Barry and Lynn have a Dali in their bedroom?" she said.

"You lie," said Gabriel, who knew this very well.

"I don't. Peter – can I go and show Gabe?"

"Of course," Peter said, wiping his finger across the screen of his iPhone. "Do you know I've got an app here that tells me the artist and album of any song that's playing in the room? Check – I just hold it to the speakers, and hey, it tells me it's Deep Purple's 'Child in Time' on their album 'Old Farts Can't Rock', circa nineteen-seventy-dinosaur."

He looked up, expecting laughter, but getting none – Gabriel and Barbara had disappeared. Down a darkened corridor, up the marbled stairs. Sweaty hands on the cool chrome banisters – nautical, Barry called them.

Into the master bedroom, dark until Barbara found the switch. Behind the bed, "The Temptation of St Anthony". Elephants with long spindly legs. Washy skies, long horizon. The horse in front rearing, snorting head turned towards a woman atop the first of five spider-legged elephants. The woman fondling her own breasts. Behind her, a tall knobbed pyramid, also on an elephant. Gabriel knew the print well, knew even the mildew on the lower-left corner of the mounting, had always suspected that the picture was from the years when Dali was signing anything and everything to pay the rent, though he'd never, of course, mentioned this to Barry or Lynn. Wanted to tell Barbara to show off his Dali knowledge, but instinct kicked in.

"Wow," he said instead, reaching a hand towards its protective glass in a kind of benediction. "It's just amazing. Signed, even," and just as his gushing threatened to ruin things, Barbara homed in, kissing him with her perfect lips, her serpentine tongue oddly warm, soft, lacking scales, flicking switches in him that he never imagined were there. Gabriel turned wooden. He folded terrified arms around her, wanting neither to take her nor to reject her, in case either broke the fragile magic. Then her hand where it shouldn't have been, her other hand undoing her own summer clothing – he would later wish that he'd taken his time, savoured her, relished her flawless body, the mole on her left breast, the almost-purple nipples rising to greet him; he would wish that he had taken over like a man. But Gabriel was a starved boy who did not realise how hungry he was until the chance to eat presented itself. He clawed off his own clothes while she lifted her top over her head and drew down her underwear. His hands were on her, all over her at first, then on parts of her, parts that he saw for the first time with his fingertips. And then the blind animal thrusting, her hands slowing him, guiding him to a place barely glimpsed, but so warmly welcoming. A collapse onto Barry's bed, then a surrender to the primordial rhythm, and it was over, over too soon, millennia of instinct and lust flaring in short minutes, dying in seconds: excruciatingly, unbelievably more than anything he'd been able to attain with his imagination and his handfuls of Kleenex.

They lay entwined for a moment, Gabriel certain that he was the first boy – man – in history to have felt this, done this. And then Barbara pushed him away.

"I have to pee," she said, her voice distant. Took up her clothes and held them to her body, closing the bathroom door behind her. And Gabriel in the half-light, looking down at his dick, limp and sad-faced, smelling not like him, but like him and something stronger. A small smear of blood – Jesus, am I bleeding, his first thought. Am I going to get sick, going to die from this? And then his finger telling him no and he wiped the jellied mucus and pink onto his jeans and pulled them up.

Gabriel walked back to the kitchen, poured another Coke. In the real surreal world beyond the down-lighters above the white counter, the white floor, the white appliances and white crockery, the old folk still sat around the braai fire. A woolly murmur of voices, a burst of laughter. The edge of alcohol on it. Why drink, Gabriel wondered, when the real world has such marvels hidden around every corner? The adults with licence to revel in these all day, all night, all week, but instead it's beer and wine and forced laughter. And Peter still poking at his phone, swiping his pink little fingers across its face, making it do its own secret, solipsistic things.

"Like it?" Peter asked, not looking up from the screen. The girl wandered in, sat next to him, her expression autistically distant, fey.

"It was beautiful," Gabriel said. He looked at the girl, waiting for her to enjoy his double entendre, but she did not hear, was not listening, instead looked at the adults as if they were very far away.

And then later, while Peter went off about an app that could show you the streets of New York, London, Cairo, so much better than Google's Streetview, Gabriel sat on his stool flicking a foot left, then right, watching the laces of his shoe switch from instep to outstep, outstep to instep, astounded at how something that had seemed as fantastical as a unicorn or the fountain of life at one moment had revealed itself the next as clearly as a hotdog, a schoolbook, a stubbed toe might do.

By the time Gabriel climbed into bed, the evening had already retreated into the mists of fable. Had the smell of Barbara not risen from the warming sheets, he'd have struggled to hold on to what had happened. The recollection itself was fragmenting, dividing, the splinters of it no longer sequential, dissolving and slipping away between the fingers of memory.

Tracy

Tracy had learned much over the past sixteen years. Learned much, even though she had only read a handful of books in her life, learned not through what marriage had taught her, but because she had kept her eyes and ears open to everything else.

She had learned what it was like to be the flesh and blood counterpoint to Chris's fantasy, for the ghost of Dalia never failed to slip between them in their most intimate moments. In bed. Walking down the aisle. Waiting for Gabriel to be born. Naming him. His birth. Driving. Discussing curtains. Shopping. From the most private, the most important, to the most banal – there Dalia was.

So Tracy learned that it is impossible to compete with a ghost. A ghost is not bound by laws of space and time, and might appear anywhere, at any moment. A ghost is not limited to the faults and flaws of the living – ghosts are perfect. You can't win against a ghost, and you can't banish it.

Tracy had learned also about the mirage of potential, its highest point the moment you held your newborn child to your chest, its skin still smeared with vernix. Everything afterwards only chipped away at that perfection, revealing the faults, and amplifying them with each passing day.

She learned that potential itself is a kind of ghost, presenting itself as hope, as desire, as ambition, at any time and in any place, and that only in the rarest instances did it come to anything.

She learned that while pity may precede love, love does not automatically replace it.

She learned to take her soft body and make it as hard as the core that it covered, for she understood that while the meek may indeed inherit the earth, only the strong could possibly survive it.

Age: you beat it by denying mistakes made over the years. If the mirror painted a picture of you as a twenty-five-year-old, surely the indiscretions of later years didn't count? What right did the mirror have to throw back at you an image marked with fine wrinkles, distorted by motherhood and gravity, flecked with sunspots, brushed with grey?

Tracy worked hard at overcoming this incongruity, and the harder she worked, the easier it was to forgive herself her marriage to Chris, to forgive herself the fact that her son was sixteen, that when Jono first spoke to her, her body had reacted as if she were still twenty-five. To forgive herself this response, she had to forgive herself also for giving in to the promise of it.

She had learned that not all potential was good potential: there was the potential for damage, degeneration. So she assembled personal trainers and a plastic surgeon as a faithful team whose task it was to keep the years of sun and the influence of gravity at bay. Now that she was thirty-seven, she was also a highly credible thirty-one to anyone tactless enough to ask.

Denial precluded acceptance, but when acceptance was no longer avoidable, there were other solutions. Botox, at first. Then a surgical sculpting of a too-thick nose. In July, the enhancement of her breasts: true paps they had become, the nipples descending, everything slipping to a point of no return. Chris could pay, would pay. He had taken her youth, and his ghosts had slowly stifled her with their ectoplasm and cold breaths. He owed her whatever it would take for her to recapture the best of her life, the part that she had given to him: she had – romantically, stupidly – married a half-man who hid behind the leg he had lost, who lacked the courage to take up his crutches and hobble away from the monkeys on his back and the spooks that shadowed him – she'd married the half-man when she herself was half in love, half in pity, and half-pregnant.

Gabriel was five-ninths formed when they were married. Pure, perfect, sinless, unspoiled, he was now few of those things; now he was moping and sulking and wanking his way through his spotty teenage years. He had his father's height but also his father's lack of spine. There was so little of her in the boy. If she hadn't been present at the birth, she would have doubted his parentage.

There was still something there, though. A chance of becoming, and at sixteen, Gabriel still had ample time. He should build his physical strength, build his mental strength, grow the confidence that Chris leached out of him. That was the only part of her that Gabe displayed – a spirit that Chris couldn't see, though, and refused to see through the forests of his own life. She couldn't be sure whether Gabe was even aware of it, understood it. Or was he just keeping it under wraps until the time was right? But there was substance and weight there, and he simply needed direction and nourishment. It was plain for all to see – except for Chris, of course.

And then there was Jono. Jono who had no ghosts, just an undeniably corporeal ex-wife who demanded monthly maintenance for her fat kids. There was no phantom between her and Jono, and no illusion of love or permanence, just the reality of giving, giving and taking, giving and taking whatever it was that the moment required, negotiated in a terse dialogue that was nothing more than the harmless and humorous residue of their time together.

It mattered little that Jono was forty-five, with a belly that slapped against her when they fucked. And what if he had loops of grey hair on his shoulders that sometimes made it hard for her to touch him? It was her he saw when his eyes were screwed shut, her alone, and that was enough. Almost *more* than enough. It was almost quite enough for her to disembark from the gravy train of her marriage to Chris. Because Jono was not wealthy, but he was easy, uncomplicated, and an easy, uncomplicated distraction.

When he first met Tracy, he'd gaped like a schoolboy seeing a real-life calendar girl. He wore a bad shirt and worse shoes. He introduced himself as the coolest man in town because he owned a small company that installed air conditioning, and she found his self-deprecation endearing, his chattiness a cool shower after the verbal drought that was Chris.

Jono drove a bakkie with his company logo on the doors. Took his kids to McDonald's every second weekend. He tumbled in the pool with them, wrestled on the rug with the boy and took the girl shopping as long as there was no rugby on. He dusted off the rusty old oil heater and played Monopoly with them in winter. He fetched and carried them without complaint – unless there was rugby on. Their round faces were always delighted to see him, and they pushed past each other to be the first to hug, and sulked when the weekends drew to a close and they had to go back to their mother's.

Jono had no expectations of them, of himself, and they returned the favour.

But Chris was a different animal entirely, him and his passive-aggressive ways. Pushing Gabe by criticising, congratulating only when his modest achievements crossed Chris's orbital path. And then there was Chris in bed, behaving like the engineers he equipped with plans which brooked no deviation. As if fucking were no more than an equation to be solved and concluded. Phase One: do this, Phase Two: do the other, Phase Three: wipe up and go to sleep. As though he'd memorised the process from a manual – mechanical pumping for exactly *so* long, like a piston running on finite energy, and then shut-down. All his imaginative powers sucked dry by his business, his buildings, his clients, himself.

Whereas Jono loved her to keep her shoes on when they fucked. And she grew to love it too, looking at her Manolos and smiling as her feet hung suspended in the air over Jono's back while he grunted and snuffled away. Initially, the pleasure lay in knowing that Chris's money – six, seven, ten thousand rand – had paid for those shoes, just one pair of them, but as she learned to move, just so, to position herself just right, so that Jono ended up satisfying her almost as often as he satisfied himself, they took on a new dimension, fetishist she supposed, completing the loop between her heart and her soul and her desire. So, more shoes, because variety added to the spice: more shoes, more of Chris's money, more of Jono, more pleasure – a perfectly virtuous circle.

She had first met Chris at a student digs – ex-varsity peers, for Tracy had dropped out, realising without remorse that academia was not for her. She found herself drawn to the handsome, tall young man who spoke little but commanded interest and attention when he did. Serious, strong: she liked that. An architecture student, a prototype Howard Roark from a prequel to some half-read book. And then the mystery that revealed itself when he stood up: only one strong, tanned leg, the end of his shorts crisply folded and pinned over the missing other one.

"What happened?" she asked him once she'd worked her way over to where he was sitting at the braai.

"What happened when?" Defensive rather than playful.

"To your leg." His eyes had turned away and his face reddened. Perhaps her question was too much.

But he'd told her, slowly at first, and then unstoppably. Two years before, New Year's Eve. A party with friends. Tequila. Flaming sambucas. By then already outgrowing the party thing, he said, but played along anyway. He was seeing a girl who didn't drink, so having to drive was no excuse for abstinence.

They had left at about two, girlfriend Dalia behind the wheel. Heading from Sea Point through town to get back to their digs in Rondebosch. A red light. Laughing and joking, Chris not as drunk as he might have been. The lights turned green, the car behind hooting because Dalia was laughing so much she hadn't seen it change. Despite the hoots she'd wiped her eyes, and then pulled out, slowly, because Dalia always drove like an old woman, he said, and that was when the missile hurtled towards them from the left. Chris swore it was on two wheels, cartoon-style, as the driver tried to control it, headlights scowling, he'd said. And then the impact. Their car was flung onto its roof, slammed against a lamp post on the far side of the intersection. Glass everywhere. In his eyes. His mouth. In his hair. Inside his shirt. There was someone between the bonnet of his car and the road. Something severed, dark hair darkening, and Chris wondering who it could be.

He was upside down, dangling from his seatbelt, but Dalia's seat was empty. And the thing under the bonnet – it wore Dalia's clothes, had Dalia's hair, her clothes all stained in dark camouflage patterns, he said, and then a steel curtain made half of pain and half of black closed on him.

After being coaxed awake, he'd been told that he had lost his leg. When the doctor felt he was strong enough, he let him know that he had lost Dalia too: she'd been thrown through the windscreen and crushed by the car and had died before she reached the hospital. If only, he said to Tracy, if only not tequila and sambuca, so that he could have driven; if only the highway bypass and not the short cut through town; if only her seatbelt, then maybe also just a leg. The driver of the other car – a boy with no licence, who vomited up his night's excesses against a wall and was driven away by angry paramedics to have his wrist set – the driver was doing close to a hundred, witnesses said, and had killed his own two passengers along with Dalia. Dalia, whom Chris had never managed to bury, even though he'd donned a graveside yarmulke that kept being blown off by the wind because he didn't know to clip it to his hair; even though he'd cried like a child for her as they lowered her into the sandy Pinelands earth. Cried for himself too, later on, under the weight of the blame from her parents, her sister, her aunts and uncles and cousins and grandmothers.

Tracy had put a hand on his thigh, the thigh of the half-leg, and though Chris had flinched, she didn't move it.

"I'm so sorry," she'd said, and her wet eyes mirrored his. "What did you do?" Another stupid question, she'd thought, but once some things are out, they're out.

Chris had looked at the back of his hands before replying.

"You're going to laugh."

"I won't, I promise."

"Other people do. Not a real laugh, just a kind of snort. Probably because they think it's crazy."

"So I promise I won't snort either."

Chris had stared at the flames flicking at the grid for a moment. "We – my folks and I – tracked down the driver of the other car. And then we arrived unannounced at his front door. A front door in some not-so-cool suburb. He was twenty-one or so, lived with his parents, had just been fired from his job at some chain store or other. His dad answered the door.

Thought we were Jehovah's Witnesses until he spotted my crutches, my leg. And then I saw that he'd been waiting for this moment, for the knock on the door, waiting for his son to be, I don't know, attacked, accused, vilified. Beaten up. Hated. What a way to live, waiting for hatred to visit you, knowing it's just a matter of time. So he started shouting at us, saying that Brett had been through enough, couldn't work, couldn't function, was a wreck, and so on and so forth."

"I'm still not laughing."

Chris had smiled. God, that smile, that happy-sad smile, she'd thought: I could eat it, I could lick his teeth and chew his lips and hold him and stroke him and make it go away and make whatever is left whole again.

"So we calmed the old man down and said that we wanted to chat to Brett. He invites us in, shouts up the stairs, and this young guy, all skin and bones and bags under his eyes, unwashed, unkempt, basically broken, slinks down. When he sees us he goes white and starts backing away, up the stairs, shaking his head and whining like a dog."

Chris's father had called him back down, and the boy came sobbing and making noises that nobody could understand. The boy's mother appeared, smelling of sweat and kitchen. She wore a polyester apron, stained with dinner. She had some kind of spinal condition that set the top of her body out of alignment with the lower half, Chris had told Tracy, as though the weight of her world had bent her sideways, an old pylon about to collapse.

Chris's dad took control.

"Brett – that is your name, isn't it?" The boy couldn't speak, sobbed, nodded.

"Brett, this is my son, Chris, and my wife, Sylvia. Now, we don't have to go into what happened on New Year's Eve, because we all know the details. We're here for one reason, which is to say that as far as we're concerned we hold no grudges. We'd like to forgive you. Everyone makes mistakes, and while some mistakes have more serious consequences than others, mistakes are made to be forgiven."

The boy had begun to sob afresh.

"Now," Chris's father had said. "While we'd like very much to draw a line under these events, there is a condition attached. There were lives taken, lives ruined on New Year's Eve, but those who are in a position to move on should do just that. And you're one of them, Brett. You've survived in body, and now you need to survive in soul. Our forgiveness is conditional on you picking yourself up and putting this behind you and making something of your life. Picking yourself up and moving forward, and not wallowing about."

By now, his parents were crying and the boy's own sobs were seismic – a discordant trio standing in the doorway as Chris and his parents left.

"Wow. That was pretty big of you," Tracy had said.

"Not even close. If it had been up to me, I would have killed the little bastard. If you meet my mom one day, you can give her the credit."

"Did you ever see him again?"

"Never."

Three months later, Tracy did indeed meet Sylvia. And Chris's father, Michael. A meeting at once happy and awkward, as Tracy had a stomach bug and kept having to excuse herself.

"It's the pipe thing," she told Chris later, "I can't do the smell of tobacco." She was pregnant, of course, the growing prawn provoking the nausea, the prawn that would soon enough become Gabriel.

And then, the wedding. Tracy in a cream dress which could not quite be arranged to hide her five-month belly. Chris watching her walk – waddle, slightly – down the aisle, watching her but seeing Dalia, she knew, Dalia down the aisle, Dalia trying to conceal the bump of his child under layers of cream. The vows, the kissing of the bride, the gossamer presence of the dead girl, sticky as a spider web as they embraced.

Gabriel arrived in crumpled perfection, hair dark like his father's, the dimple of Chris's cleft chin already visible. The young family moved into Michael and Sylvia's house while Chris finished his studies. The closeness of it all. Sylvia fussed around the baby, giving advice and half-baked instructions. Michael's pipe-smell reached everywhere, settled on everything. A cascade of half-marked test papers seemed to fall around him wherever he went. He was bewildered by the baby. He seemed scared to touch it in case he damaged it, and was afraid of its crying and its nappies. Chris too was hands-off, also afraid. Perhaps when he looked at the child he didn't see what he wanted to. Saw nothing new, just a miniature of himself.

During his final year of study, Chris had found an internship with a prestigious firm. It was an enviable placement and Chris was a promising student, at once creative and practical, an unusual combination of left- and right-brain skills.

He had almost completed his time at the firm when a brief came in for a small residential house – too small a project to warrant the service hours when there were hotels and office blocks and mansions on the impossible slopes of Clifton to be designed and appropriately remunerated. Chris attended the meeting with the senior partner, whose task it was to turn down the prospective client. Chris noticed the client's clothes, his shoes, the rare watch on his wrist, but the partner missed these cues and said a tactful no, and then the client smiled the way some people smile when they are angry.

Without thinking, Chris had said, "Let me do it."

The partner gaped at him. The anger left the client's face.

"You haven't had a garden shed built, let alone a house. You have no practical experience," the partner sputtered.

Chris had shrugged as the client stared at him.

"Maybe this is his chance to gain some," the client said, still looking at Chris. He turned to the partner. "Since I'm too small for your firm, I'm sure you won't object if I gave this young man the opportunity?"

The client had invited Chris for coffee. Picked him up in a Porsche. Explained that the house was for his parents, that they were getting on and needed something manageable, that he'd bought them a level plot in a security estate. Told Chris he'd had differences with his usual firm of architects and was looking to change. The little house was nothing, he knew; but it was a test, so it was everything.

Chris warned that he was obliged to finish his internship, that his finals were looming, and that his time would be limited.

"Do you want it or not?" the client asked.

"Of course I do."

"Well, then."

So Chris asked questions and the client answered them, and by the time he got home – Gabriel shrieking, Tracy sweating, Sylvia fussing, Michael trying to block it all out behind a cloud of cherry tobacco – a package was already waiting for him, outlining the restrictions and the dos and don'ts for architects designing dwellings for the estate.

He worked up a few concept sketches, and Chris was awarded the project. While the little house was being built – Chris going to site, hounding the builders, tweaking the plans as he went, sleeping three or four hours a night to get through his university work – the client mentioned that he was considering alterations to his holiday home, a fiddly and difficult job which Chris thought about and solved in a way that had never occurred to the owner. Who then made Chris promise that he wouldn't just accept a job after graduating, that he would start up on his own straight away; in return, he promised Chris a small retainer and future projects.

Chris told his parents that the old Austin Apache would have to move out of the garage, and with some invention and no money he spent two weeks of December converting the space into a studio.

The client kept his promise, and slowly the scope of the projects, and the income from them, grew. Six months later, the now-rusty Austin was reinstated in the garage and Tracy and her young family moved to a flat in the city. Chris took a small office a short walk away and hired an assistant and a draftsman. They planned houses for plot-and-plan estates, refurbished small shopping centres. Then other clients came knocking, having heard of this unusually smart young man.

By the time Tracy was twenty-eight and Hayes Inc had bought them a house on the slopes of Table Mountain and furniture and cars that turned other twenty-somethings green, her wardrobe had progressed from thrift-store purchases to designer labels, though by then tiny wrinkles had begun to appear on her skin. The new house with its picture windows framing the bay demanded domestic help, and Tracy employed a string of women. First there was Princess, then Angie, then Eunice and Selina and Marie, each tenure shorter than the preceding one, until Martha eventually arrived and showed surprising stoicism, even following the family to Bishopscourt later.

Tracy's breasts ballooned while she was on the Pill, deflated as soon as she went off. Push-up bras when off, industrial-strength support when on. Her curviness turned plump. And her hair, once a rich honey blonde, faded to mousiness. How narrow that window of flawlessness between the prime of adulthood and the onset of decay. And Chris was always working, and when he wasn't, he threw out little jibes that could only have had their origins with his dead girlfriend.

Pour the milk before the hot water.

Don't put a hot coffee cup on that surface.

Keep to the slow lane if you're not overtaking. Your car is a tip. Could you be so kind as to put your laundry into the basket instead of next to it? Put the milk back into the fridge when you're done. Is there any good reason why the salt and the pepper are never in the same place?

Chris's long hours, motherhood, the incessant subsidence of her body, the ever-present ghost of the dead girl between things began to have their own contraceptive affect. She seldom had the urge, and Chris seldom had the energy. And Tracy not yet thirty.

Still, men turned to look at her when she walked past. Not as frequently as before, but when they did the hungriness of their eyes on her back, on her butt, on her legs, was pleasantly sexual. Potent, too: the kind of power that Chris's money didn't give her, the kind of power that was hers alone, the kind of power that was diminished when Gabriel was in tow.

So, the first tentative squirts of Botox, at the corners of her eyes, between the brows. What was that – three, maybe four years off for a few minutes of pain? Chris didn't notice. Didn't notice it at all, in fact. Nor did he notice the lowered necklines, the raised hems.

And then the first run. Two kilometres in twenty-two minutes. Feeling uncoordinated and ridiculous as she tried to keep running, slowing to a shuffle instead. Barely able to put one foot in front of the other the following day. So she joined the gym, started spinning, swimming. But the more she swam, the larger and smoother her muscles grew. She switched to weights, worked out a programme with a personal trainer. His hands on her, positioning her limbs, her back, her shoulders. Such a cliché, wanting to fuck the personal trainer – and she would have, there and then. If he'd shown any interest, if he hadn't been gay.

Soon, she was running again. It was easier, now, and harder too as she pushed herself further each time. Two kilometres in fifteen minutes, then three, then, with an effort – a great effort, lungs burning, tearing – four. Sloughing off the weight, calves taking shape, thighs tautening. Her waist contracting. Muscle appearing where her belly button had once smiled when she sat. Cheekbones emerging. And the stares increasing, intensifying – no longer sneaky, but blatant.

And then Alex. Alexandra. Dark brunette to Tracy's blonde, Veronica to her Betty. Lunch after gym, a bottle of wine chased with a few mischievous shooters. Then Alex's flat – what acceptable reason, under what pretence? A frenetic groping in the afternoon light, a fiddling, then an intuitive understanding of each other's bodies. Illicit, taboo, dark sex – as terrifying and liberating and exhilarating as a new drug, so much so that she could not, would not allow herself to repeat it.

Next, squash-playing Jason and a series of silly liaisons. In his car on a mountain road in broad daylight. In restaurant toilets. Once, his foot between her thighs over lunch. But as soon as his wife began to suspect, he dropped Tracy and crawled off to destroy what evidence he could, avoided her in the gym, and then a week or two later quietly disappeared.

The day after she turned thirty-two, she scrutinised her profile and decided that the chin was too heavy. Worse, a shallow hammock had formed at her throat, and her nose had thickened somehow. Chris couldn't see what she was on about. Chris, the architect, who could spot the smallest imperfections in a ten-storey building but couldn't see them in his wife. His shrug of capitulation, his signing of a cheque. A day and a night in City Park Hospital, the pain of it sharp, cleansing, healthy. Concentrated in the bridge of her nose, in her chin, in the taut skin below. The retreat of time once the swelling had subsided and the bruising had faded. This time Chris did notice. He had looked at her intently, then taken her chin and gently turned her face to look at her profile. Stared for a moment, and though he complimented her, he sounded disappointed. As though he had hoped to see traces of Dalia somewhere.

The photograph she'd chanced upon: him, younger, whole, with an arm around a laughing Dalia. Squirrelled away in a bottom drawer, like porn.

He could keep his Dalia, his Jewish princess. She would have her own mementoes; they'd at least be alive, willing, grateful – and disposable. So there was Ben, Stieg the Swede, Derek, a flirtation with a Belinda she'd quickly closed off; Douglas, Richard, a disastrous one-off with someone else whose name she couldn't, didn't want to, remember. And now, Jono. Jono who had stuck, against all odds. Jono the Fat. Jono the Hardly Rich. Jono the Simple. Jono the Clown. Jono the Habit. Jono who was easy, happy, bouncy, light, cuddly, discreet; everything Chris wasn't. Jono, for whom she'd had her boobs done with Chris's money. Jono of the Shoes. The Botox top-ups, the gym work, now had a purpose, a focus.

And Jono couldn't believe his luck.

Chris

I decide to do nothing about Tracy and Jono, say nothing. Decide to keep the chin up, the lip stiff, to stick by all those things that my father told me would see one through hard times.

In reality, though, it's just too much effort to confront her. I don't have the energy to counter the denials, or for the showdown that will follow. The accusations and counter-accusations and recriminations and re-recriminations that will bounce between us, hurtful as half-bricks flung with intent, only to be picked up and flung back. All the stored, unsaid things that will suddenly surface: all the blind, snapping, sharp-toothed monsters from the deep that need never see the light of day.

And then there's Gabriel – the kid is already struggling. Struggling to read, struggling to walk upright, struggling to sit up straight. All he needs is more dumped on those skinny shoulders, thrown in his spotty face.

Then the splitting of things, because there would be no other way to banish the monsters once they'd surfaced. The splitting of the house that she thinks is hers and I think is mine. The dividing up of the accumulations of sixteen years of marriage, the things that start to crumble and flake the moment you buy them. Arguments over the valueless and therefore infinitely valuable bric-a-brac of sentiment and nostalgia. Which, actually, she could well keep, because the fucking of Jono has destroyed their worth already.

The splitting of Gabriel; how would we possibly do that?

There's the maths of it. Say I am a, Tracy b, Gabe c: If $a–b$, then

$$x = \frac{c}{a-b} - \infty$$

Find x.

But you cannot, because how do you calculate the infinity of loss when only some of it can be measured? The cash of it, the stuff, the uphill climb from Plumstead to Bishopscourt; nothing else.

So for now I will do nothing. The right time will come: it was Napoleon, I think, who said that when your enemy is committing suicide, you shouldn't lift a finger. Or in this case, when your enemy is fucking herself into a corner.

Something like that.

Meanwhile, Tracy, oblivious. I haven't tried to initiate sex with her for months, so not trying it now is hardly going to attract attention. Besides, the thought of sharing the mosh-pit with Jono, well. That intimate, private, secret place, now on time-share. Like eating off someone else's fork, only worse.

We simply continue not to talk to each other unless things cannot go left unsaid – important, practical things such as "We need milk", or "Don't forget to collect the post" or "Please chase the panel beaters; the free car-hire expires in ten days"; we simply continue to ensconce ourselves in opposite parts of the house, me in my study, she in her dressing room, Gabriel in his doorless limbo.

You can watch the age thing coming, but you can never pinpoint the precise moments of change that time brings. Take our – my? Tracy's? – plane trees, for example. They have leaves, and then they don't. And then they do again. There's no discernible mid-point. So I am unable to put my finger on the moment in the scrambled project-plan of my life when Tracy began to change. Was it at the altar, she pregnancy-plump, glowing as they say, me leaning on Barry's forearm so that I could do without the crutches during the ceremony? Was it when Gabriel arrived – beating fears of Down's Syndrome and blindness and deafness and oxygen deprivation to emerge a perfect waxy caterpillar? Or was it later, when she snuck her first Botox shots without discussion – or afterwards, when I wouldn't give her the pleasure of noticing? Or when she worked so hard to lose her femininity, her femaleness, at the gym, on the road. Her first half-marathon, a respectable 2:12, the joy of personal victory, the mounting agony of ITB like a kick to the knee with every step she took; perhaps it was then. Or did something snap or click into disturbed place during the shopping sessions, at the moment of feeling the crick in my neck while dragging shopping bags into the Land Rover, the Prado, the short-lived SLK, the buggered-up Range Rover? *Something* clicked, snapped; I don't know what, when.

I wish Tracy had laid Dalia to rest when I did. Tracy – my shrink, my lover: unable to see that my mourning was over once my outpourings had ended, when the bottle had run dry. Tracy, who every New Year's reminds me of the accident, and is then surprised at the effect on my mood. Tracy, who long ago began waving the red flag of Dalia at my advances until they petered out, stopped altogether.

Tracy, who decided not to abort or put up for adoption the tadpole that I'd implanted in her. "*I'm* adopted," I told her, "it'll be fine." Her face, aghast. "It's not an *it*." Our first fight, quickly doused by the mutual promise of marriage. And now: soft, gentle, loving Tracy, turned into cold steel on the inside, hard sinew and plastic on the outside, barely a woman, a Jono-fucking, unknown person.

I suppose the anniversary of my accident hasn't helped. If Dalia and my leg had been taken on, say, the 23rd of August or the 9th of May or the 12th of October, the date would have passed a dozen times without my remembering. But nobody forgets New Year's Eve, itself a celebration of death, the death of another year, always heralded by my observation: it's been three years, it's been seven years, it's been ten, seventeen, since. And *this* time, the nineteenth, I forgot, finally forgot all about it – until her bitter reminder. Of course Dalia was dear; I loved her as much as anyone can love at twenty. How would life have been with her, how would things have panned out? Would we have stayed together for ever? Would we have broken up by the following March? Probably. It's good while it lasts, but at that age there's always another flame to be lit, other faces that fascinate, other bodies to explore. Of course Dalia's death was painful, but after nineteen years, there have been other losses too.

Tracy, the Jono-fucker, one of them.

Yet it's Tracy the Necromancer who invokes Dalia when it's least appropriate and most hurtful, as if she's some kind of medium. A party trick that's found its way into our bed, into our hearts, into Gabriel, into everything, and stayed there.

I just don't know how, when, it all started.

I find myself wondering, at my usual 2 am wake-up, whether she's been unfaithful before, before this Jono. Which raises another question: what exactly is an affair? Do you have to fuck someone else to declare your lack of love to your partner? Or can you have an affair with the gym? Are the Ladies Who Lunch a metaphorical muff-dive? Is it an affair if you love Botox, golf, stamp-collecting more than your spouse? Perhaps Tracy has had all sorts of affairs – other men who parade sneering before my closed eyes, other pastimes, other things: inanimate objects like shoes and clothing, cosmetic surgery, needy friends who keep her satisfied.

Take her friend Joanne, divorced and broke, Joanne who lived with us for over a year and cried on the couch every night while Tracy counselled her and held her head when she puked after mixing too much of my gin with too many of her Valiums. Me squeak-thunking from one room to the next, not sure where I should be, what I should be doing. Tracy stumbling into bed with her knees tightly together and her ears numb, beyond hearing, because there was no libido-dampener or conversation-killer quite like Joanne's tears, Joanne's sour vomit, Joanne's snotty pile of issues.

But. I put my hand up.

I admit my affair with my work. My only excuse is that without it, at best I'd be working in a respectable firm for someone else. At worst, we'd still be living in Michael and Sylvia's old house with its peeling paint and leaky toilet, still be push-starting the Austin so that I could limp off to earn a buck so that Tracy could afford the odd magazine where she could peer longingly at images of the surgically enhanced. My work has been to give her everything she needs; hers has been to take more than I can give.

And what if there have been other men before Jono? If she's done it with one man, does it matter if she's done it with dozens – running partners or other women's husbands or shop assistants or fawning young pretty-boys? And what if I did confront her? Would she capitulate, cry her apologies, lift the corner of the forty-thousand-rand Persian for me to sweep the shattered bits of it all away? What if she begged forgiveness, promised to love me as she used to?

What then? Would I keep her?

I don't know.

And by now it's four o'clock.

The next day begins with Tracy bringing me coffee in bed. The rarity of this is enough to set bells ringing: something is coming – perhaps an admission, perhaps my stiff upper lip has not been convincing, or has been too apparent; perhaps she wants to move things along herself and will at last bring Jono into our bedroom.

I am wrong.

She turns her back to me, lifts up my Mr Happy T-shirt that she'd worn to bed. She parts her legs just enough for a glimpse of her labia with their cropped and spiky defences.

"What do you think?" she asks.

"Very nice," I say, thinking that this must be how Jono sees her while I'm writing cheques and drawing houses and office blocks, and I can't help wondering if she bends over and lets him take her, dog-style, goat-style, on the bed, on the couch, over the kitchen counter. What now?

She exhales, a sharp, impatient snort.

"No, *this*," she says, and under each butt cheek draws a line with her forefinger. "And this," and grabs two handfuls of buttock and jiggles them up and down, from side to side, affording me the briefest glimpse of a spider-like anus and again, the mocking labia.

This is Jono's territory, and yet: perhaps it's the sight of the forbidden land that brings on my erection.

"What am I looking at?" I ask when she stops, hoping, I suppose, for a repeat performance.

"My arse is dropping down the back of my legs," she says, turning to me and pulling her T-shirt down to cover the front of her.

I want to comment on the sudden modesty, don't.

"Looks fine to me," I say, guileless, cock-stand hiding against my stomach under the covers. I expect her to say something like, "Yes, it would, wouldn't it," but instead she swallows her retort. And then a whine, more subtle than Gabriel's – he is so much like her, has nothing of me other than his height – but a whine nonetheless.

"Chris, babe," she says, a phrase which always precedes a request for an indulgence. "Please. I can't be going around with my butt drooping to my knees. I've made an appointment with Dr Vonnegut and he's especially managed to fit me in so that he can check me out. You know how busy he is."

I don't know how busy he is. I don't know how many women's butts Dr Vonnegut – that other Dr Vonnegut, the local, lesser-known spinner of fiction and fable – is expected to peer up each day, how many pictures he must take of the bits his patients don't like any longer, how many times he has to upload them to his computer to reveal with a bit of instant CGI how those bits *could* look after he's been at them with the knife. And of course, another difficulty: the problem of Jono. My cash – a guess pegs the procedure at twenty, maybe thirty grand – so that Jono can have more booty, more fun when covering her like a husky or taking her like a missionary or swinging from the chandelier or whatever it is that the two of them get up to.

Whilst I.

The almost-confession in her phrase, "going around": evidence, but not enough.

Perhaps I need to reconsider my strategy of saying, doing, nothing. Because if there ever was a time, well. But I bite back, swallow the anger, continue innocent. "I don't know, Trace. Last year was a tough one – I don't need to lecture you on what the economy did to us architects. Maybe I'm not seeing what you're seeing, but for forty or fifty grand, I don't know how much better it could, um, turn out."

"Jesus, Chris. In December you were boasting how well the firm has weathered all that shit."

"Not as well as I thought. It was relative to what everyone else was doing. I sat with Shahid the other day, and it looks like I over-estimated things. But, hey, maybe there are other ways that you can raise the money," I say. In spite of myself. But she's not listening. She's *not* listening so hard that I could ask her right now how long she's been fucking Jono and she wouldn't hear.

But I don't.

"And then there's the thirty-five grand for the Range Rover."

That gets her attention, angrily. "What about insurance, for fuck's sake?" Reminding me of that untranslatable word in Afrikaans – skaamkwaad – as her guilt flares defensively into anger.

"The Rover is under-insured, they're not going to pay," I lie. A good, solid lie that I know she won't counter, won't know how to. A fantastic little lie.

So, silence.

Then I say, "Let me think about it." Which she hears perfectly, smiles as sweetly as she can manage, thanks me. Knows, I'm sure, that my response is a childish one because every child senses that a reply like that means no.

Tracy heads for the stairs to sort Gabriel's lunch, pulling her T-shirt down in case I am perving at her arse. After *that*. And me: the almost-confrontation, the suppressed adrenaline of it, has sustained my erection. So I hop to the bathroom, close the door, turn on the shower, hop onto the non-slip shower mat, take myself in hand. I try with conviction and effort to recall the glimpses of Tracy's secret bits but instead Murray's assistant with her coy cleavage comes to mind as I see again her short skirt, the long legs with their dancer's calves, smooth to the touch under the tights, as any clichéd male fantasy might have them. What might be beneath that skirt, beneath that top? What might be underneath all that, once it has been unbuttoned and unzipped by me, ripped off by her. What might be beneath all of that?

What might be.

Later, at the office, a call on my BlackBerry. A string of numbers I don't know and can't ignore.

"Hi, Chris, it's Alice." Not Alicia, not Alison, not Al.

Alice.

"Hi, Alice." Mouth dry in an instant, an absurd thought that she knows about the wank in the shower. I'd done the maths afterwards, while washing my hair: assume impotence at fifty-five; take an optimistic average of sex once every two months if I was prepared to share that Jono-contaminated passage; just eighty-four orgasms before everything gave in, before prescriptions for Viagra. But only if I was ever going to fuck her again, which I am not. So the correct answer to my calculations: zero.

$84x = 0$ when $x = 0$. A simple-enough sum.

While Jono, well. While Jono beavers away, so to speak.

"How's your day?" Alice asks.

"Busy," I reply.

"Shit. I was hoping that we could meet. I think our brief to you, um," a pause for effect, "needed a bit of help, so I've got something to give you."

"I have a meeting right now, but from twelve, well, I have a two-thirty, but that's internal so I can move it." Jesus. I'm babbling. I don't babble, but right now I am. Perhaps simply relief at not being bust for using her as wank-fodder, perhaps just a second injection of adrenaline that day.

She sounds disappointed. "Damn, I was hoping for two-thirty."

"Like I said, I can move it. Do you want to come here?"

"Can we do lunch somewhere? I'm running all day, I'll be starving by then."

Memory will play tricks: you don't have to be Sylvia to know this. Alice arrives for lunch – late. She's wearing jeans and sneakers that stumpify her long boardroom legs. A faded sleeveless top, high-necked, cleavage-free, with stains at the armpits. Her hair is strangely kinked, not very clean. The make-up gone. I don't recognise her until she stands over me at the table, says "Hi, Chris." I wonder what I was seeing in the shower earlier, am annoyed that I suggested this prissy place for lunch.

But still.

Still, I could so easily close my eyes to those sneaker-shortened legs and bury my nose in one of her damp armpits. Scoop her up into our shared absence of baggage, devour what I've gathered and the consequences be damned.

I start standing up. Used to people saying that I please shouldn't worry to, I don't put much effort into it. But Alice makes me go the whole way. I put out my hand, she ignores it, puts down the folder she's been carrying under her arm, stands on her toes to give me a Continental air-kiss on each cheek. I get a whiff of her juices, sweat almost fruity with a hint of departing perfume. I look at the folder as I sit: there's a dampness on the spine where it pressed up under her arm; I resist the temptation to pick it up and sniff it, lick it even.

"Sorry, site-visit day today." She flaps her hands at her armpits and blows through pursed lips as she sits. "I probably smell like a sheep."

"And you have hat-hair too," I say.

"Oh my God, now you tell me. Those hard-hats just do not make for a good look." She pushes her fingers through her hair from her temples to her crown, shakes her head. "Better?"

It's made no difference. "Absolutely," I say.

I find myself embarrassed by the ponciness of the restaurant. I'm a regular; the waiters know me by name. It's usually a good place to make clients feel appreciated; but Alice I'm not so sure about. We could have done McDonald's in the car and she'd have been fine.

A waiter appears. "Drinks, Mr Hayes?" he asks. I look at Alice.

"You know what? It's a late lunch and I think I'll give Mr Murray a skip for the rest of the day. I'll have a Heineken, please."

The waiter looks at me, expecting my usual mineral water order.

"Make that two, Smiley."

Alice waits until he's gone. "Smiley?" she says, leaning forward. "That can't be for real, can it?" Her eyebrows are perfect arches; I don't know how they shoot up so high, find myself hoping that Tracy never sees them, or else.

"It is too. And that guy over there is his brother Happy."

"No."

"Yes. They've both been here for twenty years or so. Something of an institution."

"So you come here often?"

Why do I back-pedal? I know there's embarrassment in my shrug. "Clients like it," I say. "And I like that it looks out over the sea."

"I love it. Love the kind of seventies shabby-chic. Authentic. You couldn't pull it off properly if you tried."

Alice opens the menu, skims through it hungrily. I look around the restaurant with her eyes in my head. Notice the carved, heavy chairs, the old-world livery of the serving staff – burgundy jackets with Nehru collars for the waiters, burnt orange for the wine stewards; no sniffy sommeliers here. I notice the softly fraying corners of the linen tablecloths, the tired drape of velvet curtains too heavy for the heat of the day, the view of Jeeps and surfboards and bleached blondes and the deep blues and bright whites of the wind-tossed ocean beyond.

The wine steward brings the beers. Nose upturned because we haven't ordered a decent wine instead. Walks off, stiff-legged. Smiley takes his cue and appears. Alice orders for herself, lots, foreign words spoken clearly. I order my regular meal. She pushes aside the beer glass, raises her bottle to toast me. I raise mine, aim it at hers.

"No, no, no," she says, pulling away. "You have to look me in the eyes. Otherwise it's bad luck."

"How can I clink your beer if I'm looking at you?"

"Instinct," she says.

I look her in the eyes. Cat green. We toast again. It works. "Yum," she says after she drinks.

She's managed to nail Murray down to a style, to function, to budget. To rental per square metre, turnover clauses, to parking rates. It takes her five, maybe seven minutes to relay this to me.

"And that's the bones of it," she concludes. "It's all in the spreadsheets in the file. I'll mail everything to you as well, along with a few more pics for style reference that I've got Anton to commit to. I've told him that if he changes anything I'll kick him in the kneecap and then resign, so go with it. He wouldn't dare, anyway."

Because you're fucking him, I want to say, but don't.

She takes a breath, smiles, changes key. "So, Mr Hayes," she says, dangling her empty Heineken from thumb and forefinger. "What about you?"

I drink from my half-full beer. Buying thinking time.

"Me?" I say. This girl-woman is turning me into Gabriel, into someone inept.

"Yes, you, Chris Hayes." She's teasing, smiling with those white teeth, arching those eyebrows. Her lips are full, naturally full, Tracy's before the Botox gave her a duckish pout, stopped her almost from smiling at all.

"Well, I'm an architect," I say, slowly, hamming it up, buying time to think up an answer that she might want to hear.

"And?"

"Married." A warning, unheeded.

"Kids?" she says, still smiling, asking with those eyebrows.

"Gabriel."

"And how old is Gabriel?" She catches the wine steward's eye, indicates two more Heinekens.

"Almost as old as you."

"Rubbish."

"He's sixteen."

She doesn't respond to the silly flirtation: the playfully arched eyebrows flicker into a brief frown. She may be ten or eleven years younger than me, but she is not a child.

"So you've been married, what, sixteen or seventeen years?"

"Sixteen."

She narrows her eyes, doing the maths.

"And how has sixteen years of marriage treated you?"

I'm saved by Smiley and the wine steward, who arrive at the same time. They vie for position at the table. There's a play for power at every level.

"Brilliant," Alice says as Smiley serves. "I could eat a horse."

We eat.

And talk, mostly about the development.

Alice orders more beer.

And when we finish eating, she orders two more.

The beer makes it easy for me say things that are mine to keep, mine to hide and lock away. I throw them out not because I'm forced to, but because this delightful, curious person has asked, and I find I want to let them out. They are tiny spurts of steam from a pressurised boiler. Alice orders more beer. And rephrases the question I'd avoided earlier.

"So, Chris Hayes, how does life find you?"

"Right now, pissed, actually."

"Well, you should be happy too. You have a fantastic business, and it sounds like you've got a healthy son, a beautiful wife. More cash than Jesus, I guess. I hope I'm in the same place when I'm your age."

Your age.

The abyss between twenty-sevenish and thirty-nine – forty minus a month or so, actually.

"Be careful what you wish for," I say.

"Wow," she replies, looks down at her beer. "Well, what do you want? Like, what can anyone want when they have everything?"

A Land Rover and a hut on a beach, no less than four hours from anywhere else. You.

"Whatever they don't have, I suppose. A yacht. A small vineyard. A game farm, a cottage on a Greek island. The usual."

"Not very sustainable. Financially, I mean."

I shrug. Want to say I couldn't care less. Needn't care less.

"Or imaginative." She laughs, takes a long sip of her Heineken.

I smile at this brazen, brash, happy girl. Do not lose this, ever, I want to say. So I do.

"Don't ever lose this thing of yours," I say.

"What thing?"

"Your cheerful thing. Your curious thing. Your happy, carefree, in-your-face thing. Your put-people-at-ease thing."

"That's more than one thing," she says. And then, a switch flips somewhere inside her – the too-deep, too-heavy, old-guy-full-of-beer warning switch. She glances at her Swatch. "Oh my gosh, I have to go."

"Now? To the office?"

"No, good God. I'm going out tonight so I better get home and have a beauty sleep. All this Heineken you've been forcing on me, yowzer. Need to make myself pretty for tonight – it's Phuza Thursday. Party party."

Yowzer. Phuza Thursday. Party party. Ten, eleven years the difference. So old, and so young. I see then, see that this creature has a life beyond business lunches and shopping-mall briefs, a young life when she's not bunking work for a free lunch with a one-legged old guy for the five-minute task of handing over a file. And there's a boyfriend, probably, obviously. Friends who love her frankness, her light teases. I instantly hate them all. The boys fawning, pawing; the girls bantering, full of secret code that goes back to varsity, college, high school, a time far beyond me.

Alice is digging in her purse, trying to hold up the falling curtain of hair at the same time. I tell her to put it away, that the next one will be on her.

Because maybe, that.

I hope that.

And then, a closer, warmer, slightly less fragrant hug. A kiss on my cheek, perhaps a second longer than it needs to be, but maybe it's the beer distorting the way time works.

"Are you okay to drive?" I ask. Hoping to give a lift, to prolong this somehow, though I should hardly be driving myself.

"Don't need to. I live up the road, walked here."

"Cheers, Alice."

"Goodbye, Mr Hayes," she sings.

Sassy, flippant. The formality of "Chris", the flirtation of "Mr Hayes". How different it used to be. I replay her words in my head as I leave the cool dinge of the restaurant, but they quickly lose their music and take on the sing-song cadence of a classroom full of pupils: "Good – bye – Mis – ter – Hayes."

Unlike normal people, I'm unable to check my messages and missed calls on my way to the car. So I'm sitting in its baking interior when I take a look. A pile of e-mails that will have to wait. The office, umpteen missed calls. And a missed call from Marietjie – who is–? – and I remember before I've formed the question and call her back.

"I have good news and bad news," she says when she answers. Probably my most-hated preamble. I wait for her to offer me the choice of which option I'd like to hear first, but thankfully she doesn't.

"The bad news is that your biological father is deceased. The good news is that I've traced your mother, who is very much alive."

I can hear the "But" in her voice, say it for her.

"But?"

"But there's more bad news, I'm afraid. She doesn't want to meet with you."

Gabriel

Barbara was in touch on Facebook and BlackBerry, as long as the chat was light – music, movies, their three mutual friends.

Gabriel wrote, drew. He sent her short poems:

The world walks across my dreams

My broken roots

Crushing them to dust under hobnailed boots . . .

He sent drawings too. Behind them all was the memory of New Year's Eve, or rather the memory of the memory. Love and deprivation reinforced each other, and the more he wooed her with his words, his pictures, the more he was sure he loved her. And the less she responded.

One cool April afternoon, band practice. He'd been invited as a spectator, picked up the bass that nobody else wanted to play. He didn't really know what to do with it, so George the Dog explained the basics – just watch and play the E-string wherever the bar chords go – and so he started, half a beat behind, then a quarter, then an eighth, and eventually in time. Watched, put to use the ear he didn't know he had. Took the bass home along with a small amp, was permitted to play only when Tracy was out. He taught himself scales, how to rearrange them, bend them, make them say what he wanted. Then, a memorable day: Chaplin – a moniker in honour of his upside-down mouth and droopy eyes – Chaplin fucked up on the lead riff, got lost, stopped, so Gabriel took over with a roaring, rumbling bass solo, fingers flying, stopped for four beats to take in the silent gaping, began again in the style of cheesy eighties' slap-bass, Frankie Goes To Hollywood. Loved the astonishment of the other band members.

He called Barbara to share his triumph. She listened until the apathy of her murmurs slowed his gushing to a trickle.

"What's up, Barbs?" he asked, and wished he hadn't; the question invited Barbara – Barbara the Flame, Barbara of New Year's Eve – to come forth with a new bit of information. She was tired of arty types, she said, quite liked buff guys these days, jock types with big shoulders and six-packs. She used words like ripped, pumped, shredded, and told Gabriel that she had in fact met someone just like that. She was sure he'd understand, and what with the distance between Cape Town and Joburg it couldn't really last anyway, could it?

And then she said progressively less until she said nothing at all and the phone went dead.

Then she quietly disappeared from Facebook, from her cellphone that rang unanswered every time Gabriel called, until later a recorded voice said – in an unnecessarily cold way, Gabriel thought – that the number he had dialled was no longer in use. The girl had vanished, had erased herself from the digital universe, from Gabriel's analogue life.

So Gabriel sulked for a few weeks, certain that he could cut into the girl's silence with his own, that by saying nothing he would be telling her everything.

He invoked her memory whenever an erection prompted, whenever a wisp of braai-smoke drifted his way. He tried to remember her touch by

106

staring at the postcard-sized "Temptation of St Anthony" stuck to his wall. Once, forced to accompany Tracy to the mall, he smelled Barbara's perfume and homed in on its source – a middle-aged woman in pearls and too-tight jeans. Did Barbara share perfume with her mother? The thought was disturbing, though he wasn't sure why.

Then one Sunday morning he woke up, convinced that his pining must at last have reached her in some telekinetic way. He checked his phone and Facebook, but there was nothing. He went to the bathroom, took off his shirt and stood in front of the mirror. Was met with a violent rash of acne. A skeletal body topped by a large head on a thin stalk. Stark ribs, no pecs. Tent-pole arms, the girly wings of protruding hip-bones. A spill of fine hair issuing from his navel and falling to his groin. Happily the reflection ended there, did not show his broomstick legs, his large pale feet.

But it was enough.

He announced to Tracy that he wanted to join the gym. Her eyes widened for an instant and he wondered if she was going to laugh. She didn't, though. Instead, she drove him to the gym, and saw to it that forms were filled out and signed and a year's membership paid in advance. Took him to a sports store and had him kitted out in trainers, shorts, bright slimy-feeling tops which, she carefully explained, were made of high-tech fibres designed to fleck the sweat from his body.

Driving home with his mother, he felt stronger already, as if this was the first step in winning Barbara back, as if it would help him reach into her silence to connect once more.

He began on the treadmill, managing five minutes of hang-headed heavy breathing, watching his feet in their too-clean trainers slog along the rubber runner until he simply had to get off – shaking, rasping, embarrassed.

In time he managed ten, then fifteen minutes.

Twenty. Forty.

A month on, the trainers had lost their novice look, had taken on a bit of character, his head no longer too heavy for his neck to bear.

A magical retreat of the acne, not total, but substantial.

And then a few weights to build bulk. The flush of embarrassment and the red of effort indistinguishable. They're not watching me, he intoned: on the up "They're not" and on the down "watching me", until the burn and the pain of it left him with no option but to stop. But he came back for more, always came back for more. Until one day a personal trainer, blonde and short and strong and blue-eyed, smiled at him pleasantly, came over and gave him a few pointers. Looked back and winked as she walked off. A wink that drove Barbara into retreat, even if only for a moment.

It took his father ages to notice, of course, not that Gabriel was doing it for Chris. When he did notice he tried to correct what Gabriel was doing, giving advice, instruction, without first investigating the objectives. Gabriel wrote the shortest of poems:

My Father

My father is trying.

Very trying.

And then, muscle – not buff and bulging, but strong, ropey. Pecs chiselled, tight and neat, deltoids broadening his shoulders, the lats adding their own visual appeal. Abs so close to the skin you could see their striations. Body fat ten, maybe twelve per cent.

Despite the early winter chill, he took to playing bass with his shirt off, at once appreciating the looks from the girls who came to watch the band jam and deflecting them: every flattery threatened to sever the connection to Barbara, to betray the fidelity that was by now nothing more than a matter of personal pride.

He planned longer runs on the neighbourhood roads, powering up steep inclines, a lazy lope downhill to recover, a few steps of flat, and then another incline. Each imperfection in the surface, each change in the wind or the temperature was another small dragon to be slayed: treadmills, he decided, were for beginners and huffing old men in baggy shorts and gym moms in Lycra. He began to rise earlier than his father, far earlier than his mother. Ran in the morning, through the morning cold, through sheets of rain and luminous dawns when, if he ran far enough up the mountain, he could see the snow on distant peaks to the north, and the agitated ocean to the south. Started running to the gym as a warm-up to his weights session, running home to cool down. Schultz barking his demand from behind the high wall to join the run.

An overheard conversation that made him smile. Father: "I think it's becoming a little obsessive." Mother: "It's good for him, don't piss on that parade as well." Father: "So an hour of running and two hours of gym five, six days a week is okay?" Mother: "Works for me. You should try it."

And one Saturday morning, the automatic instruction from his father: "Close the gate behind you." The words dulled by their many repetitions, and Gabriel stretching, opening the gate and running off. His return a few minutes later, tears streaking his face, the bloodied body of Schultz in his arms. Sensing freedom, the dog had slipped through the unsecured gate, scampered on his old legs after the scent of Gabriel, was hit by an X5 hurrying home from the shops.

The warmth of the dog, perhaps not dead after all. Gabriel dropped to his knees on the lawn, set down the dog, bent over it, lifted its head. The unresponsive weight, the hazed and unfocused eyes told him what he needed to know. He lay Schultz's head down gently, raised his bloody hands to his face, let out a howl.

"Jesus, Gabriel," his father said from the portico. His mother appeared, looked at Gabriel and the blood on his white vest, leaned against the doorway for support and put her hands to her face and began to sob.

"I'm so sorry," Gabriel howled, scrubbing his bloody hands through his hair, a silvery rope of snot sliding from his nose. His tears, the dog's blood. "I'm so sorry," he said again, and again and again. Then his father by his side, hugging the boy, hugging until Gabriel's resistance was overcome, hugging until the boy's taut body folded into his own, shook with the effort of his tears.

"It's okay, it's okay," Chris said, holding Gabriel while he heaved. "It's not your fault."

When, of course, it was.

His father put the last of Schultz into a garbage bag, hoisted the surprising weight into the Range Rover, took it to the vet for disposal, returned to find Gabriel showered, changed into jeans and a sweatshirt, sitting at the kitchen counter with his forehead on his arm. Fresh tears, then his father's hand on his back, rubbing it.

"Where did it happen?" he asked.

Gabriel raised his head just enough to look at his father. "Silvertree Avenue. I didn't know he was behind me. Just heard brakes and a thump."

"It's a blind rise. People always drive too fast up there even though they can't see what's ahead."

Gabriel sat up. "I'm so sorry, Dad," he said, looking down at the kitchen counter. "I should have closed the gate." And Chris not disagreeing, patting his son's back briefly and clunking off on his crutches.

And then Tracy, Mom, *the* Mom, began agreeing to every arrangement, any plan of Gabe's, no matter how loose – the kind of plans that would have elicited a flat negative from Chris – as long as he was occupied, it seemed to him, so that Tracy could growl off in the Range Rover. And Dad, *the* Dad, the über control freak, noticing nothing, somehow with his head so wound into himself – work, Gabriel supposed, always work – that if the house had fallen in, if Schultz had reappeared reciting Shakespeare, if a protesting Buddhist monk had set himself alight beside the swimming pool, Chris would not have noticed.

On an unseasonably warm July afternoon, Lynn gave Gabriel a ride home, earlier than usual and in a rush because Peter had a choir recital. Lynn all tunnel-visioned and racing because precious Peter was on the verge of being late for his squeaky Handel harmonies, not waiting for the Hayes gate to open, simply letting Gabriel out of the Cayenne and roaring off with her nose almost touching the steering wheel. There was nobody home. It was Martha's day off, Chris was at work, Tracy somewhere else. Gabriel walking along the garden wall with its ramparts of electrified fencing that kept the family safe, knowing he'd be fried if he tried to climb over, and even if he managed it, knowing he'd still not be able to get into the house. So he sat down on the verge, locked out of the castle, scratching through his lunchbox and found bits of biscuit, a hot mouthful of sour juice in the water bottle . . . and two hours later Tracy coming home, make-up not so made up any more, so terribly sorry that she rubbed calamine lotion on his sunburned face and fried him a steak herself – rare, just how he liked it – and let him drink Coke until he shook, and then did the reverse-bribe by casually suggesting that his father needn't know about this. And Gabriel, dyslexic but not stupid: the cogs of Tracy's strategy falling into place, his own strategy one of secrecy and silence.

Chris and Tracy

And then we celebrate my fortieth, even though it's only July, even though the actual day is months down the line. Me pretending to be okay with the non-date. And besides, when the day does come: $2012y - 1972y = 14{,}600d$. Find the true value of d, of each and every day of a life: find the weight of it in kilograms or bushels or feathers.

We'd discussed a week in Tuscany or Thailand to mark this surprisingly achievable milestone, but eventually decided that something with friends, something local, would do. Would do because it meant only two or three hours of travelling together, Tracy and I, not the fifteen or twenty a more exotic location would require. And between the lines: the presence of others would provide the necessary padding between us. So Tracy confirmed a booking at an exclusive lodge, conveniently during school holidays; with the date sorted, there was one less thing to worry about.

Tracy organises everything; all I have to do is pay the bills, instruct Gabe on how to pack the Range Rover, drive them both for the few hours it takes to get to the Cederberg where we'll meet Barry and Lynn and Tony and Julie La Vita. We leave an hour later than I'd planned – Tracy packing and repacking, dressing and undressing and re-dressing – and we are already silent, the three of us, before we have left the driveway, Gabriel with his iPod, Tracy Facebooking and messaging and whatever else – to whomever else – on her BlackBerry.

Me turning over Marietjie's news: a fire-heated rock that I can't grasp, can't put down – I am angry with *Her*, of course: but more than that, I don't understand why there is no desire to close the circle *She* opened – along with her legs – forty, almost forty-one, years ago. I suppose I expected eagerness and excitement, willingness at worst.

But.

I turn on the radio, flick through the lather of talk shows and commercial music and religious broadcasts and dull little community transmissions, switch to the CD player where I'd had the good sense to replace the Madonna and Mariah Carey schlock with my music before we left. Audioslave, Chris Cornell at his choleric best. Tracy doesn't look up from her phone, reaches out, turns it down. I turn it up again – though just a notch – on the steering-wheel control. Don't have the heart for a silly battle; there are others more serious to wage.

We pass through the wealthy suburbs that lie in the cool shadow of the mountain, head through lower Observatory where the wind always blows, past the shabbiness of Valkenberg mental hospital, its hundred-year-old design and dim windows and streaks of pigeon shit a movie cliché, the deranged trees in its grounds bowing at forty-five degrees before the southeaster, symbols of a determinism that has bent some people into madness and others not, has seen some certified while the rest of us are allowed to roam free.

We pass the ugliness of industry marring the shoreline of Table Bay, the lower reaches of the mountain behind us hidden behind a skirt of brown diesel haze. Through a rash of new urban sprawl, cloned homes on sandy plots, dripping details of misinterpreted Tuscany – Jerryspringerville, Ivan calls it – a place where Tony's pizza outlets thrive, and then on to Blouberg, where we eventually shake off the tentacles of the city and ascend the hills of the hinterland. Hills shorn after the harvest, awaiting the heavier winter rains. The earth black and rich: the Swartland.

We are five minutes past a filling station, its red-and-blue branding having announced fuel and hamburgers and rest rooms, when Tracy looks up from her BlackBerry and blinks at the bright reality of the world beyond.

"I need to pee," she says. I wonder if she does this on purpose: perhaps her plan is to drive me mad, have me committed to the pseudo-Gothic confines of the hospital we passed earlier so that she can claim her inheritance and with Jono can rollick and gambol and fuck on a bed made up of sheets and duvets stitched together from my money, the cash and the share certificates cosy enough linen. I slow down, pull onto the shoulder, stop to check the traffic before I swing around. There are sheep in a stony field beside us, dusty and dirty-bummed, gnawing at the soil.

"I'm not pissing out here." Pure class, my Tracy.

In the mirror I watch an oily old Opel approach, wait for it to pass. There are easily eight or nine people squeezed into it, bulging through the open windows, fighting with their fellows for a gulp of winter air. The Opel is an old red GSI, dangerously powerful in its day, and despite the load it carries and the smoke that billows from its exhaust, the driver is making the most of its remaining kilowatts. I hear the stressed engine and bass beats flattening in pitch as it passes, check the road ahead, do a U-turn, head back to the petrol station. Stop under a stretch of shade cloth. Open the door into the windswept day. Give Gabe money and send him to the shop to buy water and a few soft drinks. Watch Tracy totter towards the Ladies' on her heels, the crisp wind tugging at her filmy skirt and threatening to blow it up over her hips.

Fifteen kilometres further on, I see the carcass of a blown tyre in my lane. I move our cool cocoon of steel and leather and tinted glass into the oncoming lane. Beyond the tyre, torn rubber lies like a trail of breadcrumbs. Then, a number plate – an old yellow one, metal, twisted – on the barrier line as we head up a rise. Something else ahead – a bumper, along with part of a fender, perhaps. I slow to sixty from a hundred and forty, then to thirty. Tracy and Gabriel sense the change in momentum. Tracy looks up, Gabriel leans forwards between our seats. Broken glass litters the trail of debris in the road, a wing mirror. I slow down a little more, and as we crest the rise I see the remnants of the old red Opel smacked up against a tree on the opposite side of the road. It is on its side, the driver's side; the roof has moulded itself around the trunk of the tree. Smoke emerges from its undertray, fluids ooze from its injured shell, the raised rear wheel spins slowly, eccentric on its hub. Some of its occupants lie on the road, some on the gravel of the shoulder. Cheap luggage, plastic bags, a lone shoe – there are always lone shoes – a doll, I hope it is, swaddled in a white cloth; disconnected debris, items meaningless, morbid in their banality. The music is still pumping, some repetitive dance track, the heavy bass causing the speakers to buzz.

There is a Traffic Department vehicle in the shade of a eucalyptus on the left – the road is notorious for speedsters, and so also notorious for traffic officers who hide out around corners and over blind hills to catch the unwary. One of the officers is in the road. He darts this way and that and reaches for something at his hip that isn't there and darts back to his vehicle from which a second cop is emerging. He holds the handset of a radio to his mouth. Coffee slops onto his trousers from the Thermos cap in his other hand. I imagine the officials only minutes ago sitting quietly waiting for offenders to offend, sipping coffee from shared flasks, talking family or rugby or fishing, and then the shock of a cartwheeling Opel, broken glass and baggage and passengers and then just smoke and screams and blood and lubricants and fuel and the back wheel spinning to the bass beat.

I slow to a crawl, pick a route through the mess. None of us says anything; we have silently agreed that it would be pointless to stop. Not one of us with any medical training, after all; a man on crutches and a blonde in heels and a pale teenaged boy would be more of a hindrance, surely, than a help. Then a wild howl, an unfettered scream that penetrates the insulation of the Range Rover. Tracy reaches out and turns up the last of Chris Cornell. Once clear of the carnage, I accelerate gently to a hundred and twenty, stay at the limit. In the mirror I can see Gabriel twisted in his seat to look out of the Rover's rear window. Tracy is back at the BlackBerry, back to her tweeting or SMSing or messaging or Facebooking or whatever. Gabriel turns to face the front again, says "Jesus," puts his earbuds back into his ears. And as she turns the music down again, Tracy says, an automatic throwback to something long lost: "Don't say 'Jesus', Gabriel."

Is that the best this little family can manage – a one-word prayer that is uttered as an expletive and not as a prayer at all? I suppose it is. Beside me, Tracy is poking at her phone; in the rear-view mirror I see Gabriel slump down in the seat and fiddle with his iPod.

All back to normal, then.

I am agitated when we arrive. The almost-silent journey, punctuated only by toilet calls, with Gabe's mild expletive, the accident scene – the fragility, the sudden finality of it: people barrelling along with their hips and elbows pressing against each other, happy to sweat it out to get to where they are going, then a weakness in the tyre wall. And me and accidents, well.

Barry and Lynn have already checked in. They sit on the veranda of the lodge, Lynn with a perspiring rock shandy at her elbow, Barry with a gin and tonic. I can tell from the shine in his eyes that it's not his first. A brief flash of irritation – this is my invitation, my treat; it would have been polite to wait, but. This is Barry, for goodness' sake, not some freeloading stranger. Then the sight of his drink makes me want one too; the thought of the sharp, sour coolness of it pushes away the silence of the journey and the lingering images of the accident, so I leave Tracy to bark orders at the porter and go to the rooms with Gabe and do whatever it is they each have to do there.

I'm considering a second gin when Gabe shows up with Peter in tow, towels flung over their shoulders and wearing board shorts, despite the cooling evening. Gabriel looking rangy, wiry, a residual sprinkle of pimples across his back; Peter pink in the evening cold, fat little-boy tits with inverted nipples, a deep dark hole where his navel should have been. They wave, head for the pool.

An hour later, Tracy emerges – showered, dressed in white, freshly made up. I'm on my third gin, and feeling it. Barry has slowed down, drinking only to keep himself in the tipsy zone; Tracy orders a double, and so does Lynn. The drinks have just been served when the La Vitas arrive. They apologise for being late, explain that the road had been closed for an hour because of an accident.

"An accident?" Tracy says. "They closed the whole road for an *accident*?"

I look at her, but she is looking at Tony, then at Julie. I know she can feel my eyes on the side of her face, but she doesn't give in, doesn't turn to me.

"Looked bad," Tony says. "I think people died. They had to do a forensic thing and clean up before they could let anyone through. Ambulances and rescue vehicles and cops all over the place."

"That's awful," Tracy said, sipping her gin and tonic. "Those poor people."

Julie has her eyes closed, a hand over her mouth, looks like she's about to cry. Lynn stands up, but Julie flaps her away. "I'm fine," she says, "fine." But then she begins to sob and Tony leads her away and the rest of us sit and stare at our drinks.

Tracy brightens in her brittle Tracy way. She looks at me, challenging. "Well, we can't let that spoil Chris's birthday, so bottoms up, everyone." She raises her glass in a cursory toast, then takes a sip.

"I'll drink to that," Barry says. "Here's to the big day tomorrow." We drink. We talk about nothing in particular; I am distantly amazed at how words, so many words, can be contrived and woven and strung together to say so very little.

The La Vitas return; Julie has composed herself. Lynn chases the boys from the pool; they are blue with cold, and she sends them off to change for dinner. We eat, a subdued meal – Barry manages only one bottle of wine between himself. We agree that with the game drive early the next morning, it will be a long day, one to remember: we should all get a good night's rest.

There are no lions here, no hyenas, just the rare mountain leopard, an elusive and nocturnal creature that for the most part has been shot to near-extinction by the local farmers; it's more myth than flesh and fur. We have no hope of spotting one from the back of a grumbling game vehicle in broad daylight. There are no other predators, nor elephant, hippo, rhino, buffalo, but still the ranger has a rifle mounted on the dashboard of the vehicle. It's a modified old Land Rover 110, topless, with metal tubes that support a canvas canopy, and a windscreen that folds down. There's a CB radio set, mostly silent, also bolted to the dashboard. The vehicle even has a tracker's seat, for God's sake, attached to the bonnet. The ranger drives us around pretending excitement at docile zebra and skittish bontebok that we come across. He is of Khoisan descent, he tells us, his eyes and prominent cheekbones bearing witness to his claim. He introduces himself, his name a collection of clicks that sound like a pebble clattering down stairs, and he laughs when we try and pronounce it, suggests we stick with "Jonas". Asks us how things are in London, and when Barry tells him to watch more Sky News to tune in to the accent he looks baffled and doesn't believe that there are people from Cape Town with accents as larney as ours. I sense that his words are rehearsed, that at some point it had been an honest mistake that led to the discovery that some locals find it flattering to be taken for Britons.

Then he stops the vehicle, a little more suddenly than necessary, invites us to alight so that he can show us the spoor of gemsbok in the sand. He takes up a stick, draws a circle around the larger of the prints. "Adult male, five years old, a big one, about two-fifty or two-seventy kilograms. This one here" – another circle – "female, three years old. And here – a young one, born last spring. They're going for water; come, we'll find them." He could be talking complete shit of course – how would any of us know? – but his showmanship is rewarded with a trio of gemsbok at a watering hole three minutes further on. The antelope hear the vehicle, raise their heads, stand still as the guide turns the engine off; only their withers twitch, their ears independent radar dishes scanning for danger. The watering hole is man-made, fed by a pipe that leads from a low concrete structure housing a borehole. Access to the dam is spoor-dimpled, with scat peppering the sandy beach. Barry coughs; it's enough to make the gemsbok canter off: they don't wait to investigate.

"We got them from Namibia," our guide says as he drives us away. "They're still very nervous – there's lions there, desert lions. Maybe in a year's time they won't be afraid." He turns to look at Gabriel, wedged with

Peter between Tracy and Barry in the middle seat. "They will 'chill'," he says with a wink at my son. The man's eyes are red; I wonder if he is completely sober.

We get out, stretch our legs. In the dawn light we have seen a couple of zebra, the promise of a giraffe in the distance, various antelope. It's Africa, of course, but not: it's a sanitised slice that probably provides enough to keep the real Brits happy, but I am disappointed. Up north, one's enjoyment is sharpened by the genuine prospect of seeing lions, perhaps even a kill; the possibility of a herd of buffalo engulfing your vehicle like a rank black river, or elephants appearing out of the moonlight, silent grey ghosts moving through the mopani trees. But here there's just fynbos scrub; here there is no acacia. Here, in this pretend-Africa, the night brings a thin damp northwester that threatens rain; in the bushveld, winter nights are still, crisply cold. And there's seldom a moment when you don't hear the faraway yip of hyena, the rhythmic grunting of a lion.

But, here we are.

The guide has unpacked a folding table from the back of the vehicle. He spreads it with a white cloth, and from various boxes and containers conjures filter coffee, milk, sugar, croissants, jam, rusks. Crockery and cutlery. And with a final flourish, bottles of fresh orange juice and two bottles of Bollinger. I remember that it's my birthday – my un-birthday, my pretend-forty years on the planet – and suddenly, so do the rest, hugging and kissing and back-slapping and asking me if I've broken my fingers or am I going to open the fucking champagne already. I do, the pop of it frightening birds from a nearby bush. Pour for everyone, Gabe and Peter too. Gabe sniffs, sips, pulls a sour face, quietly puts down the drink; Peter sips, sips again more deeply, holds on to his glass. One bottle would have been enough, but Barry opens the next one – again, that pinprick of irritation at the guest playing host – tops up everyone, inverting the ratio of champagne to orange juice so that the champagne is only slightly discoloured. The guide begins to pack up; we're ready to leave but Lynn needs to pee, so Barry escorts her behind a cloud of bushes – and comes hurtling out, screaming something about lions. Then Lynn, terrified, hopping desperately along behind him, trying to run and pull up her panties and her jeans at the same time and as she gets them up a dark stain of wet between her thighs, spreading to her knees. Barry by now helpless with laughter, his butt on the running-board of the vehicle, hands on his knees. Tony laughing but not meaning it. Tracy saying, "Jesus, Barry, grow up," and pouring the last of her champagne onto the ground. Julie handing Lynn a blanket from the vehicle to wrap around her waist. Gabriel not knowing where to look, Peter pinching the bridge of his nose, eyes squeezed shut, facing the bush on the other side of the vehicle. Jonas, whom I was beginning not to like, efficiently completes the packing, climbs into the vehicle, shouts, "All aboard, ladies and gentlemen," as though nothing has happened. Lynn, clumsy in her blanket, takes Barry's seat, points wordlessly at the seat next to the guide and the chastened Barry moves to the front.

Halfway back to the lodge, we're still silent, bored with antelope and awkward with the residue of Barry's prank, when Lynn raises a hand high above her shoulder and brings it down to clobber Barry on the back of his head. Barry almost plants his face into the rifle on the dashboard. Tracy snorts; there is a moment's silence and then she starts laughing uncontrollably. And then Julie starts, and Tony and I can't help it either, and then the boys join in and we're all laughing because we're relieved and because Barry's reaction to his wife's slap is brilliantly and candidly comic as he turns around in his seat and kneels on it and takes up Lynn's hands and kisses them and says, "I'm sorry, Lynnie," and turns back without milking forgiveness. Soon enough our laughter fades, but it's not long before Tony can't help himself and says, "Lions? My God, Lynn," and everyone starts up again and Lynn turns around to try to slap Tony too and for a few minutes life is simple and good and light and innocent and easy, and I wonder whether Barry's genius lies in risking everything to bring us together, because even though we're old friends there has until now been something that's come between us all, a cold and transparent something thrown up by forced companionship; perhaps after all these years of being friends we have nothing new to share and have become tired of, tired by, tired with one other. Or perhaps the tension between Tracy and me is more obvious than I'd thought. I don't know, but whatever it is, it's my party, this.

Barry and Tony take the boys for a hike along the river; the uniform is strops and board shorts and lashings of sunscreen and hats. It may be mid-winter, but it must be around twenty-seven degrees. Peter has a towel around his shoulders, and I marvel at my son, at his newly developed muscles: he is walking tall, swaggering almost.

The women appear in white towelling gowns and walk down to the spa, built discreetly into the overhang of a rock to look out over the valley. I take myself and my book to a poolside lounger and for a while sleep off the early-morning champagne and the mid-morning brunch, and when I wake up I hop over to the pool, dive in, the coolness of it shocking me, the water and the weightlessness freeing me. I swim a few laps, push hard; I haven't swum seriously for some time, and I can feel where muscles are being used in unaccustomed ways. She – *She* – is in the pool with me, though; an evil water-sprite who rides on my back and diminishes the joy of swimming, but at the same time drives me to swim harder so that my triceps burn with the rage of it and I am unable to continue and flop onto my back to float as best as I can while the cool water draws the pain from my arms and the warm air calms my lungs. And then I get out of the water with a heave and a twist to sit at the edge of the pool, and then hop to the lounger where I discover that it doesn't take long for the sprite to transmute from water to air, because there she is, sitting on the lounger beside me, staring at me, her presence making me re-read words, sentences, paragraphs, sucking sense from the pages.

I am awoken by a hand on my shoulder. A female form cuts into the setting sun: tracyalicesylvia, perhaps – but it is Lynn: in her touch more affection than I have felt on my skin in months.

"You're burnt," she says. I can feel it, the winter sun still clear and bright at – what is it? – almost five in the afternoon, the temperature still in the early twenties. Lynn is right; I can feel the tightness in my skin.

I blink, raise my hand to the sun to block it out. "How was the spa?"

"Unbelievable. Imagine, three middle-aged chicks, starkers on a rock, having the hell pampered out of us."

"Don't let Tracy hear that."

"Starkers?"

"Middle-aged."

Lynn sits down next to me on the lounger. I wriggle over to make space, she lifts a thigh onto the mattress, puts a hand on my chest, pushes her gown down between her legs, but it's gaping at the top, revealing a breast – unaugmented – its soft pink nipple relaxed, disinterested, oblivious maybe, I don't know. I try not to look, try to focus on her eyes.

"Chris, are you okay?"

"Sure. I've had a fantastic day – you don't understand how precious a day like this is, just me, my book, absolutely nothing to do that I don't want to do."

She looks away into the middle distance, over the stark and beautiful valley below. I can't ignore the opportunity, sneak a furtive glance at her breast again, look away when I realise that if I keep doing that I'm going to get a hard-on in my board shorts, and then what.

"You just seem – Jeez, Chris, don't take this wrong, we've been friends for years – you just seem a lot more serious than you used to be."

"Old age," I say.

"And a lot more flippant as well. Hiding behind sarcasm."

"I'm sorry, Lynn," I say, but I'm thinking how good it would be to tell her about Tracy, about Jono, about *Her*, to tell this sweet, kind, normal woman everything and get it all shared, halved, lightened somehow; but she doesn't deserve it, doesn't deserve to be entangled and entrapped because I know what knowledge does and I know that it's not like a boil you can lance or a subscription you can cancel, it's nothing like something you can make go away, because once you know things you know them for ever, can never shake them off. And I'm also thinking how good it might feel to be with this sensible, sensitive person and then I'm instantly disgusted because I've known her and Barry for years and I held their rings for them and made a silly speech on the day they were married, just as he did for me.

"I suppose there have been a lot of things on my mind," I say. "The business has been a bit stressed over the last eighteen months. I'm worried about Gabe; he's just growing up too fast, in unequal parts that make him think he is more capable and independent than he is. And Tracy and I, well –" and it almost comes but I swallow it down: "We've been married, how long, like centuries, and sometimes it's hard work."

Gabe: Don't say 'like', Dad.

Lynn strokes my chest, looks down at her hand, I at her tit and away just in time as she looks up at me again. "Okay, Chris," she says: she hasn't bought a word of it. "If you want to talk about it, you know where we live."

We.

Of course it's "we". What was I thinking – hoping: that this is some kind of glorified pick-up process, that Lynn is about to throw her lot in with mine, throw everything else away in the process?

"Thanks, Lynn."

She pats my chest, stands up. "See you later. And get out of the sun, okay?"

Tracy is sitting on the toilet, bent over, legs apart, plucking errant hairs from between her spread legs with a pair of tweezers. She is humming.

"Good day?" I ask.

"Stunning," she says. Plucks.

I shower. The water scalds, even though it is barely warm. Get out, dab my burning skin dry. Look at myself in the mirror. "You look good with a bit of sun," Tracy says. "Healthy." She walks behind me, runs a spidery hand across my shoulders as she passes. I feel a breast brushing against me; it makes me arch my back, away from her. "Wear the white shirt tonight," she says, tosses me a small container of moisturiser, "and use this."

We've agreed to meet for sundowners at six-thirty, but of course it's a ruse and they're all waiting for me as I get there at six-twenty and they all burst into "Happy Birthday", Barry as off-key as ever and none the shyer for it, Peter warbling in his choir-boy voice and Gabriel looking like he wants to die quietly as a few other guests join in.

Despite the singing, the closing lines of the old Talking Heads song plays in my ears: "Same as it ever was, same as it ever was". We're two hundred kilometres from home, but I feel a wave of déjà vu, have a glimpse of Sisyphean toil: New Year's Eve, the same people, but for the known Unknowns – now it's the unknown Unknowns of the lodge who are trying not to look at my leg – the same procedure, the same effort of rolling the rock of sociability up a hill only to watch it roll down again.

"Ah, look, he's blushing," Barry announces. "Er, no he's not – ladies and gentlemen, may I introduce Mr George Hamilton." He shouts the name like a boxing announcer; I wonder if he is a little pre-loaded. The adults laugh, Gabriel and Peter look at each other, shrug, not knowing who George Hamilton is. The fickleness of fame, not to mention the political incorrectness of the perpetual suntan, the permanent cigar.

"All right, friends and family, tonight we're doing things in reverse," Barry announces, claps his hands. On cue, a waiter appears bearing a tray-load of tequila shots. "Tonight, we're going to get the unpleasant formalities out of the way first." And again, the brief flare of irritation, like a match just struck, hot and angry, burning down, burning out. And at the same time, a thought that flickers, dies: what was Lynn thinking when she? – and then gone. Barry is just the MC, I remind myself; Tracy is the hostess, I'm merely the bank; this will work, but only if we remember our roles.

We down the tequila. It's surprisingly smooth, without the reptilian bite of the usual stuff. Expensive. Then, gin and tonics, bloody Marys, Johnnie Blacks, whatever it will take to force the sun down to the horizon. Tracy vying with Barry for the starring role, Tony laughing at everything, Lynn sipping a drink where Tracy and Barry are attacking theirs, Julie silent. Then, gifts, although the strict instruction was not to do them. Ridiculous, costly things I'll never use, hardly wear – the re-gifted old bottle of Chivas from Barry aside, handed over with much ceremony and a little laughter, another loop destined to loop and loop and loop until one of us dies – these expensive things will pile up in drawers and cupboards with all the other ridiculous and expensive things my blessed life has brought me, unused, still wrapped. Tracy's tactical wait before she presents me with hers: a Breitling big as a cathedral clock, all knobs and dials and bling and reminding me of Anton Murray, and as I hug her and gush my surprise and delight I wonder which of my credit cards she used to pay for the thing.

And then dinner. Ice buckets never empty of the bottles of white that Barry orders, reds lined up on the table like an alien city skyline. I allow Gabe a cider, or something that is marketed as a cider though I doubt an apple has ever been near it. Lynn follows my lead, allows Peter one as well. Through the talking and laughing I see Gabe taking a sip, not liking it very much, catching the waiter's eye to trade it for a Coke, and I feel a swell of pride in the boy: all the edgy music, the silly drawings – at least he isn't a drinker.

Tony tastes his starter, a little nibble. Julie looks at him. "Okay, baby?" she asks. I want to slap her for her timidity. She is intelligent, turns heads wherever, but on her forehead are the vertical frowns of worry, across it streaks of subservience, over her shoulders a shawl of solemnity: when she draws it around her she can slink through a crowded room without a soul noticing her. You can see it in her shoulders, broad and bony, but poked upwards like the wings of an unhappy bird. Tensed, even after the spa session.

"Magnifico," Antonio "Tony" La Vita – godfather of the South African version of pizza – declares. Tony the Italian who visited Italy only once, after his third pizza place had taken off; Tony who told me on his return that he hated the place and would never go back; Tony who speaks three, maybe five, words of Italian.

And so, from one course to the next. There is a new fire in the old anecdotes: they are told with a different spin, making each funnier, more outrageous, than they've been before, the participants forgiving the teller any exaggerations, all complicit in the embellishments. Matt on his windsurfer in the Plett waves, fine when the wind came from starboard, absolutely fucked if it swung around to port, Matt who had to be rescued by the

NSRI halfway to Rio; Jonty pulling out an enormous silver revolver in a Cape Town pool bar, threatening to blow the white ball off the table if he kept getting hustled; Lorraine, who put her stepfather in hospital after cracking his skull with a frying pan when he tried to feel her up in the kitchen. None of the protagonists present as their stories are unravelled and embellished again, the mythologies elaborated and entrenched over the years; once amusing, by now outrageous, Pythonesque. Thus do religions begin, I am certain.

Dessert is preceded by a cake, contrived to represent a building. The tower of it falls over as the waiter puts it down, Barry and Tony blaming years of shit architecture for its failure. Tracy gets up, tries to right it, lights the remaining candles; Lynn rises to allow her access, comes around the table, sits in Tracy's seat beside me, puts her hand on the thigh of my stump and squeezes, looks at me as though I have just lost a family member. "I know you hate birthdays," she says.

"What would probably be worse," I say, "is not having birthdays." I put a hand on her soft thigh, squeeze it, smile happily, my hand on her leg making me even happier.

But.

But the maths of it, the potential loss: if I am c and Lynn is l, and I stand to lose so much: then $c + l = cl - x(t + g + b) \therefore$ probably a mistake. The unknown of x, multiplying the loss of Gabe, Barry, Tracy, x with its own value for Lynn, its own value for me.

Tracy brings the cake, leans between Lynn and me, almost dropping it into Lynn's lap as she puts it down. Our hands on our own thighs until Tracy steps back again.

"Way to go, Trace," Barry shouts, drinking to the narrowly avoided misfortune.

There is a lull as my guests watch and I am about to blow out the candles when Julie lurches forward, elbow on the table, plants her chin in her palm.

"So," she says loudly – uncommonly loudly for Julie, loudly enough to make us all look up. "So, guess what." Guessh. And then she waits, rocking gently to and fro, making sure she has the attention of everyone, and I wait too, not blowing out the candles, expecting a drunken blessing, hoping it won't slur into a speech.

But no.

"Tony'sh having an affair," she announces. Loudly.

Silence, not only from our table: indiscreet unknown Unknown heads at other tables turn to gape at her.

"Ah, bella," Tony growls and can't find more words than that and shuts up.

"Fucking some pizza mana – manager – person. Some divorshed franchisee something, I don't know what the fuck she is, probably has big tits and a tight fanny. Tony I'm sure can tell you more," Julie pronounces.

"Jesus," says Barry.

"Christ," says Tracy, and I look hard at her but all I get is the side of her face.

"So, tell us, Antonio," Julie continues, "tell us, Italian Stallion – does she have great tits, a fantastic young cunt? Does she suck your dick, take it up the arse for you?"

She grabs her glass, swills the contents; a drop runs from the corner of her mouth and onto her top. Tony stands up. Goes around the table and pulls her up, gently enough, by the arm. Says something quietly into her ear. She stands, wobbles, Tony wraps an arm around her, shepherds her towards the door. She tries to pull her elbow from his grasp, fails. "Stupid fucking pretend-Italian," she shouts on the way out. "All dick and no balls and definitely no fucking backbone."

Barry, the ineffable Barry. Offers apologies to the unknown guests, offers tequilas, champagne, twelve-year-old whiskies as compensation, drinks many of them himself. For a change, I concur with his expenditure of my money because his magic restores equilibrium and also because I have Lynn's hand on my thigh and her eyes in my face and the memory of her fantastically feminine left tit with its gentle pink nipple in my mind. I squeeze her leg, could swear she responds by moving it closer to me. I don't counter Barry when he orders another round on my tab, enjoy Lynn's smiling collaboration when I pour my drink into Tony's half-finished cup of coffee while the rest swallow theirs.

"So?" Lynn says, asks, eyebrows up.

So I know how Julie feels, I want to say, but I don't. Am tired also of staring at Tracy who will simply not look back at me. Instead I say, "So can I blow out my candles already?"

I blow out the candles, attempt to cut the collapsed thing of a cake into something one might want to eat, but it's hardly worth it. More tequila arrives, we make a show of drinking it, a show of enjoying it, and then dessert, coffee. The boys excuse themselves as soon as they've finished their mousse. Julie's words lie like a damp sheet over the four of us left at the sad table: Barry tries to reanimate things, gives up, slides down in his chair, his head tilted backwards. His eyes hood; I am certain that he will fall asleep here, now. Then Tracy suddenly sits up, hands palm-down on the table like a medium's, back straight, staring at the salt cellar in front of her.

"What, Trace?" I ask, but she ignores me, stands up, sways, turns and runs out with a hand to her mouth.

"Uh-oh," Lynn says. Stands up too, and in doing so takes her hand from my thigh, shrugging my hand from hers. Hurries after Tracy. The warmth of her palm cooling on my leg.

By the time I've crutched to the room — a little erratically, I'll admit, though I'm good at making it seem I've had more to drink than I actually have — by the time I've hobbled to our room, Tracy is sitting on the toilet, dress hitched up around her waist. Around one ankle is her thong, lacy, curled around itself; she is clinging to a plastic bin on her lap, heaving into it. Lynn at the door, hand over her mouth and nose, squeezes my shoulder as she leaves, says something I don't hear over the noise of Tracy.

"Are you okay?" I ask Tracy.

"Fuck off," she says. Fuggoff. An elastic strand of drool stretches from her mouth to the dustbin.

"This is not my beautiful wife," the Talking Heads sing to me.

"So you're okay, then?" I ask.

"Just fuck off, thank you." And retches, spewing a mix of dessert, wine, tequila, coffee into the bucket. Simultaneously shits a wet stream of partially digested main course, Moët, gin, whisky, Jägermeister, whatever, into the toilet bowl.

I listen at Gabriel's door; it's quiet. Lift my hand to open the door, decide rather to let sleeping teenagers lie: with the noise and the stench across the corridor, well.

I look in on Tracy again, but she gurgles and gives me the finger. So I leave the noise and the funk of the chalet, wander around in the moonlight, consider a nightcap at the bar, decide otherwise. Here, far from the city, the night is cool and the glare of the moon subdues the stars. There's a lush smell from the damp landscaping, green and rich. I think of Tracy alternately throwing up and shitting; I am happy not to be holding her head, happy to have been told to fuck off — hope, actually, that the whole event feels as unpleasant to her as it looked to me — happy to be here in the sharp, clear air. I find my lounger at the pool, lie down on its dewy cover, the hotel lights now dimmed, only a few still on in the surrounding chalets. I prepare to slap mosquitoes, but there are none. Am surprised at the silence from the dark, none of the usual chorus of insects, birds, frogs. And then from the far side of the pool a familiar shape appears, hugging itself against the chill, stopping to look out over the moon-silvered valley.

"Psst," I hiss.

"Jesus," Lynn says. "You gave me such a fright." I decide not to make a comment about lions. She comes closer, sits on my recliner like before, hand on my chest. Barry has passed out in his clothes, she says, is snoring like a yak, she would never be able to sleep, didn't even bother trying. I put a hand on her thigh; it edges closer to me. I place my other hand on her waist, stroke the softness that breaks like a wave over the top of her skirt, feel its warmth through the fabric. And then she leans in to me, smears her mouth against mine, rips through the buttons of my white shirt, holds me like she means it, this real, warm woman who is not a ghost or a phantom or a fantasy future or past, she is mine at the moment, she is mine to be held and kissed and fucked in the cold Cederberg night while Barry lies snoring and Tracy pukes and Sylvia slips further away by the second and *She* hides in her web of denial, safe from her role in the genesis of everything. Lynn is mine but she is Alice too: the warmth and closeness of her could be Alice, could be anyone, any woman other than my wife, would be Alice if I could make her so, but she is Lynn and for that I am happy enough.

And afterwards, a strange absence of regret: Lynn in my arms on the narrow poolside lounger and I can't any more so I tell her everything, the Sylvia and the Marietjie of it, the *She* of it, the Alice of it; the Gabriel and the Tracy and Jono of it, and she holds me while she listens, holds me until I'm able at two-twenty in the cold morning to fuck her again, to do my best friend's wife again until she moans and whimpers so that I have to place my hand over her mouth to silence her wanting and she bites into the edge of my palm and gently releases it once it's all over.

Chris and Sylvia

By the time you are within a shout of forty, thirty-nine and three quarters, how do you define yourself if not by your past? At twenty, you define yourself by your future. By the great things you will carry out, by the experiences that will enrich you, by the great sharing you will do. You do not foresee Dr Seuss's Lurches and Slumps. At twenty, you are in a state of becoming, oblivious to mistakes yet to come. So you forego your condition of human *being* for human *doing*, because you cannot *become* without doing: you cannot become by merely being, so you *do*.

But you also *don't* – you don't do so very many things because you're doing a few others. When you look back over the messy canvas of forty years, you evaluate the choices you've made, the use of colour, an inappropriate brush now and then, areas where your sense of proportion has been distorted by what's going on around you.

Yet even then there is a vague but ever-present sense, a tugging, which whispers that things might have been otherwise. All you can do is paint over what has been committed to the canvas, but no matter how you work to perfect the picture of your life, the ultimate measure of success or failure is down to how little mess you leave behind.

The doing of marriage: such is time, either suspended indefinitely, or passing so swiftly that the present is instantly the past.

The doing of fatherhood: and look, look at me – I share advice, hard-earned wisdom, and still Gabriel kills the dog, will kill many more meta-phorical dogs in years to come.

Son-hood: undone by Sylvia's disease, negated by *Her* unwillingness to face her past.

And then the fucking of your closest friend's wife: so stupidly counter-intuitive, complicating instead of simplifying. But when the itch is so per-sistent, present so long, the scratching of it, well.

The silence at breakfast the next day: Barry toying with a piece of dry toast, green-faced, not brave enough to eat it; Tony without Julie, as though that were the norm; Tracy absent, again at the toilet bowl in our room, now fearing dehydration; me, Gabriel and Peter with plates piled high – eggs, bacon, sausages, mushrooms, croissants drowning in jam, juices, coffees. And Lynn, picking at a few small pieces of fruit as though still satiated from the night before, looking at me with her open, candid look, me hoping that Barry won't notice, won't decipher. What is she trying to convey – an apology? A forgiveness? A collusion? Some kind of understanding? The promise of a next time? The reassurance that it need never happen again?

I don't know.

And then, on check-out, a complicit clerk hands me a note when I ask for the bill: "Happy birthday, boet – your best friends, B+L."

Barry has paid for everything – our accommodation, our meals, the hectolitres of expensive alcohol thrown down various throats only to be thrown up again. Thrown up by him too, no doubt, while I was doing his wife in the garden.

Whose presence follows me home in the Range Rover, hovers about Gabriel next to me, weaves around Tracy lying on the back seat, her head on a stolen hotel pillow, allegedly goose-down. Lynn here, now, so close that I almost open my mouth to talk to her, not about the sex of it, just the *it* of it, the *it* I have missed so much for God knows how long. A presence at once free of guilt and laden with it, but so tempting, so accessible – all it would take is for me to fabricate a meeting, drive to their house while Barry is at work and Peter is at school, and then. Then more: more Lynn, more deception.

So.

So I can't. Won't.

I'm about to leave the office at the end of the next week when Ivan passes my door on his way out. He stops, backs up, and invites me to his Shabbat dinner even though he knows I'll turn it down. I wonder if the spontaneity of these invitations is intended to catch me off-guard, if he enjoys my floundering for excuses. Before I leave I give him a moment to catch the lift so that I don't have to elaborate on my lies.

Then, a casual message tossed out by the Solitaire junky outside my office. Sam, slack-jawed as she clicks, too inert even to get up and begin her own weekend, is jolted by a distant memory as I crutch by.

"Oh, Chris," she says, her voice dusty with inactivity, "someone called for you earlier, but you were in a meeting." She begins rummaging for the message.

"A client?" I ask.

"Don't know. Some home or other." She scratches through a mess of paper.

I sigh. "My home, Sam? Was it Tracy?"

"No. The Something Home for the Something. Oh, the Something Home for the Aged. Ag-*ed*, they said."

Sylvia.

"When?"

"Around eleven, I think."

I stare at her. She blanches, understands that perhaps she should have said something to me in the six hours that have since elapsed.

"Fuck it, Sam." I never swear at work, least of all at the staff.

"Sorry, Chris," she whispers.

I crutch back to my office, call the place where my mother has been in limbo for the past five years, that well-meaning, tragic place of unliving, un-dying, where you drift along in a bubble of drugs and diapers until it all bursts, finally and conclusively: then you slip beneath the tides of institutional timetables, to a place where their ebb and swell subsides and no longer means anything.

Barry and Lynn attend the funeral. Barry gives me a rough man-hug, Lynn's a gentler, better-fitting version. Sylvia's friends from the home who are able to attend are wheeled up, and stopped a safe distance from the graveside. They stare at the proceedings, beyond grief, probably wondering how long until it's their turn, what it might be like in that cold, tight cavity, wondering what awaits them there, and beyond. Death can happen at any moment, as Dalia might testify, but when you know it is so close that not medicine nor anti-slip mats nor eating your greens can stave it off any longer, surely Christian, Muslim, Hindu, Jew have to question, have to interrogate all they've been taught? Or maybe not: perhaps that's exactly the time you cling to what you've been led to believe, any challenge to this far too upsetting to consider. Yet all the while wishing it was behind you already, wishing it was over – the ultimate exam, job interview, bungee jump – as it now is for Sylvia.

While the old people gape at her open grave, dug as close as is permissible to Michael's, my mother, my not-mother, lies in a shiny dark wooden box with brass handles I know she'd have approved of, suspended for the moment on chrome rods. A priest I don't know is intoning, a caricature of a Monty Python caricature. Ashes to ashes, dust to dust. The all and the nothing.

There are three mourners I do not recognise. Possibly old teachers who'd once taught with Michael, nurses who'd once nursed with Sylvia. A tall, upright old man wearing a cravat, a shrunken woman, another, somewhere in between. The tall man silently weeping; I don't know him, can't picture him at our house, cannot recall his name, can't imagine why the emotion. Perhaps years ago he and Sylvia did to Michael what Lynn and I have done to Barry, what Tracy is doing to me; or perhaps his sadness is that they never did any of it. And Gabriel, dry-eyed, probably thinking that he can finally bury the torture of the Endless Bath along with his grandmother. Barry and Lynn appropriately sad-faced, respectful. And Tracy sobbing. Holding on to my shoulder with one hand, on to my forearm with the other, she heaves and pitches so that I struggle to balance the two of us on my three legs – always have, the thought occurs. I marvel at her distress, the depth of it, but cannot fathom it. Cannot fathom, and am furious with her for being able to cry like this, for her ability to let go of whatever it is that is inside her, because I cannot. I am twisted inside, a hosepipe with a kink, a nausea with no release, afloat and awash on the inside, dry on the outside.

I am furious with Gabriel for his frown and his dry eyes because I am furious with Sylvia: the boy should know that I alone have the right to fury. Gabriel should be sobbing, for without her he would not be standing here, whereas without her I would simply be standing somewhere else – maybe, even, on both my feet – maybe in New York or in an Indian ashram or as a participant in a Bosnian military parade because who knows what might have been if, if not.

I am furious with Sylvia, not because I might have found myself somewhere completely else. I am furious because some illogic which is not bowing to reason blames her for her disease, and the same illogic decrees that the responsibility for not recognising me was hers alone, not recognising me either in the flesh or as her son, denying me both.

I am furious with her for everything else her long dying took away – the smallest things: a greeting, a sensible conversation, a smile that might have meant something so small and then so much.

I am furious because I never discussed my adoption with her – or with Michael – during all our years together as a family. It was a subject tacitly understood and taboo at the same time. Like going to the toilet: you may announce that you are on the way to powder your nose, but you do not discuss the details of it.

I am furious with her because any chance I may have had of extracting these details from her expired years ago, and she gave me no warning of it, or at least not enough of a one.

I am furious with her because she allowed those idiots at the home to let her die before they found it in themselves to make a second call to my cretinous secretary, before making any attempt to contact me directly: when I have a cellphone, a home phone, two e-mail accounts, Skype, SMS, BlackBerry Messenger, Twitter and God knows how many other means of contact – how many other fucking ways would anyone need to announce the impending death of my mother before they let her die without me? I want to kick the nurse under her fat kneecap because I am furious with her, not personally but institutionally, immensely and totally, for she represents all the red tape and yellow folders and white string and brown paper that could not get a message through to me when I needed it most; I hate her officious, desk-bound uselessness as much as I resent her snub nose and her doe-eyed sympathy and her shameless breasts.

I am furious too with myself, at my own indignation at Sylvia's death: as at my adoption, she has once again gone ahead with no consideration for my opinion or counsel on the matter. I am furious with Sylvia that *She* refuses to meet me; a perverse reasoning convinces me that if it wasn't for *Her*, there would be no Sylvia, and so no me, which can only have been Sylvia's fault for rescuing me from *Her* in the first place.

I am furious at the finality of Sylvia's grave being covered with indifferent soil, at the two expressionless men in overalls, spade-blades shiny with so many graves dug and filled, dug and filled; I am furious at the efficient way they go about their work, the neutral expressions they bear: neutral for the sake of respect, or because of indifference, I don't know, but I want to leap across the fast-closing trench and throttle a little feeling out of them, shake them by the shoulders simply because their blank faces are so very blank.

I am furious at the aeroplane that passes overhead, off to Amsterdam or Miami or Perth, merely for passing overhead.

I am furious that Sylvia died with the cold, practised words of a paid nurse in her ear while I was busy squeezing out constipated ideas for Murray's development.

I am furious that she has died.

Furious that she is so completely, absolutely, irretrievably dead.

Tracy and I are the only ones who have a drink at the wake – the same Tracy who'd forsworn alcohol after the Cederberg, mere weeks before. Even Barry settles for coffee, Lynn for a glass of water. The old people sipping tea and munching biscuits and the porcine nurse wiping their chins when they drool. The tall man not here, escaping my interrogation. Tracy with a glass of wine, me with a double whisky: we are both looking at an old woman in a wheelchair when we see her suddenly glance around, feral, wily; as we watch, she empties a plate of biscuits into her lap, covering her booty with her blanket. Our eyes meeting and laughter escaping in snorts,

Lynn and Barry staring, looking at each other, back at us, then Tracy help-ing me to my study where we close the door and laugh openly, loudly, childishly, holding on to each other as we rock. Tears from the laughing, diaphragms in spasm.

Shortly after our sober re-emergence – the bereft son comforted by his loving wife – the small party of mourners takes its leave. Last condolences from the shrunken little teacher, from the nurse, her hand on my arm a fraction too long, her grip a fraction too tight. Barry with another man-hug, Lynn with a light hand on my shoulder. I watch them walk to the car, angry now at Barry for having her, when I only have guilt.

Surprisingly, Gabriel helps Tracy clear the plates and cups, hugs me un-prompted before he retires to his grotto, and I hug him back and want to warn him that I'm next, that soon enough he'll be the only one to carry things forward – but I don't; besides, what are these *things* I have in mind? One single generation of genes, sprung from nowhere, a belonging that is no deeper than a coat of paint? I don't know.

I am sitting on the couch, strangely exhausted, slouching, eyes closed, when Tracy comes to sit next to me. Snuggles close, puts her head on my chest. Something she last did in the dying throes of my Dalia-mourning. And the once-familiar smell of her scalp, her shampoo a reminder of how the world used to be. Before this. Before Jono and Botox and cosmetic sur-gery, before that thing in her turned cold and went hard, before it turned me to the fantasy of Alice, the reality of Lynn. Before. And then my tears, falling onto the top of her head. She not moving to save her hairdo. Reach-ing an arm across me, holding me as I weep. And later, in bed, my hand on the crescent of her hip, and she not moving away.

Sylvia's life is handed to me in two cardboard apple-boxes by her nurse, who thrusts her tits at me while I pretend not to notice. One box contains

Sylvia's clothes. I don't want them: they have nothing to do with her, and I don't want the soured old-lady smell of them. Ask the nurse to give or throw them away.

I take the remaining box home, sit on the floor of my study, open it. Inside, a few romance novels. A pasteboard box of jewellery that Tracy would hate. A book of poetry, all frogs and peat, by an Irish poet I'd always detested. Sylvia's and Michael's birth certificates, ID books – Michael unusually bewildered in his photograph – long-expired passports, their marriage certificate, Michael's death certificate: cancer. A small photo album I've never seen, shiny patches on its suede cover, sad and frayed at the corners.

And a tiny earthenware pot that commands my attention.

Unglazed brown, poorly turned, a flat waxed cork sealing it shut. A label taped to the cork with the words *Cassie Hayes*. And in a different hand, in black marker, on the side of the jar: *Cassandra Hayes, 7 Jan 1965 – 19 Aug 1967*.

Who the fuck was Cassie Hayes?

Michael's mother was a Cassandra, but too strong, too feared a matriarch ever to be a Cassie: no diminutives in her life.

And then the dates, well.

I pick up the album, flick through crimp-edged photographs held loosely in place by little paper triangles.

Sylvia as a girl, her father proud beside her, a drab block of flats behind them, Jesus thorns threatening from flower-boxes lining the walk, both father and daughter in austere clothes, both smiling despite. I remove the photograph: written on the back in careful script is a place and a date: Kenilworth, 1948.

Another photograph: a small boy in blazer and cap, a smudge of Gothic behind him – a chapel or cathedral in the rain. Michael in York, maybe, or Leeds; I don't know, I don't recognise the building, I never visited the Yorkshire of his boyhood. No date, but I guess 1943 or '44. Two formal wedding pictures: Sylvia petite and pretty, the stain of something on the image – ink, perhaps – over her heart; Michael already schoolmasterish, bearded, finer-featured than I remembered. A few pages on, the young Michael and Sylvia in the gardens at Kirstenbosch, unposed, laughing, a tiny girl between them, laughing too, the shadow on the mountain behind putting the time at mid-afternoon. On the lawn, the remnants of a picnic: white cloth spread on the grass, a wicker basket, leftovers of lunch. They are each holding one of the child's hands, her feet are forwards, her bum back, her body pulling down on the adult hands. I get the impression that if they were to let her go she would sit down on the comfortable padding of her nappy – she seems far too young to stand on her own.

Cassandra after her grandmother, Cassie my almost-sister.

"I never had a *son*," Sylvia said the last time I saw her. I don't know if the emphasis is hers, or mine, and when I try to replay the words in my mind they're like words in a badly remembered dream, so indistinct that I begin to wonder if she even said them at all.

On the picnic cloth: two plates, the leftover food mummified by the chemicals of the photographic process. Two wine glasses, one on its side, and between them a something, at first glance a shadow or a crease in the picnic cloth, on closer inspection a baby's bottle.

Of course there are questions, the hows and whys and whats of this child, this sister, this not-sister. But there is nobody left to answer them, so I let them die, stillborn.

There are other photographs too. A close-up of both of them, me between, six or seven months old at the time. Pictures of the beach, couples and children in old-fashioned swimwear and laughable hairstyles, women in bathing caps with rubber flowers attached. Michael standing proudly next to a new, or new-ish, Morris Minor. Me with both legs bent, about to dive into someone else's swimming pool. Then, two more pictures with me in them: one where I'm standing outside the house, already needing a scrape and a coat of paint; another with Michael and Sylvia on either side of me. Lost frames from a forgotten past. Cassie present by her absence: there are no more images of her.

I try the words again: Cassie, my sister. Cassie, dead before I was born three years later, almost to the day. Cassie, the daughter Sylvia and Michael had never mentioned. Cassie, the skeleton in the closet, squirrelled away in a secret corner of the little Plumstead house she shared with her father and mother and adoptive brother. The latter never suspecting, never given a reason to suspect. I pull myself up off the floor, crutch to the kitchen to make coffee. Cannot watch the face in the kettle, the face that may not have been there at all if Cassie Hayes hadn't died; am drawn back to Sylvia's small legacy and forget about the kettle.

And then.

Then there is a baby picture with my name written in the corner, in painfully penned letters trying to be neat but not succeeding. "October '72" under my name. The picture is not mounted, lies loose between the leaves of the album. I turn it over. On the back, in the same careful, untidy script: "Our gift from Debbie B."

It takes me a moment to understand: that is *Her* name.

Debbie. I'm disappointed.

The name strikes me as thin, flimsy, once fashionable but now insipid. It has no resonance. "Deborah" has more gravitas, more character; it is the name of a princess, while "Debbie" is the name of her chamber maid. "Debbie" is meagre, mean, fragile. Like rice-paper, easily torn, instantly dissolved by a few drops of water. And that belittling diminutive, well.

Debbie's surname, her secret name, starts with a B, it seems. But a B for what – something as generic as Baker? Was – is – my mother Debbie Baker, and is she herself just as forgettable as her name, a mousy librarian who made one bad decision? Or is her name exotic, such as Buñuel, or is it interesting like Bismarck, or elegant like Balantine, or comic like Barrow?

Disappointment at the "Debbie", frustration at the truncated "B". Knowing that I will never know. The knowing, also, that I know so much less about my parents – my adoptive parents – than I'd believed. Cassie but one shaft of refracted light – how many more are there that I don't, never will, know about?

How easy it is to be an architect, with the materials and tools at hand to throw down foundations and build what you need; how much more difficult to be an archaeologist, trying to reconstruct history from a broken wheel and three rusted arrowheads.

Ivan with his Roy Lichtenstein yarmulke has insisted that I take a few days off. As though it were up to him. I know that for the rest of the working week he'll be posturing and pontificating, offering clients unprofitable deals just to secure the business, marching around the office with his chest puffed, irritating the staff with pointless but insistent instructions, unable to differentiate the urgent from the important, instead of simply being the excellent architect that he is. I couldn't much care – the damage he causes is usually transient, irritating more than fundamental, like rain on a car you've just had washed.

But.

As always, Shahid will keep an eye on him.

There is a text message from Alice on my phone the next morning: *So sorry for your loss. All strength, thinking of you. Some things will always put shopping centres into perspective. Love Alice.*

Love Alice.

Well.

"Love, Alice" is a greeting.

"Love Alice" is an instruction. One that I would not find difficult to carry out, because since our sharing of unseemly laughing fits when I wept for Sylvia – and for myself – since all that, Tracy has drawn down the veil, retreated back into her more recognisable self.

I hop to Tracy's dressing room to tell her about the photo of the little girl. Tracy has a bra on, nothing else – her tits hurt, she says, and a bra helps – as she ponders what to wear. She's moving quickly, keeps looking at her watch. Has a date, clearly. My mother's been dead for less than a week, and despite your public outpouring of grief at her graveside two days ago you're already off to fuck your boyfriend, I want to say, want to shout, but don't.

"I found some interesting stuff in Sylvia's things," I say, leaning against the doorway, both attracted and repelled by the spiky Brazilian that she doesn't bother to put away.

"Good," she says.

"There were some photographs."

"Hm."

"And an urn."

"Uh-huh."

"Do you know what they keep in urns?"

"Soup? Coffee?"

"Ashes, Trace. The cremated remains of dead people."

Tracy stops, looks at me.

"Did you know that Michael and Sylvia had a child before they adopted me? A daughter who died, that they never told me about?"

She bends to pick up a pair of red shoes, looks over her shoulder at me without standing up. Shakes her head, exasperated. "No, I didn't," she says. Puts down the red shoes, picks up another pair. Turns and bends a leg sideways and raises the foot to put on a shoe. No panties yet – perhaps she won't even bother with them – all the better to fuck him, I am sure. And everything pulled open as she pulls on the shoe, hopping to keep her balance, folded pinkness exposed. Who puts on shoes before the rest of their clothes? "What makes you think so?" she asks. Changes legs, picks up another shoe, bends the other leg out.

"A named and dated urn, filled with ashes. A pic of them with a little girl, taken way before I was born."

Hopping, angry. The shoe won't go on. She sits on the floor, leans her back against a shelf. Opens her legs like a dancer, bends the bare foot towards herself, knee out. The fleshy flower between her legs, carnivorous, beguiling, fatal. Vagina dentata. It's like a traffic accident – I don't want to look, but can't help myself. How did she ever grow so fucking insensitive? She gets the shoe on, crosses her legs prudishly, hiding it all, reminding me in a gesture that it's effectively out of bounds – now you see it, now you don't – that I am no better than Tiny Tim, slavering at the pastries through the bakery window.

Tracy stands, heels together, arms folded. "Chris, maybe it's time you went to see someone. Your parents were the most honest, straightforward people I've ever known. And you – seriously. Just listen to yourself now. Jesus." She stands up while I wait for more. Slips on a clean-cut grey dress of raw silk. Still no panties.

"Tracy, an urn with a name and a photograph is pretty much empirical. I'm hardly hallucinating here."

She stops abruptly with her back to me. "What are you actually looking for?" she asks. "All these fucking ghosts everywhere, when here we are."

I don't have an answer, leave her sanctuary. Still do not know whether she will head out of the house with panties on or not. Don't care. I recall an earlier attempt at making coffee, am in the kitchen staring at the morphing face in the kettle when she rushes by, closes the door to the garage without saying a word. The electronic garage door grinding open, squeaking unhealthily, I notice, the growl of the Range Rover, the whine of a high-speed reverse down the long driveway, the garage door closing. And then silence, but for the growing rumble of water coming to the boil.

I go to the cemetery.

Aptly, it has begun to rain, softly; the cemetery looks as though it has been prepared for a Gothic movie. Low black clouds, the grey of the drizzle sharpening the green of the lawns, dulling the cypresses almost to black. Fat cold drops falling from the bare plane trees, the oaks.

Sylvia's grave is still a mound of earth, the gravestone yet to be completed, yet to be set above her. Such a large stone to mark such a small life: obscene, almost. The rain falls harder, taps a matrix of little fingerprints into the soil of the mound, erases the indifferent cuts of the spadesmen. Michael's grave untended – ungroomed as he himself always was. I let a crutch fall, hold the other by the shaft, bend down and pull guilty weeds from the gravel, shake dead stems from a glass vase, pour out the foul-smelling dregs. Pull myself up, hop over to a tap, rinse the green crust from the vase as best I can. Wish I'd brought flowers. Absurdly look around me for something – a long, heavy-headed stalk of grass, perhaps, or even a daisy or two left by a recent mourner. Replace the empty vase.

I suppose you're expected to pray at the graves of loved ones, but I can't find the right words for prayer; the only words I have frame accusations, demands, pleas – nothing that is supplicatory.

I stop trying. Admit that I'm here only because if they went to the trouble of being buried side by side, Baby Hayes should not be left out. I take the urn from the pocket of my coat, struggle to dislodge the cork, end up cracking the neck of the little jar on Michael's gravestone. Knock off the top, sprinkle the ashes onto his grave, onto Sylvia's. How much of the ash is Cassandra's, how much burnt coffin-wood, who knows?

There you go, Tracy, I say out loud. All ghosts laid to rest now.

Almost all, anyway.

I go home. It's Thursday. Gabriel is at school, will, according to Tracy, be heading for the gym afterwards – running there and then back afterwards. Just six months ago, my floppy son, and now would you believe. And Tracy is, well, on her way out, as she puts it.

I go through Sylvia's boxes again, hoping for something more, finding nothing. A few years ago on a three-month project in Bahrain, after weeks of meetings in Arabic and dust and the haze of the Gulf, I began to miss home. Not my house, my city, my family, but *lions*. I hadn't seen a lion in the wild for a decade, but the knowledge that I was so far away from them made me long for them terribly. That's how I'm missing Sylvia right now. I miss her like the lions I haven't seen for years.

I check my calendar. If Sam has done things properly, I only have one meeting on Monday. Anton Murray. And, of course, Alice. So I do the sensible thing and crutch up the treacherous stairs and retrieve my prosthetic leg from the back of my closet. I prepare the cup with a thick pad, strap it on. Sit on the bed, pull on the matching sock and shoe on the dead-rubber foot. The shoe is new, shinier on top than the one on my right foot, the sole clean and unworn, still with the sticker on it. Lever myself off the bed with my arms. Take a tentative step. The pain is like those pin-prick blood tests they take from the end of your finger where the nerve endings are concentrated; it's just a bigger version. I was told by the physio that it would take a while to get used to, that the stump would have to build up a bit of a callous, a bit of toughness. She likened it to learning the guitar, when one's fingers start off soft and sensitive where the strings cut into them, but soon enough become hardened to the task. I've never played the guitar, so her analogy was lost on me, but I'm sure "Kumbaya" never felt anything like this. I make it out of the bedroom, take three times longer to get down the stairs than I would on crutches. Afraid, like an old person, of falling. Lean against the banister at the bottom, sweating. Go out into the garden – a gap between winter showers – take a turn around the lawn I haven't been on for months, years perhaps. Find myself surprised that it is so vast, so manicured. Barely make it back into the house, remember that I've left my crutches upstairs.

Hobble to the couch, tear the Frankenstein piece off me. Turn on the TV, flick to Sky. South Africa has made world headlines for the wrong reasons once again: over thirty dead after police open fire on striking miners. The anchors, a middle-aged man and a young woman, are judgmental in their comments. I want to take it up with them, rail against their moralising, because even though I don't yet have the facts, I want to defend this ridiculous country.

But.

Chris and Alice

It takes me a few days to regain my focus at work, then more than a month to draw up detailed plans for Murray's development.

Alice arrives ten minutes early. I would usually let the client wait until the appointed time, but ten minutes without Murray, well. I have left my crutches in the car, am trying the prosthesis again. Perhaps knowing that I would be meeting her today is the reason, I suppose. I limp to the reception to greet her; she is office-dressed again, a simple and not-very-long dark dress, hair – blonder than before, if that's possible – held in place by a plain black band. Black stockings against the winter chill, heels. She stands to greet me: "Hello, Mr Hayes." The green eyes of it. The music of it. The music I'd forgotten: nothing like a roomful of school kids at all. Alice ignores my hand, hugs me formally, if such a thing is possible.

"Anton can't make it," she says, "so it's just us, I'm afraid."

"Damn," I say, but she is too preoccupied to appreciate the sarcasm.

I take her through my concepts. They're well-formed, at last; if approved, the next steps will be technical: the drafting of the details, the engineers and quantity surveyors, costings, planning permissions. I know something of the vision will be lost – it always is; there's always a chasm between a concept vehicle shown off at an auto show and the version of it that finally ends up in the showroom; the trick is to keep the gap as small as possible. If it ends up not too far from the original, I know that it will stun, strike, work well for Murray, be a strong addition to the firm's portfolio. There's an excitement to it, almost sexual, which swells with Alice's appreciation of what she sees. Swells for me, in any event.

I haven't yet finished when she takes her phone from the table, dials. Waves away my quizzical look. Holds the phone to her ear, frowns after a minute or so, ends the call.

"What are you doing?"

Puts up her hand without looking at me, redials, waits.

"Anton?" she says after a while. "Yes, hi. Okay." She waits. I'm shaking my head, holding up my hands like a parking attendant trying to stop a Fiat from reversing into a Bentley. She rolls her eyes, swivels on her chair so that her back is to me. "Yes, I'm here. Listen, you have to have to *have* to see Chris's work . . . I know you'll see it sooner or later, but sooner would be better . . . No, like today."

I can hear Murray's attenuated voice across the room.

"Okay, let me check with Chris. Thanks, bye." She turns to face me.

"Check what?" I say. Suspicious.

"Anton is tied up all day. Can you take him through the work over dinner tonight?"

Today is my fortieth birthday.

The real birthday, the no-more-thirty-nine day: such a difference a day makes. A supermarket greeting-card from Tracy on the kitchen counter this morning, signed "Best, Tracy. xxx". A small bottle of Hugo Boss after-shave and a hand-drawn card from Gabe. They had both already left for school, no celebratory plans discussed – I suppose the celebration has already taken place – but dinner with Alice, well. I look at the large-format papers spread across the boardroom table. "It'll have to be a big restaurant."

"Laptop, Mr Hayes. It's 2012."

Of course I'd far rather present to Murray the proper way. Paper, my environment. Laptop images are somehow transient, look like they've been quickly Googled, PowerPointed, seem too easy to be taken seriously. But the tactility of paper makes the images real, gives them a mystique and a romance that a screen can't convey. Because paper is tangible, it's a smaller mental leap to the finished product. And then there's Murray's inability to chew and focus at the same time; there will be other patrons, the distraction of waiters. But, then. Dinner with Alice. Weigh the risk of the project being rejected. Alice, project; Alice, project.

Alice sees me vacillate, probably picks up a few volts of my low-level agitation.

She puts a hand over mine. Squeezes, I think.

"Trust me on this, Chris."

So Alice wins.

"Okay. But if he bombs it the next dinner is on you."

"I owe you, anyway. So if he doesn't, it'll be on you."

Alice books a private room at Plan B, the latest favourite restaurant of tourists and moneyed Capetonians. The kind of place that sees you at home later on lunging for the white bread and peanut butter or opening a can of tuna to make up for the tiny portions served with jus and foam and minute sculptures of things that may or may not be edible. Vegetables in unrecognisable shapes. Precious combinations: quails and figs, salmon and dark chocolate, mussels and blueberries and ripened Camembert. There is something ancient Roman about the menu, a decadence that goes beyond the prices; it's not my favourite place.

But.

The private room is a relief, although the enthusiastic lighting undermines the privacy. Murray is late, not surprisingly, so we sit.

"I thought this place would make a good backdrop for your presentation," Alice says.

Pretentious and overpriced? I want to ask, but I don't. "It's great. I'd just hope that the development will be successful for a little longer than Plan B."

She orders a rock shandy. I am disappointed, had imagined – hoped – that she'd have a few glasses of wine, and that the evening would relax and become as easy as our lunch on the Sea Point beachfront. Remember, through my little fantasy, that Murray will be around. Remember, in time, that this is work.

"Good idea," I say, and order one for myself.

She leans forward, puts on her teasing face, smiles with those eyebrows.

"So, Mr Hayes, I see you've ditched the crutches?" she says, her voice a little nasal with the joke of it. I blush, can't help it, the reason I've been hobbling around in pain for the past few weeks exposed by her tease. Of course, it's because of Alice, because I want to appear whole in front of her, complete, and I blush because I think she knows it as she would have known the reason for a trendy new haircut, a younger man's ironic T-shirt or a sudden pair of North Stars. Because I knew she would notice, comment, where Tracy would have done neither.

"I've been trying to get used to this thing for years. Paid a fortune for it, and most of the time it lies around gathering dust in the back of a cupboard. So."

"So?" she mimics, still smiling.

So I want to lean over the table, kiss you, take you home – yours, not mine – insert myself into your life, be part of it, lose myself in it because

153

I'm lost in my own, and being lost in yours would be infinitely more pleasant.

"So how did you get Anton to commit to a direction? Your brief was great, easy to get a grip on, easy to work with."

"Psych 101. Once you know Anton, he's like a puppy."

"And I suppose the only trouble is the crapping on the carpet every now and then."

"Okay, so he's a bit attention-deficit, maybe a bit bipolar too. Irritates the hell out of me sometimes, drives me nuts – 'Naughty Alice!'" – and she slaps herself on the wrist – "'You shouldn't be talking about the boss like that. Just think of the pay cheque, Alice dear, think of the CV.'" She raises her eyebrows and her rock shandy and says, "Here's to Anton."

Sips.

And then says, "Once you get to know him, you can tell when it's the right time to raise things. So right now, he thinks dinner was his idea. And when his wife calls after an hour or so, he'll think it's his idea to go home too."

"So his input on your brief was –?"

"Substantial. Fundamental. Seminal." Her sarcasm is light; it is also a cue for the way I should put my proposal to him.

"And you think this is the 'right time'?"

"He had some good news this morning. Got an outrageous offer on one of his developments by some pension fund or other, and of course accepted immediately. He doesn't come across as the most polished, old Anton, but he's shrewd. Street-smart. Got some kind of clairvoyant thing going. I bet that within a year after you've built the new thing it'll be on the market, at a sixty per cent premium to what it cost him. I guess we're a good team."

Just exactly what kind of team, I want to ask, but even if Murray hadn't arrived just then, I wouldn't have.

"Hey, Chris," he says. All jovial, a high-five instead of a handshake. And "Chris" this time, not "Craig".

"Howzit, Al." Shakes her shoulder, sits down between us at the table. "Now what can you kids tell me?"

From my bag I take a folder of A4 printouts, open my laptop, boot up.

"Apple – nice," says Murray, "weird but nice. Creative types, huh," and he looks at Alice and gestures at me with his thumb.

"Something to drink before we get going?" Alice asks him.

"Jeez, do I look like a sick person? As for you lot, it's time to lose the cooldrinks." He snaps his fingers and orders a double Jack Daniels, so I do too; Alice orders a vodka and tonic, gives me a look that suggests I allow her to take the lead. I am concerned about the possible effects of the booze on Murray – three sips and I'm afraid he will be lost to us.

"So, Anton," Alice begins. And reiterates her brief, has him nodding, agreeing, before she hands over to me. I hand him the printouts that I've brought, go through the presentation on my Mac. I can see him loving the paper mock-ups; after a while the images on the screen become superfluous, so I stop clicking through the presentation and simply talk him through the sheets of paper.

"Nice watch," he says halfway through.

And then I finish, and he sits back, takes a long gulp of the Jack he's hardly touched.

"Wow," he says. "Fucken wow." He grabs each of us by a shoulder, shakes hard. "Fucken bloody damn wow. Let's eat." And raises his arm and clicks his fingers again, and without consultation orders for us all from the more expensive menu and then says, "Wine?" but before we can express a preference he says, "Bugger the wine, in point of fact." This time he waves both arms to summon the waiter and orders a bottle of Veuve, and once the waiter has skulked off, he looks at me.

"Just one or two things, though," Murray says, and my heart sinks because those are the very words that usher in the hunchbacked Spirit of Compromise, the capricious God of Ego who is invoked when clients want to stamp their own little boot-prints of authority all over the work, and before you know it you are left with something banal at best, at worst a salad of incompatible ideas. But Murray has uttered the words, has ushered in the demons.

He riffles through the papers I've given him. Shuffles them again. I sit back, open my mouth to say something. Alice catches my eye, warns me off by shaking her head in tiny little stiff-necked shakes. So I pick up my Jack and take a sip. Murray peering at the elevations, running a middle fuck-you finger over the plan views as if it's helping him to see, as if there's a scanning device or an eyeball in the tip of it. And then he goes through them again.

"Don't you think," he says finally, reaching for his Jack and finishing it off, "that the typeface you've chosen for the signage is just fucken horrible?"

"It's not cast in stone," Alice says, and I shut my mouth. "We can get a graphic designer to sort it out."

Murray nods, slowly, focused and serious in a way I haven't seen before. "And don't you think," he continues – and I think, here it comes, the killer blow after the first sortie – "that the pillars you've indicated in the retail area will be a right royal pain in the arse for shoppers? I'm thinking trolleys here, mothers with prams, gangs of families having to bob and weave like Joe Frazier to get around the place?"

Alice's eyes are wide, looking at me.

"The pillars are a cost-saving measure," I say. "The alternative would be to span the area with arches. Expensive, because they'd have to be substantial. But if we put in arches, no pillars."

"Jesus. Have you ever been to Dubai Airport? It's a disaster with all those pillars in the way, like a fucken forest. So, lose the pillars. They'll de-value the place by millions and nobody will know why, except the three of us. It's – what's the word? – instinctive. Tenants will hate it and won't know why, so I'll be shitting Twinkies trying to get rentals. Customers won't come because of the bobbing and weaving and the way that groups of them are split up every ten steps. They'll never be able to tell you the reason be-cause they won't know *why* they don't like it – but that's exactly it: it's a shopping mall, not a fucking slalom course."

He gulps his Jack. I see there's more coming, am sure it will be on the same theme, say nothing.

"Thing is, if the shoppers stay away, I'll have a lot of tenant churn. We keep the pillars and in eighteen months I'll get offered x instead of x plus fifty per cent if we lose them. My God, imagine all that space, just float-ing, without all those horrible fucken pillars. Fuck the money, let's do it right."

He is agitated, and he's correct.

"Brilliant idea. So we lose the pillars, done," I say, sounding like Ivan.

"Just like that?" he says.

"Between me and the engineers, we'll sort it out," I say.

"Fan-fucken-tastic. New drawings by Thursday?"

"Friday," I say.

"Good enough for me. Cheers." He raises his glass; Alice's shoulders re-lax and I am thinking to myself, how on earth am I going to make those fucking pillars go away, least of all by Friday, when the waiter arrives with three enormous plates, each containing something the size of a dog pellet surrounded by squiggles of sauce and some green stuff, which is an-nounced as an amuse-bouche, on the house, to keep us entertained while we wait for our starters.

When the waiter opens the next bottle of Veuve I go easy because the amuse-bouche has not amused very much and has had little effect against the double Jack; when we toast I take a sip and Alice drinks the stuff half-way down and Anton finishes his off in a swallow and the world is good and kind and the goodness of it is made real by the adrenaline that flows when your work is accepted, appreciated, loved even.

Proudly announcing that he has to piss, Murray gets up. The waiter lets him exit before replenishing the glasses.

"Très slick, Mr Hayes," Alice says, hand raised in a Murray-style high-five. I lean forward and we are clumsy with the slap; our fingers slip into the other's and for a long moment we are holding hands, and when I check to make sure that what I feel is actually what has happened, I see she has stubby thumbs, the last joint of them half the length they should be, the nails wider than they are long.

"What happened to your thumbs, Miss Client?" I ask.

She retracts her hand and I want to retract my words but it is too late, so I meet the disconnection, the parting of hands, the squeezing of hers between her legs under the table, by saying, "Thanks for your warnings while I was presenting. And thanks for a great brief."

Alice ignores the platitude, pathetic as it is. "The thumbs are genetic, some throwback in the family tree, thanks for noticing." The age difference – so absent, then so apparent.

"Sorry," I say, "gormless."

She raises her eyebrows. "What are gorms, anyway?" she says lightly. I'm not following, perhaps the Jack and the half glass of Veuve, so she explains. "The expression is 'gormless'. That's a negative. You can't logically define things by a negative, by what they're not. So it has to mean having no gorms. Therefore, there have to be things such as gorms. It's like incapacitated – have you ever heard of someone who's capacitated?" So quick to move on from my tactless observation, this Alice.

"And here's Anton," I say, "definitely a capacitated man rich in gorms."

"Rich in what?" Murray says as he slides into his seat. And between us we try to explain, laughing, but he gets bored, twitches in irritation, pours more champagne without calling the waiter, declares that he is so fucking hungry that – and on cue the waiter appears with an assistant, I suppose the effeminate sidekick might be called. The assistant explains the intricacies of what we're about to eat – which won't be a hell of a lot, I'm sure. I suspect that, like me, Murray would be far happier with a plate of steak and chips, but then Alice reignites his enthusiasm with visions of the new development, firing him up again, and then we're served a tablespoon of bisque in bowls the size of Monaco. The edges are decorated with two small prawns, three slivers of fish and a mussel; the waiter pours white foam into the puddles of orange bisque, barista-style, making leafy patterns. Murray glares at him as he fiddles, and when the waiter steps away Murray consumes the concoction in all of thirty seconds.

Then his phone rings and he goes to a corner of our private room to take the call, speaks meekly. Alice looks at her watch – and just the way she cocks her wrist and the way it hangs, the strap too big, off-kilter: well. When you're besotted, the simplest things appeal.

"Told you," Alice says.

Murray returns, holds up the bottle to see what's left, fills his flute and downs it, all without sitting. Takes out his wallet, gives a credit card to Alice, points at me and says to her, "Do not let this man pay, or else," and on his way out he talks to the waiter, who backs away in tiny steps until Murray slips him a banknote. He waves at us, walks out the door.

"The wife," Alice says, "you can't believe."

"I thought –" I start saying, then shut up.

"What?" Alice says.

"Nothing, really."

Her eyebrows shoot up again into their perfect arches. "You thought we were having a thing, didn't you?"

"Well. Sort of, I suppose."

"Sort of nothing. You were either thinking it or you weren't. You can't sort of think something, that's not how the brain works."

"Psych 101?"

"And common sense. I mean, really, me and the boss? I don't do bosses."

"Nor do I," I say. It's a lousy rejoinder and suddenly I want to tell her about Tracy, about the limbo-ness of it, but the waiter returns, opens another bottle of Veuve, refills the glasses.

"See why I deal with him?" Alice says as she toasts, and I make sure to look into her eyes as I raise my glass, and then we talk small easy stuff, and when we finish the Veuve the waiter tops up our glasses and we look at each other and laugh and say no more after that and he pours and we talk and we drink and I go to the loo, trying not to limp, and when I'm there I unplug the prosthesis and massage the aching end of me for a minute or two.

Me and Alice, Alice and me; how could it be? Say I am c and Alice is a, surely $c + a \neq c + a$? Surely the sparks and cymbal-crashes will diminish and she'll tire of the squared-up edges, the tedium that is Chris Hayes at forty; surely the pull of her party-party, Phuza-Thursday friends will prove stronger than the one-legged old guy? And what do I want, anyway? Her approval as much as her body, her love as much as anything? I wash my hands, control my limp as I walk back to the table.

I don't know.

I've barely sat down when Alice says, "Jeez, you took your time, bye," and she uncrosses her legs and runs off to the loo, and when she returns she doesn't sit in her seat but comes around to my side of the table and pushes me back in my chair and straddles my lap and says, "Mr Hayes," and takes my face and kisses me so that Dalia's, Tracy's, Lynn's kisses seem like soda where Alice's are double Jacks – rich, tarry, warm, edible almost. And while we're drinking each other in, the waiter creeps up and drops a couple of shooters on the table – Jägermeister, I suppose: I don't much care, they're not able to compete with her kisses – and then he discreetly leaves, and Alice; well, Alice, the flavour and the love and the warmth and the humour of her around me body and soul, the zenith and the apex and the summit, like a dream I never thought I'd ever have.

We kiss for ever. My hand up, up her skirt – and then she stops, pulls back so sharply that I swear I can hear our kiss pop. Leans back, breathy, knocks over an empty champagne glass, gently pushes my arms away. Hooks her hands behind my neck, tosses her head to throw her hair back over her shoulders. Says softly, "Dammit, Mr Hayes. Two things wrong here: you're married, and I'm having my period. Time I left."

I drive home, though I shouldn't after all the Jack and all the Veuve, but I feel immortal, indestructible, all the more so once I've safely parked the Audi in the garage.

It's late, but Tracy is still awake as I limp into the bedroom. She is standing at the mirror, creaming and massaging and rubbing, in the nude as usual – the T-shirt she sleeps in lying on the bed, but her stringy body and its plastic augmentations are mere abstractions. She says nothing, doesn't ask how I've spent my birthday evening. On my thighs I can still feel the warmth and the pressure of Alice's legs, still smell her humanness on me, still taste her, and the lingering presence of her makes me feel wildly alive, impervious to the sight of my naked un-wife, happy to keep my silence. But maybe it's time to raise the Jono thing with her, to propose our un-marriage, because Alice's period won't last for ever, and this union of mine, this pretended thing, ended months, perhaps years ago: a few simple formalities and a barrel of cash will make it all go away, and Gabriel, well, other kids have survived the long division of their parents' marriages just fine, have survived the quotient, the remainders. And Gabe so much more in his skin these days, so much stronger. The high risk of Alice, where I will have to put everything on red alert and close my eyes and *will* it all to work out. And then, Tracy speaks without turning from the mirror.

"You're pissed," she accuses, as if she still holds some kind of dominion over me.

When.

I am amazed, feel a flash of anger.

"And you're fucking some guy called Jono," I say quietly.

Tracy stops dead. Grabs the T-shirt from the bed, storms off to the guest suite. Or at least I think it's the guest suite: I lie listening for the garage door, the Range Rover, but the Jack and the Veuve, well.

In the morning, I am irreversibly forty, and my wife is gone. I can't tell whether anything is missing from the boutique-sized dressing room, can't say if she has taken anything, packed a bag; don't know if she's moved out or simply gone to gym.

I check my phone before I leave for work, am hoping for something from Alice, but there's nothing, and I don't know whether I should call or text her because I don't know what to say – thanks for last night; I'd like to repay my bet and take you out tonight, tomorrow, Sunday, all of the above, every night until I hopefully die before you; you left me feeling like I haven't felt for years; I want to move in with you next week, tomorrow.

There's nothing from Alice, but there is a text message from Marietjie van der Westhuizen. *Please phone soonest*, last night's message reads, but it's barely seven-thirty now, too early to call her.

162

Gabriel trots down the stairs, school uniform looking like it's the end of the day rather than the beginning.

"Hi, Dad," he says.

"Hi, boy." I have never called him "boy", not sure where it comes from. He gives me a look, heads for the muesli and the yoghurt.

"See you later," I say.

"Dad?"

"Yes?"

"Where's Mom?"

"Out somewhere. Gym, maybe. Why?"

"It's a helluva walk to school."

I wait for Gabe to eat his breakfast so that I can drive him there. He chats all the way. Tells me he's benching sixty kg's these days, runs four kays in fourteen minutes if he pushes, ten in forty-seven. Tells me that he's joined a band – plays the bass, he says, forgetting that I've suffered through his solo sessions; happily it only has four strings, he says with a laugh.

I have a stranger in my car.

An awkward boy on New Year's Eve, a young man I barely know just nine months later. Alice, Tracy, Lynn, Marietjie, Sylvia, even Debbie – all these women clouding my view of my son growing up, and I feel nothing of the elation of the previous evening, just the tugging of guilt at my gut and a sadness that I have allowed this, this slipping away of my son. All too soon my child will no longer be my child, and the more I crave his company as he grows older, the more of a chore it will become for him to spend time with me. I've instead allowed others to paint all over my canvas; and the small dark corner of a corner allocated to Gabe that he's busy re-painting with brightness and light – I've been too caught up with everyone else's bullshit to notice. The theory behind this thing called life so simple: there's sex, you are born, you grow up, you love, there's sex, you work, you stop, you die. But there are so many lifetimes in between, running parallel, running transverse, running diagonally, and no religion, philosophy or self-help book has uncovered the simple theory of everything that holds it all together.

A thought occurs, its barbs cutting deep: Gabriel is doing better without me.

"Gabe," I begin as we pull in to the school drop-and-go.

"Yes, Dad?"

I don't actually know what I've planned to say. Or maybe I don't know how to say it, I don't know. I put my hand on his leg, rub and pat it as I used to rub and pat Schultz's head in the mornings.

Gabe looks at me oddly, pats my leg above its wound in return. "You be good now, Dad," he says. Grabs his bag from between his legs, climbs out the car, slings his bag over a shoulder. Slams the door with unnecessary force: the same as it ever was.

Before I drive off, Lynn pulls up next to me in her Cayenne, smiles, blows a kiss, waves, then pulls Peter's head towards her for a kiss, waits for him to get out, smiles and waves at me again as she pulls off, smiles and waves as though nothing has ever happened between us.

$c + l = 0$

It may be that she's right: perhaps nothing did happen, or perhaps what happened was nothing, I don't know, and I realise that I'd forgotten all about the event – such a non-event it must have been, or was it? Because at the time, well – whatever, since then, there has just been Lynn, Barry's wife, and Barry the Generous, Barry the Boet, a comet whose trajectory flits through the centre of my life from time to time.

I am about to drive away when my BlackBerry rings and this time it's Marietjie van der Westhuizen herself, singing her name as if it were a question: "Hello, Chris, it's Marietjie."

"Hi, Marietjie."

"She's changed her mind, Chris. She wants to see you."

And then some woman behind me in a Discovery, hooting because she has a child to offload and a gym to go to and hair to have done and friends to meet so would I please be so kind as to fuck off out of the way.

Chris and Debbie

"I don't have a lot of money, you know," is how she – *She* – greets me.

I'm in a soulless coffee shop at OR Tambo Airport. I've flown up to Johannesburg, the airport the most convenient meeting point for both of us. I left my book untouched for the two-hour flight, watched instead, through the lens of hair product on the window, the dawn breaking over the Cape's soft greens and its grey mountains with their dusting of late snow. Wondered what I would find in Joburg as I watched the scarred Karoo pass by ten thousand metres below, the desiccated Free State with its empty dams turned to the heavens like begging bowls, the flat fawn Highveld with its black bushfire scars as we dropped from the sky. Joburg with its perennial blanket of smog. An ugly city of sprawling malls, red dust, pot-holed tarmac, expensive cars. It quivers in the morning haze, tensed for its daily pursuit of money. "Cape Town," Barry once said on returning from a Johannesburg trip, "is the lipstick on the pig of South Africa."

I'd been expecting Debbie for almost an hour, had begun to think she'd stood me up, so her arrival startles me – she is suddenly *there*, there after forty years of not.

I stand up on my good leg, knocking my crutches off the chair beside me; my prosthesis is back inside the wardrobe.

"You must be Chris," she says, extending her hand. It's shaking slightly, but the grip is firm. Cold, papery.

"And you must be Debbie." I sit down again, bend over to retrieve my crutches.

"I must," she says. She removes her jacket, drapes it over the back of a chair. Unwinds a light scarf. Shakes out her hair. Sits, places her bag on her lap. Takes out a pair of spectacles, puts them on, appraises me.

"I'll pay for coffee, then," I say while she examines me.

"Oh, I have money for coffee. What I mean is that I'm a futile blackmail target. You'll get nothing out of me, you know, because there's nothing to be had."

After forty years, this her opening gambit; and she is smiling. Perhaps this abrasive introduction reflects her humour, or is it possibly a defence? Or neither.

"I'm financially fine. That's not why I'm here."

"Good. Now, how did you lose your leg?"

"Car accident," I tell her, shrug as though it was nothing, which of course it wasn't; it was everything at the time. I'm not going to give the details, the New Year's of it, the Dalia of it; I am irritated because I am here for me to find out about her, not the other way around. I am here too, I realise, to see her weep with joy at the reunion, with delight and relief at the fact that her rejected progeny has struck a reasonably solid path through life, did not become a drug addict or a criminal or a tramp. But I expect too much. Or too little, I don't know.

"You look a lot less like Pete than I'd imagined. Just the chin," she says after a moment. And removes her glasses, puts them back into her bag.

"So I suppose this Pete was my father."

"Heavy word that, father. Your sire, perhaps, as I was your dam." I dislike the self-denigration, the glib mea culpa behind her comment.

"I hear he's dead."

She tells me that he died young. A pharmacy student with an unhealthy interest in the chemicals he had at hand. Overdid some home-made substance one night towards the end of his doctorate year, and then.

"He was Afrikaans, you know." How could I, but anyway. "Petrus Jacobus van Deventer. 'Pete' was our joke; he had an accent as thick as a tree-trunk. Was from Potchefstroom or Pietersburg or somewhere like that. Family tree going back to the earliest Dutch settlers. He was very proud of that – I often had to tell him to stop talking about it."

The first dribble of information stuns, a fat drop of water from nowhere, hitting my forehead – hard, cold, wet.

"Well, anyhow, the way you're looking at me." She shrugs. "I was nineteen, finding my independence and I took it a step too far. Couldn't bear his accent. But such a beautiful boy; that was enough then."

I can find nothing to say, but Debbie does.

"Do you know that I think of you every year on your birthday?"

I smile to hide my scepticism.

"Every fourth of October I find a quiet place somewhere to have a little private moment."

"Every fourth of October?"

"Without fail."

"Debbie, my birthday is on the twenty-seventh of September."

She looks at me blankly. Confusion clouds her face; I want to turn the screw, want to hurt her, but there is nothing to gain. Look away from her frown, her blinking. "Happy birthday for last week, then." Almost whispered; she's still puzzled, unconvinced. I decide to turn us away from this impasse.

"And what does life hold for you now?" I ask.

She brightens. "After I left my first husband, I married Lewis. We have two kids, much younger than you, of course. A son and a daughter. But —"

The waiter arrives. We order the coffee we haven't come here to drink.

"Why the change of heart?" I ask.

"Change of heart?"

"You didn't want to see me and then you changed your mind."

She scratches in her handbag as if the answer is in there, hidden by a hairbrush and a purse and a cellphone and a compact. She stops, looks up. "It was a shock, at first. That phone call from Martie or whatever the woman's name is. I mean, you can imagine, after all these years. I had to think things through, get my mind right, and that took time. We all have things on the shelf that need a good dusting off before we can see them clearly. I'm sure you understand."

I don't; it's all crap. Curiosity alone won out over her fears — what I might have wanted from her, might have imposed on her. But I don't push her. Am still trying to digest that I have a brother, a sister. Half, at least. Half, like everything else I have. People I may have passed in the street, sat next to on an aeroplane, shouted at in the traffic. Blood half-shared; what else?

Debbie doubles back and revisits the facts of her family in greater detail, offering me a flood of information that is of no use. I catch only the odd word: I am too busy trying to imagine my siblings, my drug-addicted and cleft-chinned father. Do they look like me, this half-brother, sister — tall, dark, vaguely Roman? Like me, like Debbie? She is tall, slim, dark hair elegantly cut. A silver lustre on the ebony. I look for a glimpse of Gabriel, of me, but the identikit doesn't measure up.

"But, you were saying earlier?" I prompt her once the prattle about her family dribbles to a halt.

"But you have to promise me never to tell them. They don't know about you at all, and I'd hate to think how they'd react if they found out."

"I've been through this with the agent," I say. "I am not here for your money, to disrupt your life, to have you thrown onto the street, to compromise you in any way at all."

She picks up on my tone. "I'm so sorry, darling, I just had to hear it from you."

Darling.

Jesus. What fucking right?

Debbie carries on about herself. Lives in the plush north of Joburg where, I know, the tan veld has surrendered to green lawns. Her husband is a something in some mining company or other, I don't care enough to seek clarity. She looks at me, senses something, interrupts herself.

"And what do you do, Chris?" she asks. Seems amazed that I'm an architect: her kids are not creative – she can't understand where I came by the ability to draw, to visualise. And Pete a pharmacist, a pure left-brainer, so where did I come from? She starts again with her husband, her children, but I feel a mist descending; again my senses retreat to a fraction of their normal powers, retreat into themselves as I try to decode things she has said thirty seconds, a minute previously. She blurs behind an opaque film, her words a low bubbling porridge. I feel I am having coffee – which the waiter finally brings, spilling it from the cups into their saucers – I feel I am having coffee with a younger friend of Sylvia's, a friend who has nothing very interesting to say. Because there is nothing in common between us other than the table we share.

I am being polite, nodding, not connecting or engaging with the babble, hoping that my gestures are congruent with what she is saying. But that hungry part of me cannot be satiated by stories of Debbie's wonderful life: I don't much care about her loves or successes or disappointments or her pride in her unknown family. It is a post-history, a follow-up to the movie, when what I want is the prequel, to know what happened *before*. Before me. Before biologies conspired to suck me from the void and to give me bones and hair and teeth. Debbie's information is useless, like trying to satisfy a starving man with images from a glossy cookbook.

I shake off the curtain between us, cut across her.

"So, that's all very interesting. But where do I come from?" Immediately disliking the petulance.

She stirs her coffee, drinks. "Chris Hayes," she says, shakes her head, laughs. "What a name you've ended up with, my goodness." She shakes her head again, looks at me. "My maiden name was Barashenkov." And waits.

"Yes, and?"

"My mother's maiden name was Jozwiak."

I feel there's more coming, but I can't foresee what it might be. Can only taste and see distant lands of eastern Europe, the Caucasus, in the names. Potatoes and rough bread and earth-browned snow cut to mush by wooden wheels. Cloudy beer, home-brewed vodka. Wood stoves. Fiddles and concertinas. Cabbage. The grassy smell of livestock. Stumpy-legged women in headscarves, old before their time, leading donkeys past diminutive houses, hay or beet or the nothing of hunger on the creaking carts behind. Names like an unknown music. Hard, dissonant sounds. The most secret of secret names, each bearing its own protection, like a tortoise or an armadillo.

"Well, Chris Hayes, this is how it is."

And she tells me the little she knows of the story of Sara and Mendel.

"Your grandmother was rescued from the pogroms of the Ukraine by a South African businessman in 1921."

"Pogroms?"

"Yes." She lifts her coffee cup, puts it down again. "You're a Jew, Chris Hayes. Without the rescue, I wouldn't be here. Nor would you."

Another splash of cold water, hard on the forehead.

She sips her coffee, lets me digest. So, not English then, not Albanian or Greek. I am of Ivan's people, should perhaps be wearing pop-art yarmulkes and not eating pork or prawns.

"And the businessman?" I finally say. It's not the question I mean to ask; it simply comes out. What the right question is I don't know.

"Isaac Ochberg. He rounded up almost two hundred Jewish orphans, brought them to South Africa. Sara was one of them, came on the boat, grew up in the Jewish orphanage in Cape Town, met Mendel, got married. Had me. I had you. And there it is."

She looks away, shakes her head, laughs a short laugh.

"It's ridiculously ironic," Debbie continues. "I had to fight so hard to shake off the old ways, to deny my history, my genetics, my parents, I had to change my name, and here my long-lost son ends up – without asking – the ultimate Wasp. Oblivious. Easy. And," she laughs, "to top it all, 'Chris' – is that short for Christian or Christopher?"

Her smile is tight, a hand fluttering about while she talks, as if it is blessing the neglected coffee cups, the sugar, the scum-skinned milk. Is she envious of the ease with which I slipped into my upbringing, into my life, this woman who handed my heritage away the moment she handed me, the meat and soul of me, to someone else? I am a Jew, and running through my veins is blood that precedes Moses, Noah, reaches back through the ages to one of the twelve tribes, and perhaps all the way back to Eden itself, if things are to be believed.

I am Jewish. I am a Jew. I would have been no less surprised than if she had told me I was a pine tree, an eel, a bar-stool.

And I am also Afrikaans, the child of Protestant settlers, who before that were the children of Holland, pushing back the sea with their dykes and polders as the Jews began new lives in the Diaspora. The snobbishness:

perhaps I should be one of those who own a Hilux, live in Durbanville, have a braai built into the patio of my face-brick house.

I consider my hesitancy at celebrating a little Jewish something with Ivan. It is the Jewish thing that gets me, grabs at my chest, shallows my breathing: we white South Africans are bastards of the most diverse sort, and to discover that you are part Dutch, part Malay slave, part Xhosa, part French – that is no surprise. But to discover that you are a Jew, well.

Jews do not let go, unless, clearly, they are Debbie. There is a mountain to climb in becoming a Jew, in being one, I think, and it's a hard balancing act to remain on the summit. One look at Ivan and you know that Judaism is blood, as much a race as a religion, a full-time occupation.

Whereas, after a splash of water on the forehead and a lifetime of denial, one can still claim to be a Christian.

"Christian," I tell Debbie.

"Christened Christian," she says. Smiles her tight smile again, shakes her head, peers into her coffee cup as though it might present a divination.

But I want to know more. About Sara's parents, about Mendel's mother. Debbie shrugs.

"It's all so long ago, I don't remember all the stories. Sara lived in a village, a shtetl, somewhere in what's now Belarus. It was not a good time to be a Jew – never is, come to think of it. One day news arrived that a group of Cossacks were heading towards the village, so the adults sent the kids to hide in the forest. When they arrived, the Cossacks raped and killed the adults and plundered the little houses. Sara once – once only – told me the story of pink snow flying on the wind when the children returned to the village, and how soon enough they discovered that it wasn't snow at all, that it was feathers from featherbeds stained with the blood of the dead villagers."

I'm holding my cup above the saucer, scared to move in case she stops.

"Nobody came for the children, so they upped and left and marched for weeks, got to some big town – Minsk or Pinsk or something, I don't remember, and ended up in the local Jewish orphanage. That's where Ochberg found them. Applied his criteria of intelligence and health, and had the lucky ones shipped to Cape Town. Sara was one of them, and twenty years or so later, she married Mendel and they lived happily ever after."

As if they were fairy-tale characters and their lives fables and fancies from Grimm. But there could not have been a happily-ever-after when their daughter turned away from them, away from five and a half millennia of heritage.

There is a silence. I have now bitten off too much. The starving man has over-eaten. I am struggling to digest but still I want more, want to stuff every cavity of my body with the untasted bits of me.

Debbie sips her coffee, offers me another morsel. I don't know what to do with it. "I used to be Dvorah, you know. Changed it to Deborah, then Debbie just stuck." The tight smile again: is she apologising this time, apologising to me for her choices? I don't know. Assimilation, Ivan calls it: the worst thing a Jew can do, to become a chameleon, to change his colours to suit circumstance, for as soon as he denies his faith he will lose it, like a muscle that weakens and atrophies when not used. And then he will become one of *them*, a Gentile, a not-Jew, and another of the precious number will be lost.

"Why?"

"Cape Town – South Africa, I suppose – in the seventies. Christian, Calvinist, narrow, Nazi almost in its own way. Jews were good to have around as lawyers and accountants, just as blacks were good to have as cleaners and labourers. Neither were good to have as friends. And all I wanted was friends, normal friends who spent Saturdays at the beach in summer or at the movies in winter. And bacon, they couldn't excuse bacon." She laughs. A society laugh, practised, mirthless.

"What of Mendel and Sara?"

"Mendel died, late seventies."

"And Sara?"

"She's still alive." Debbie – Dvorah, Deborah – my mother, my betrayer, my informant, my Pandora, my coffee guest – Debbie roots around in her bag once more, retrieving not more of the answer, but her purse.

"Please don't," I say. I am afraid that if I let her pay for coffee, she will take my indulgence as absolution, misconstrue our meeting as a ritual of forgiveness where, by sharing a few bits of my past and then paying for coffee, she can finally forgive herself the life she gave me, the life she took away.

"Oh, really darling, but I must."

But you mustn't. You mustn't presume that a bombshell and a handful of scraps give you the right to a clear conscience. You owe me so very much more than coffee, so much more than money or love: you owe me answers, can't just walk away without giving them to me. I want to tell her all these things, but I don't. Don't know how to pry the words off my tongue.

Debbie glares at the waiter, willing him towards her. I do the same, am pleased that he has been trained to believe that men are the payers. He hands a sticky blue folder to me. I put it at the corner of the table, out of Debbie's reach.

"You were telling me about Sara."

"Was I?" Her eyes fall on the folder at my elbow. She allows her handbag to settle back into her lap, takes a deep breath; it would be rude even for Debbie to leave before the bill is settled. "She's alive, but not very well. We've had to put her in a home – we couldn't cope with the care any more. Alzheimer's is so very destructive as it progresses. One is simply helpless."

Oh, I know, I want to say, but I cannot give her a reason to deflect the conversation now.

"Which home is she in?" I ask.

Debbie flaps a hand at the door, at the wall, at the window opposite, indicating a multitude of homes out there. "There's a good one down south," she says.

"South?" I ask. "Joburg South?" To anyone who comes from the north of Johannesburg, the south and its tough inhabitants exist only in rumour, are seldom visited.

"Cape Town, actually," she replies, irritated.

"I'd like to visit her. You've told me so much and so little, maybe she could add more. Fill in the gaps, bring a bit more colour and texture to things."

"It's impossible, Chris. She's ninety-three and can barely remember who I am; she's in no state to have a cosy fireside chat with someone she's never met."

"Okay then, in that case it won't matter if I visit her, just to see her, look at her. See if there's anything there that I can spot of Gabriel, of me."

Debbie's face, I'm sure, sharpens as I look at her. Something, I can't say what, happens to her eyes, the blue of them gone cold and angry.

"No, Chris."

"Debbie, I have two living links to a past I never knew I had. Now that I've met one, why are you denying me the chance to meet the other?"

She turns her head to look at the harried airport crowd, shakes her head, a sudden wetness in her eyes, blinks it back.

"Do you visit her often?" I ask.

Debbie cocks her head, cups an ear. "Beg pardon?" she says. That trick of liars, to feign deafness or incomprehension, buying time for their thoughts to gain traction.

"How often do you visit her?" I repeat. Debbie, Dvorah, whatever, fiddles in her bag, finds nothing, looks up at me.

"Whenever I can," she says, looks up, breathes deep. "It's hard, you know."

"What, the travelling or the visiting?"

She looks away, shrugs, doesn't answer.

"Sara never knew about me, did she?" I ask.

The tiniest shake of her head. "No," she says. "Nobody did. Does." And she consults her wristwatch, Rolex Oyster, platinum and gold, the daintier woman's model. The society voice returns. It is an alarming shift, as though she is suddenly channelling Joan Collins. "Good heavens, darling, is that the time already? Everyone's going to be frantic; I told them I was going to the shops for an hour, and now just look."

She takes her car keys from her bag and places them on the table. They are Range Rover keys, I notice. Then she stands up, the unpaid bill no longer enough to keep her seated. I begin to stand up but she waves me down again.

"Please don't, darling," she says. Comes around the table and puts a hand on my shoulder and pecks me on each cheek. Looks me in the eyes before she removes her hand. Drops a note, far too much for the coffee we've barely touched, onto the folder: the pay-off, the forty-year penance, the pieces of silver squirrelled out of her purse, snuck up on me despite. "And please don't contact me again. You now know as much as I do, not that there's much to know other than the facts of it. This has been harder for me than you might think, Chris. I've lived with you on my mind for forty-odd years, and then this. We're both seeking closure here and this is pretty much it, this is closure, this is it, this is as good as it gets. So please don't."

There is no emotion there any longer. Back straight, blue eyes dry. Blue

eyes, dark hair, pale skin: the perfect disguise for a defector, an assimila-
tor, an assimilationist, whatever. And then, out of the coffee shop and into
the airport herd, in her movements more suppleness and grace than her
fifty-nine years should allow. Places the scarf around her neck, releases
her hair with a flick of her hand and a shake of her head, and then she is
gone, heading back into her clearly blackmailable life.

Which took more of her time, I wonder: the coupling with Petrus Jacobus
van Deventer or this meeting with the issue of it? I look around the coffee
shop; surely someone must have noticed us, the oddness of our encounter? But people continue sipping their coffee, chatting. The young couple
amorous over their Americanos: are they reconnecting, or are they about
to part? Among the elbows and the coffee cups and half-eaten muffins on
the table tops lie crumpled napkins and empty sugar sachets. Briefcases
and hand luggage at their owners' feet, ready to trip up the heedless. The
man to my right speaks low, urgent Czech or Russian into his cellphone,
the consonants like angry bees trapped under a tooth-glass.

  I leave Debbie's money for the waiter, a too-big tip, but I am not going to
pocket her change.

  Try to get on an earlier flight. Buy a *Time* magazine, can't focus. Wait.

So I flew to Joburg that day a lapsed Christian, and returned an under-
qualified Jew. Flew out with everything I wanted and little that I needed,
returned with a mother, with a half-brother and half-sister, with brief and
broken stories about a grandfather and grandmother, a father. Flew out
an empty vessel, flew back filled with half-truths and mixed feelings. The
knowing of it all, and the danger of knowing: I could not un-know *Her*
now, denialist Debbie, denying her name and what was hers for almost six
thousand years, denying everything else that was hers for forty more.

Say I am c and Debbie is d: If $c + d = x$, solve for x – which may or may not be the answer you're looking for.

You get everything, or what you think is everything, and then there's always more.

There's an infinity between "simply everything" and "absolutely everything": absolutely everything is the *addition* to the everything of whatever is predictable, planned for, anticipated – an addition that comes from nowhere and everywhere at the same time, and feels like a punch to the face, a kick to the groin. It might take the form of an accident, or adultery uncovered, or dug-up roots that twist in unexpected directions. And there is nothing simple about it. The more furiously you seek simplicity, the more tangles you encounter.

The *addition* – it might take the form of questions unasked, or questions that occur too late in the day: What *do* you think about every twenty-seventh of September, every fourth of October, whatever the date of my actual birthday is?

Who held your head when you sweated and cried and panted your way through it all forty years ago? What did they say – there's always a *they* – what did they say when you went into Joburg General with your belly preceding you, when you emerged with nothing more than your overnight bag and some painkillers? Did it hurt, the passing of this unwanted thing? They say it's like pissing a watermelon, but I can't imagine doing that either.

I don't much care if you bled, tore, or whether or not they had to stitch you up afterwards; I want to know if it hurt down to your soul, and if so, exactly how much, in whatever units they measure pain. How much hurt was in the handing over, the finality of that post-post-partum, nine months of potential resolved after a few hours of screaming and pushing – or perhaps a sedated C-section. Was it a relief, the comfort of an emetic suddenly working, a 3.5 kg burden miraculously expelled, instantly eliminated? And the burden that dropped from your shoulders, your heart, even greater?

Bitter, sour, acid questions, all the more so for not being asked, for the lack of answers.

You think you know yourself so well, but what you end up knowing is the simple things. How to negotiate a contract. How to buy a house. How to use a pair of crutches. How to beat the rush-hour traffic. How to make instant coffee palatable. How to get married, have a child, how to fill a bank account, write cheques, swipe a credit card, crowd your space with expensive, fragile things. How to be cuckolded, how to cuckold, how to use Google to find someone who will trace the dead-end of your past. You know that you're a detribalised person living in a borrowed country which you're only passing through. And then you discover you're twice detribalised – a detribalised member of a nomad race whose shallow roots are thousands of years deep and whose tendrils curl across the branches of the world like fairy lights or lianas, right to the very far ends of it. How many times can you be disowned, how many times can you trace roots that go nowhere, how many times before you float up off the face of the earth like a helium balloon, up and on, eventually to pop at an altitude once the pressure in you is too much, to burst where nobody can hear you, see the falling remains of you?

I don't know.

When I get home I hear Gabriel grunting away in apparent agony. I hope he isn't wanking, peer through the thumb-tacked curtain at the entrance to his nest. He has dragged our old organist's bench up the stairs. He is lying on it, his feet on the floor on either side, doing flies with a pair of twenty-five-kilogram dumbbells that I've never seen before. I know I'd struggle to do what he is doing. Am pleased that he's not hiding behind the garage with a pack of Camels or a joint of Durban Poison.

"Your arms are a little too bent, Gabe," I say. "Straighten a touch and you'll work your pecs better."

He sits up. I can see the effort has made him dizzy, his eyes aren't quite focused; he sweats a smelly teenage sweat and what remains of his acne glows.

"I was trying to do my triceps."

"Then you need to bend a bit more."

He shakes his head. The shake says what it always says: I cannot ever fucking please you. Then he lightens up. "Guess what, I ran, like, eighteen kays this morning."

"That's fantastic, Gabe. Really good aerobic stuff."

"Well, it was on the treadmill, so I know it's only good for, like, ten or twelve on the road. But the rain this morning, wow, like, insane."

"So? That's ten or twelve kays you wouldn't have covered any other way."

"I suppose."

"What are you aiming for here? Bulk? Fitness?"

Gabriel looks at me, "Jeez, Dad, I'm, like, an ectomorph, you know, so I'm never going to look like a wrestler. I just feel good doing this stuff. Run a bit, get into the weights a bit. Whatever."

I want to crutch over to him, hug him. I want to sweep him up because what he is doing is good, because I am proud. I want to feel the hardness of him in my arms, a hardness I hope has seeped into his spirit, because the world, well.

But I know he, I, would be embarrassed. "That's great, Gabe," I say instead. "And try it with your iPod, it'll seem like a lot less work."

He unplugs the white earbuds from his ears, shakes them at me, puts them back in. I roll my eyes, acting the stupid one.

"Like, thanks, Dad," he says. And smiles.

"Just be careful out there, okay?"

That look once more, as though he's expecting me to call him "boy" again.

"Okay, Dad."

Half an hour later, Tracy arrives home. She barks orders at Martha about the dinner the poor woman has already prepared. Brushes past me; I sniff as she does so, instinctively, checking for a whiff of – a whiff of what? Semen? Old Spice? Fish? I don't know.

"Hi, Tracy," I say. She doesn't greet me back. Nor does she ask me anything. Despite the fact that she knows where I've been today, why.

And then, in bed. My stump still itch-hurting from its recent adventures with the prosthesis. Tracy once again hugging the far edge of the mattress as though it were a cliff, ready to fling herself off if I come near. And the knowledge that she knows that I know about her secret life, can never unknow it, that she is faking the mechanics of our marriage – for what? Because she fears admitting guilt, the fallout, the cutting off of the cash-flow? The power of knowledge, almost as great as the pretence to knowledge: she will believe that I know so much more than I do – who this Jono is, where to find him, where he works. And today I found out even more about Tracy herself, about her son, about her husband. All the knowing at once purgative and constricting; and now that I know so much, I know so very little.

In my dreams pink feathers fall against a black sky, and I am running around, frantic, desperate to collect from their clouds those that have my blood on them.

Chris

Are you obliged to *be* a Jew if you *are* a Jew? And if so, just how do you go about being one when you've never been one before? Where do you start? Do you begin by going somewhere – I don't know where – and buying a collection of art-inspired yarmulkes? And the next time you're at the office, should you say, "Shalom, Ivan, guess what?"

Do you look up a rabbi in the Yellow Pages, explain that you have the blood but not the wherewithal, the history but not the faith, that you might need a bit of your dick cut off to qualify? And what would he instruct? That you begin to learn Hebrew, the calligraphy of it, learn to read backwards, learn about the absence of vowels and what the dots around the letters mean; then, learn thousands of years of history, mythology, somehow climbing the mountain of unbelief to the summit of revelation as you acquire the technical knowledge of it all; then book a date with your newfound rabbi and bite down as he slices off the offending piece of you? What of your right to a bar mitzvah with a disco party and gifts from friends? And how will you ever grasp the difference between Rosh Hashanah and Pesach, the penitence of Yom Kippur?

I don't know.

The secret codes of it all, so much more than the bookwork: the comments, gestures, the chatter peppered with Yiddish; the secret community of it, and me the newcomer, never to be quite invited in beyond the polite outer circle of the community, over the threshold; the duality of loyalties – Israel, South Africa – so much stronger, more visceral than the faded duality of settlers in former colonies and their distant provenance. The smart Jews are wanderers, swallows, it seems, leaving the gathering winters of pogroms, concentration camps, inquisitions, revolutions. Air plants, all of them, comfortable wherever they might land, as long as they can reach back to Temple Mount, reach to the deep and ancient core of it.

And inside of me, beneath me almost, a suspicion of anti-Semitism never examined before: do I not like Ivan because he is Ivan, or because he is a Jew? Have I instigated investigations through Shahid because Ivan is, quite simply, a greedy Jew? Have I avoided his regular invitations to Friday nights and festivals because of a bigoted throwback part of me, a gene of denial I have inherited from my mother? Because the truth is I would rather not do the ancient incantations, the hocus-pocus of religion. Because the accents are resonant with differentness, an alien semi-Eastern aesthetic of dunes and dust rather than England's familiar misty meadows. Is this bigotry in me? Jews appearing in my imagination like Nazi propaganda cartoons: thick of lip, large of nose, squat of body, short of sight, hairy of forearm, praying strangely to a half-shared God while keeping one ear open for the next good deal, the money changers in the Temple, the Jesus killers – or am I merely imagining my prejudice?

I don't know.

It would be simpler of course not to be a Jew at all. To laugh it off, Dvorah-Deborah-Debbie-style, as you might laugh off a long-ago lunatic perching in the family tree; to do what my school friend Dom Hares did by claiming Scotland as his heritage, claiming his name to be *hares* as in rabbits instead of the *arrez* of the Algarve, because it was easier and cooler and far less isolating to be Scots among the Wasps than to be Portuguese.

The secret names of it all.

Perhaps to do what Dvorah did when she became Debbie, except in reverse: to change my name from Christian to Mordecai or Isaac or Moishe, a new secret name, in the hope that, in itself, it might plumb the depths of the Mount, an automated drilling rig burrowing into the heart of it, bringing whatever riches it finds to the surface. But the idea makes me instantly tired, fills my limbs with heaviness, sucks the energy from me.

So, to do something, or nothing. Or half of something. Or half of nothing, but $\frac{1}{2}0 = 0$. To do something other than waiting for roots to spring out of me, bury themselves in the ground of belonging. There are no clues, no nudgings in any direction. No divine signs or recommendations or revelations. I've never needed anyone to tell me what to do, and now, well: now there *isn't* anyone who can tell me.

I put it all on hold, wait for a flash of light, a bolt, a voice.

Or nothing.

And then, a Friday afternoon weeks later, Ivan.

We've finished reviewing the final work on the Murray project. I am pleased with it. With Alice's help, I have managed to develop, and get Murray to commit to, a final plan, one without pillars, at a far greater cost. The result is crisp, simple, practical, original, and it bears Murray's signature.

"Fantastic," Ivan says. He slaps the boardroom table. "Great for the portfolio, even better for the bank account."

"Thanks, Ivan." I can no longer call him Ive, can no longer enjoy his dislike of it.

Ivan begins to roll up the large-format printouts. I watch him and realise I'm hoping for one of his Shabbat invitations.

"There," Ivan says once he's put the plans away. He pats the protective tubes. As if he'd done the work. Stands, looks at his watch, raises his eyebrows. "Oops, have to run."

He walks towards the door.

"Ivan," I say. He stops and turns to me. "Do you have a spare seat at Shabbat tonight?"

"What?" he says. I can see he's wondering how serious I am. "You're kidding."

"No, I'm not."

"Wow." He blinks. "It'll be a late night; we'll only get going after shul. Lots of people, family."

"Okay, no problem. Another time, then."

"Not at all, my God. I'm just a little surprised. It's been – what? Six, eight years? Just trying to give you an out here, in case you were pissing about. We'd love to have you. Love it."

Gabriel doesn't want to come, of course, but he does see a free lift to his friend, George the Dog. Tracy tells me baldly that she has book club that night, can't get out of it. No Jono at the book club, from what she says; no Jono anywhere: she has said nothing about my accusation, not a word, after returning home silently that same evening. I hear Gabe making plans on the phone – he and George plan to get up early, to run the five or six kilometres from Camps Bay to the summit of Suikerbossie, past Llandudno, back again. I am beside myself with pride; envious too: with two whole legs, well – but it is a difficult route, uphill all the way there, downhill back, tough on the thighs on the outbound leg, hell on the shins and the toenails on the return. I am proud of him because he has made a choice that does not involve sneaking out of George's house late at night to attend some party or other, or ploughing through George's father's liquor cabinet, or swallowing pills that the vendor promises will make you feel good.

Tracy applying her make-up with care and concentration, half-dressed as usual, when I say goodbye: tight top and G-string – now I notice the slightly sagging bum, smirk. Skirt and heels put to one side, ready to slip into. An overnight bag left in full view, as though she wants me to challenge, wants me to question the appropriateness of the outfit for a book club evening. It crosses my mind, but of course I don't, won't give it to her.

Ivan's house is high up on the slopes of Fresnaye. I crutch up the many steps, look back across the ink of the bay before I ring the bell. Ships at anchor like floating tea-lights. At my feet, the lights that delineate Sea Point, Bantry Bay, Fresnaye, bounded by the sea and the black mountain behind, like a hole in the sky. Above it, a few stars poke through the light pollution, far fewer than in the moonlit Cederberg sky on the night that Lynn and I, well. A passenger jet leaving the city, winking its taillights in farewell. Another arriving, bringing relieved Capetonians home, giving weary foreigners a glimpse of the city that lies between the black of the sea and the mountains like spilled diamonds, broken glass.

A woman half-opens Ivan's front door. Headscarf and matching overall. Looks at me through narrowed eyes. I explain myself, she shows me in. Everyone still at shul, she says. Points to the lounge without offering me anything to drink. Although Ivan had said eight o'clock, I am the first to arrive. I sit on the leather couch and look at the mosaic of paintings that fill the wall, go all the way to the ceiling: Ivan's art, disparate pieces collected not for their aesthetics but for their value, not all of them straight on their hangings. Books with arcane cyphers and the Star of David on their spines; a dog-eared John Fowles, *A Maggot*, its black spine cracked white from many readings: I cannot imagine that this will bear on the evening's proceedings. A scatter of half-tended post on a sideboard, some of the envelopes opened, with their contents stuffed back inside; a white Chinese-style vase with converging veins of yellowed super-glue cutting through the soft blue images. A scratch here, a scuff there; silver candelabra, teapots, goblets, their edges and corners tarnished with the liver spots of age; a boxy old television set silently mouthing a local soap; the smell of fish frying, the phone ringing, unanswered. Bohemian. So unlike the prim suburbs, so unlike the anal Ivan I know.

And then a deluge of people, so many that I cannot keep the faces named. No Ivan or Janice about, but everyone helps themselves, seems to know where to find soft drinks and snacks. They sit, stand, chat, laugh. The front door left open to admit the guests: one of them is Ndumiso Ndlovu, a vaguely familiar black woman on his arm, beautiful, Ndlovu mingling confidently, singling out individuals for greetings and a chat as he goes.

A man offers to pour me a whisky, hands it to me, sits down. The tight curls of his grey hair threaten to unspring and fling his yarmulke across the room.

"What's with the leg?" he asks.

"Car accident," I say.

He shakes his head, says "Oy." Then raises his glass and an eyebrow. "Well, here's to the other one," he says. I am unused to the candour, the eyes that don't slide away. We toast, talk. He is a property lawyer; I tell him what I do. "So it's *the* Chris Hayes I'm talking to? Nice work on the Century Plaza. Very neat."

And so on.

Others come, introduce themselves, spot the leg, insist that I don't get up. A woman in black sits down opposite me, her little blonde daughter – blonde, green-eyed: Aryan, I catch myself thinking – sits on her lap and stares at my stump, my crutches. She clutches an ancient stuffed toy under her arm.

"Where's your leg?" she asks. The mother looks up, smiles at me for the answer.

"I lost it," I say.

"Silly!" the little girl giggles. "How can you *lose* your leg? Mine's joined onto me, look." She kicks out her leg and twists the foot on the end of it from side to side. Her mother laughs too, leans in to her and explains the expression. Then she introduces herself – Leora, I think – and lightly apologises.

The familiarity of it all, the intimacy. Foreign, like the squared letters of the Hebrew I can't decipher on spines of books, like the many-branched candelabra with no candles, the chandelier with its dangly crystal adornments.

Ivan and Janice arrive, greet their guests with handshakes and hugs. Janice is a large lady, large horizontally rather than vertically. A second chin wobbles as she stomps about the house greeting her guests. Then Ivan dishes out multi-coloured yarmulkes from a pewter bowl. Calls us to the table for prayers, some of which are read, some recited by rote, some sung – Janice tapping her foot during an especially upbeat interlude. The sounds of the language, rolling and guttural. Sweet red wine, mouthwashy, a shared cup rimmed with lipstick. Bread torn into small pieces and salted and passed around on a plate. More prayers. Then the food, stodgy, under-spiced, an antidote to icy middle-Europe. There's enough of it to feed three times the number of guests: an over-compensation, perhaps, for leaner times, for the historical hungers in the old country.

We eat. There is talk, laughter; everything loud.

And then children either hyper-active or asleep in parents' arms, no in-between; a trickle of departing guests providing the excuse for others to follow. I take my leave; Ivan takes my forearm. We've hardly spoken during the tumult of the evening.

"Where's Tracy?" he asks, and what I mean to say is that she is not feeling well, that she had another commitment, but what comes out is, "I have no idea." Ivan's eyes narrow and I evade any questions by hopping around him and down the steps, doing so carefully because it's dark, the stairway steep.

I feel no more Jewish than I did last month, last year, a decade ago. It must take more to be a Jew than a biological connection, than a Friday night dinner.

I check my phone in the car. An SMS from Gabe – *algood* it says, but I understand. Another from Tracy: *too much to drink can't drive staying over at Denise.* Denise aka Jono; what else. In spite of myself, I reply: *Don't rush back tomorrow, I have some things to do.*

Why am I giving her permission, why the out, why give her the excuse to do Jono tonight and again before breakfast and probably afterwards as well? Resignation, abdication, justifying Alice, perhaps simply the luxury of being home alone? I don't know.

The empty, early-Saturday-morning house. Squirrels gnawing away at the roof-trusses once more, waking me: I have my hand on my dick, hoping for a hard-on, but. Half-hearted, both of us. And forty years old: I suppose it's time to begin accepting the intermittent stalling, the final cessation.

Stale Coco Pops that Gabe doesn't eat any more, revolting and artificial, with sweet flavoured yoghurt instead of the Bulgarian because in amongst all the fucking Tracy cannot get it together to buy milk or muesli. So, coffee, black, burnt by the hot water: the kettle again, the hall-of-mirrors of it.

And then, a whim in answer to the tugging, a whim that starts with a shower, a crisp white shirt, dark trousers, a black shoe – no, two, one on a foot and the other on the end of the prosthesis. A hobble to the car, a drive to Gardens. Park. Limp to the gate that leads past the Holocaust Centre to Gardens Synagogue. Am sure that the guard at the gate will recognise me as an imposter, will throw me out, tell me to take my half-Jew bastard pretender self and go away. But he doesn't, so I ask him what time the service begins and a shadow of confusion flits over his face as he says he's not sure but it's not a big deal because people come and go as they like. "It's not church, you know," and he laughs at his joke, stops suddenly, probably wondering whether I'd get it. But I do, of course, smile back at the Christian guarding the Jews, Saturdays on, Sundays off, a wage at month-end.

I walk across the small square, grateful for the even travertine, into the atrium of the shul. Three old men are standing, talking. They hold books under their arms and have white cloths across their shoulders. One of them has tassels hanging below the hem of his jacket. Of course they're wearing yarmulkes: I've forgotten about this most fundamental part of my disguise, so like a fool I stand patting my pockets – it's the perfect excuse to step away from this thing, this unknown ritual; it's the perfect excuse to leave for the coffee shop up the road, just read a newspaper over a latte. But one of the trio of old men sees me and points me towards a man at the door to the shul who hands me a yarmulke and a book I can't read and asks if I need a tallis.

"Please." I accept, with no idea of what a tallis is, and I take from him a narrow white cloth with tea-towel stripes across its edges and I drape it over my shoulders as he has done. He hands me a yarmulke which I balance on my crown, although I am not certain I'm entitled to wear any of it. The man hands me a book and I step towards the door, hesitate. I suppose I was expecting the place to be laid out like a church, am surprised to find that there are no benches facing an altar, that where I expect the altar to be is deserted except for a young man with a long beard facing the wall and bending rapidly backwards and forwards from the hips, a low murmur like that of a shy auctioneer issuing from his lips.

In the middle of the open space, a raised wooden dais is surrounded by a carved railing. Like the bridge of a galleon, in constant readiness for the tide of circumstance that might threaten at any time, might force yet another journey to the safety of distant shores.

Above it is a gallery where I see women, only women in fact, who sit separate from the men because of I don't know what. Perhaps their elevation represents something: a promotion because of motherhood, matriarchy; or would the proximity of the sexes lead to mutual distraction, temptation? Or maybe they are second-class citizens, allowed in grudgingly, with separation the condition.

The sexton, or whatever the man at the door is, leans towards me, cuts through my trance, says kindly, "If you're from out of town you can sit at the back." It takes me a moment to figure out where the back is, and once I've done so I limp towards it. My prosthesis hurts; I hope that Jews don't kneel every two minutes as the Anglicans do.

I find a seat, and just then the men on the dais start singing, a capella, words I don't understand in a tune I struggle to follow, with harmonies that seem always to be on the verge of clashing, melodies that are woven into meaning only to unravel an instant later. The men may as well be singing about the weather or lost loves or sore feet, but I know they're not; they're singing about five-thousand-year-old things so far from me in syntax and in sense that the futility of what I'm doing settles on my shoulders like the tallis – which itself is threatening to slip down my back. The Hebrew of their songs could be Nepalese, Sioux, an endangered Amazonian language.

I am aware that my cover can at any moment be blown, so I pull the tallis closer around my shoulders and open the book I've been given. The page is numbered 658, and it takes me a moment to realise I've turned to the back. I flip the book and open it at the other front but it's still the back, only upside down now, and I feel the prickle of sweat on my neck as I have a Rubik's Cube moment with the thing and finally get it the right-wrong way up and open it the wrong-right way around. I have no idea where the correct place is, because even though the Hebrew is mirrored in English, the English is no help as everything is happening in Hebrew, and anyway six-hundred-odd pages to guess, Jesus. I glance around, sur-reptitious, expecting any moment that the entire congregation will point and give a collective alien-identifier scream: the un-Jew, the pig's trotter, the half-breed, the infidel in their midst. But nobody notices anything; per-haps there's enough of the Jew about me, after all, to avoid suspicion.

I estimate from the men near me that we are about three-quarters of the way through the book, so I turn to the approximate page and hold the thing as if I know what I'm doing and am thankful that I'm in the visitors' seating with nobody next to me to raise an eyebrow, to correct, to observe the half-baked petri-dish of me.

The choir changes key and begins another hymn or psalm or song or whatever it is, sounds of the West entwined with chromatic Eastern scales, the familiar interlaced with the strange. Just as a melody takes shape and invites my ear to follow it, it is undone, unravelled, collapses, a tonal synop-sis, it seems to me, of the history of the Jews: briefly melodic, then broken and tumbling; now rambling and seeking, then building towards a new melody.

The men in the pews ahead of me chat openly among themselves. Some sing, some are silent, while others rock backwards and forwards in their seats, rapidly muttering to themselves – as if the speed of the prayer is proportional to the speed of the prayer answered. The women and children on the mezzanine above are chatting quietly too. All this talk with these people – these unknown people – so much to say, but about what? About themselves, about each other, about those not present, about things to come and things that have been and events that may or may not come about? The constant movement: congregants arrive, stand up, leave as it suits them.

I sit when everyone else does, stand when they do, turn pages when they do, try again to match the Hebrew characters with the corresponding English, but of course it's useless; there's no marker, no departure point. The thing is a runestone in my hand, and I do not have the key to the code.

I am watching the mysterious proceedings when a woman in a wheel-chair is pushed in. The men in the front rows turn and nod little nods or wave little waves; she smiles broadly, inclines her head. Her attendant, the man who helped me complete my disguise, wheels her between the pews and with a practised pirouette spins her around to face the dais, parks her beside a row of seats. She is ancient, the skin hanging in thin curtains from her cheekbones, a mottle of different shades. But her eyes are sharp and alive and bright under the shadow of her Sabbath hat, her head erect on its long neck. The man on the seat beside her bends towards her, puts a hand on her shoulder, she a hand on his forearm, turning to him, saying some-thing, leaning in again with a smile, the something she says making him laugh; he touches her shoulder gently before she sits upright again.

Another man, on the way out, stops, drops to his haunches, talks to her briefly while holding her hand in both of his. Royalty, clearly, spared the upstairs banishment because of her infirmity, her greeters pleased that she is here to grace them with her presence. Then she puts her hands in her lap and looks towards the men on the raised platform, her head set a little to the left, waggling slightly as she listens to the singing and praying.

Whereas I.

And then a thought.

What if the old woman is Sara, my grandmother – here, present both in body and mind? Perhaps it really *is* her, ancient but lucid, respected and loved, bringing to this faraway world a thread of ancient tradition.

I indulge in the idea for a while, for other than this flight of fancy, there is nothing here for me. That half of my blood which is Jewish fails to respond to the singing, the prayers, the congregation. There is nothing in my cells that responds in revelatory goose bumps. There's no lodestone here to guide my soul, no lens to focus the tugging, no flash of illumination – no light to enlighten the Gentile. I screw up my eyes, admit the failure of my timid Jewish experiment.

I gather my tallis about me, clasp the prayer book to it, press the rebellious disc of the yarmulke to my head as I limp out, squeeze through the gap between the old lady's wheelchair and a pew. Look down at her, hoping for something, a marker in her face. She looks up at me, smiles. She is even older than I had thought; the sharp blue eyes surprise, make me want to say, "Sara?" But of course I don't: she would only shake her head, and then there'd be the indignity of explaining that I'd mistaken her for someone else.

And perhaps I have dug deep enough.

What good would it do to scratch beyond the first level of artefacts?

I smile at the old lady. Other than the blue eyes, I see nothing of myself, Gabriel, Debbie. And by her expression I can tell she sees nothing of herself in me.

When I stop to pick up Gabriel at George's house I realise that I still have the tallis around my shoulders and the yarmulke on my head and the prayer book wedged between my thighs. I roll them into a rough bundle and stuff it all into the cubbyhole before Gabe gets to the car.

The Jew of me scrunched up, back in its box, put away.

And then, that Wednesday, Tracy off into the arms of Jono again, under the guise of the city's most active book club. I retrieve a one-man dinner from the microwave when a slip of paper catches my eye, just a corner of it, poking out from under a fashion magazine: it's a post office notification, almost two weeks old, about to expire. Tracy fetches the post – one of the few chores she still manages to carry out between trips to Durbanville; she has forgotten or chosen not to tell me about the notice, that it's in my name.

The next day I stop off at the post office on the way to work. Pick up a shoe box wrapped in brown paper, tied with string, sealed with wax at the knot as though an older person has put it together, no return address. Posted anywhere – the origin is blurred, the box dented where a worker has thumped it with a rubber stamp; I hope that it contains nothing breakable. Leave it on the passenger seat when I reach the office; I will open it later.

I go through a day that is mostly a final meeting with Murray and Alice before the project commences. Alice and I awkwardly formal, wary of maintaining personal space, her hand covering the top of her shirt when she leans forward to look at the plans, wary of comments that may be ambiguous. Murray, of course, the usual oblivious and imperceptive social buffalo. He signs off small revisions to the plans, the additional costs; I should be relieved, excited, but each signature means less time with Alice. Time I want to spend with her and can't see how: Alice the player, Alice with her one-legged puppet.

I find the forgotten parcel on the passenger seat, open it before I start the car: its anonymity, its unexpectedness, demand attention, and there is nobody I can ask for any kind of explanation.

Inside the box, a short note:

I thought you might be interested in these.

XX Debbie.

PS: Your grandmother puts in an appearance about half an hour into the movie, or so she used to think.

Beneath the note, photographs and photocopies, a commercial DVD titled *Ochberg's Orphans*.

What is it with my mothers and their secret histories in cardboard boxes? The rounds and rotations and cycles of things, perhaps, I don't know.

I flick through the papers. The photographs are mostly old, some frayed and showing yellowed cracks over their formal blacks and whites; some are modern and snapshot-ish and amateurishly candid. I shuffle through them, select one – old, white-veined, the blacks and greys of it faded to motley browns. It shows a group of children, the boys in trousers and jackets too short, the girls in sack-like dresses; all with heads that had been shaved some time before the photograph was taken, the scalps covered with shadowy new growth. The pin-points of the flash reflected in their eyes make them appear feral, frantic in their stillness. As though they are all about to leap, scream, burst apart. One boy moved as the shutter opened, the action smearing his face, and the ghost of a third ear has replaced his nose. Someone has taken a pen – fountain, not ballpoint – and circled a small girl. She is pretty, grave, a fuzz of dark fluff framing her head, pale eyes evident even in black-and-white. Another image: a serious little boy in a sailor suit and yarmulke, with the same small girl – older now, her hair a neat bob – sitting on concrete stairs leading up to a triple-storey building. Behind it, Table Mountain with its summer cloud.

A more recent image, in colour, with a bluish haze where the yellow has faded from the print: a young Debbie holding a baby. Her hair bouffant, her dress a geometry of browns and oranges. A Post-it stuck to the photo identifies the baby as Alistair.

Lest I might have thought.

Colour Instamatic pictures of two children, an older boy on the lawn, spraying his younger sister with water from a hosepipe, she laughing, arms blurred like wings as she flaps them up and down. Hanging over the high white wall in the background are clouds of purple jacaranda blossom.

A snap of Debbie and a man, older than she: their cheeks are pressed together, squashing their smiles.

Alistair in a Speedo holding a trophy at a school gala, grinning with big new teeth.

The daughter in a formal Matric pose, against a mottled backdrop.

I close my eyes, searching for a match, try to see me, or Gabriel, in their faces. But there is nothing there.

There is more: photographs and photocopies of old documents – copies of a ship's ticket or bill that confirmed Sara's passage to Cape Town, a copy of a group passport with its photograph of thirty kids arranged in tiers, copies of lists in an old-fashioned script presenting foreign, lumpy names: Cwengel, Treppel, Sagatkowsky. The photographs and photocopies lie in my lap, on the seat next to me, in the passenger footwell; they lie there as I sit in my car, as I try to connect them all to the roots of me, try to connect myself to them.

But their paper faces are flat, bloodless.

I do not feel these people, do not feel them in me, me in them, do not feel them at all; their only value is the conundrum they present: if $a^2 + b^2 = c^2$, then why does $a^3 + b^3 \neq c^3$? Pythagoras so simple, Fermat rather less so.

I gather up the papers, the documents, place them back in the box.

Put the lid on it.

Gabriel

Gabriel lay on his bed with his earbuds screwed deep into his ears – all the better to hear the bass – and if he'd allowed himself, he would have wondered if the discord of Rammstein outweighed his enjoyment of it, but the answer might not have been the right one and may have poked at the fundamentals of his musical taste. So instead, he rubbed a thumb idly across a prominent and painful zit on his cheekbone: they popped up far less frequently than before, but still, every now and then, there they were. Gabriel had pinned an old sheet over the doorway, and while it gave him privacy from prying eyes it did nothing for sound, so every now and then he removed a bud and listened, surprised each time at the silence of a house that had once carried the chatter of his parents or melodies of his father's whimsical music – rock, opera, jazz, reggae – or the whirr of his mother's hair dryer. It occurred to him that the house had, save for the secret sounds of his iPod, grown an invisible fungus of silence that had, over the past what? – weeks, months, years? – spread over everything, silenced its machinery. Every now and then, the fungus allowed a short burst of words to escape, terse and sharp as radio static, and then it closed over again, and there was just the white noise of the wind in the plane trees, the click of the switch opening or closing the garage door. And underneath it all, the cracks and creaks of decay.

If he had asked himself another question, whether the goal of his running or gymming had swung from the hope of once again attracting Barbara to escaping the fungus, the right answer may have also been the wrong one. And meanwhile, life – or what was passed off as such: the treadmill of school, the same friends, the band, the doorless bedroom, unexpected and therefore suspicious acknowledgements from his father, a mother who no longer was very much of a one, seldom present, even when she was at home. The slow accumulation of dust, and frayed edges, and light bulbs that had stopped working, and other small but big things ceasing to function: the top right hob of the gas cooker, the water filter in the fridge, the drain in the shower, the once-reliable gardener seeking liquid refreshment from a brown paper bag while the manicured foliage grew roots, crept up around his too-big gumboots.

And death: that crazy old woman, his grandmother – any affection or pleasant memories of her erased by what he had come to think of as "Bath Night", a B-grade horror movie title, when she wouldn't let him out of the tub and scrubbed him raw while the cooling water froze him to the bones. The wooden coffin, solid enough, he hoped, to contain her, the hole deep enough to bury the memory of that night. Six years later, Gabriel still shunned baths, would rather remain unclean if no shower was available. His father angry at the graveside, as if dead Granny Sylvia could have done anything about anything, the mad old bat. Later, cookies munched by a few strangers who had no connection to him, none to his parents, and not a great deal more, he imagined, to his grandmother. And later, his father angry no longer, crying instead.

His father brought home a box a few days later. A smallish box, with contents that rattled when Gabriel carried it to Chris's study, a box not quite full. Stuck to its folded flaps a jam-jar label – white, with blue edging: *Sylvia Hayes (Deceased)* it said in large girly handwriting.

Life, and then death, and then so little in between that it all fits into half a box.

On a day when band practice was cancelled because George the Dog had tonsillitis, Gabriel arrived home early, went to his room without greeting his mother because she was on the phone, heard her speak in a way she once used to speak to his father. Gabriel deciphered tones, chuckles, implications rather than actual words: the flare of a damp match rather than a blinding epiphany – his mother was having an affair. His mother was having an affair that his father either didn't know about or care about. Gabriel lay on his bed, waiting to be shocked at the revelation, but the shock never came. Held his breath as Tracy walked down the passage towards his room, passed by, turned towards the stairs, still on the phone. Her words clearer, thrilled as a child's: "I'll be there in half an hour, big boy." He held his breath, heard her rush down the stairs, open and close the door leading to the garage. The metallic sounds of the Range Rover's diesel engine. The creak and squeak of the garage door opening and closing, a door that never used to creak or squeak. How much space would the bits of his mother's lover take up in her box one day, the boy wondered; how much space would his father, he himself take up? Then he put on an old Def Leppard CD from his father's collection, turned up the volume and lay staring at the ceiling until he fell asleep.

Early winter, and his father's birthday in the mountains. Gabriel was pressured to attend because forty is a milestone, even if it wasn't quite forty, even if über-nerd Peter was to be his only company. The mountains a rocky chain, scrub and stunted plants amid weather-carved yellow stone, like a scene from a Western. Peter distraught: no cellphone reception for his iPhone, and his new iPad kept dropping the wi-fi.

After Lynn had wet her pants and Barry and Tony had walked with him and Peter a short distance along the river while his father lay at the pool reading and yawning, he persuaded Peter to join him on a mountain-bike ride. Pointed out that the day had cooled. Lowered the seat for him, showed him how the gears worked. Filled a water bottle and placed it in the cage of his bike. Insisted that he wear a helmet, adjusted the straps under his chin. Not four hundred metres from the house, as they crested a short rise near an earthen dam, Peter said, "Hey, I'm done," sweat pouring from under his helmet as he turned around and headed back. Gabriel went on alone, rode along the dam wall, stopped to look out across the valley. Heard a snort behind him, a lip-flapping snort. Across the dam, a gemsbok, big as a stallion, dun body and a black face with symmetrical white flashes above each eye, one horn rising into the air like a sword – a metre, a metre and a half long – the other broken off above the hilt. The animal snorted again, looked at Gabriel blankly. Lowered its head and shook it once. Lifted it up, turned, walked away from the dam, slid silently into scrub so sparse that it seemed incapable of concealing anything. Gabriel dropped the bike, ran around the dam, tried to find where the antelope had disappeared. He scrambled up a shamble of rough boulders, stood at the summit, looked around, saw nothing. The gemsbok had dissolved into its world.

Gabriel returned to his bike, rode away from the dam, the lodge, and soon he had lost sight of both. Stopped to drink from the water bottle, listened in amazement to a silence shaped by birdsong, leaves in the wind. Then he rode further, chased a small herd of springbok across a flat sandy plain, knowing he didn't stand a chance, laughing aloud at the silliness of even trying, at the knowledge that nobody could hear him. Felt the sweat and the heat and the dust and the burn in his muscles from fighting the bike through the soft, sucking sand. Rode back to dive, clothes and all, into the cold water of the pool, changed his mind when he saw Lynn in a dressing gown sitting with Chris on his recliner, her hand on his chest, went off and took a cool shower instead.

Drinks, dinner. Gabriel could feel the tightness in the air, the desperation for everyone to have a good time, the anxiety that something might derail the evening. Barry gave the tension voice – loud voice – and tried to break it by ordering tequila, tried to break it by ordering all sorts of other drinks as well. When his father offered him a cider, Gabriel accepted, but he didn't like the sour tang of alcohol beneath the sweetness of the fake apple and ordered a Coke instead. His father watched this with a smile, his mother chatting, her voice growing shrill and her eyes already glassy. He and Peter ate as though they seldom saw food, asked to be excused after the gluey chocolate mousse – Gabriel embarrassed at the growing volume of the conversation, Peter anxious to beat his best score on a new iPad game. Later, Gabriel woke to the sounds of his mother and sandwiched his head with the pillow as he tried again to sleep.

Early November: the long wet winter had dried up and tourists were headed out of Cape Town by the busload, swamping the winelands. Runners were out on the roads, cyclists had dusted off their bikes, pink legs and cleavages were making nervous reappearances after months of hibernation – when, one evening, a storm came out of nowhere and so did an SMS, from a number Gabriel didn't know.

Call me. Barbara.

He took his phone and locked himself in the privacy of the bathroom.

She answered immediately. "Hello?"

"Hi," he said. Croaked. Filled a tooth mug with water, gulped it down.

"Hi, Gabe," she said. A small, flat voice.

Silence, but for the fat skeins of rain flying against the window and the electronic shush of the phone.

"Where have you been?" he said, his voice still strange. There was too much hurt in the question, he knew.

"Growing a baby." The words almost whispered, mechanical.

"What?"

Rain. Wind. She said nothing for a while, and then: "Your baby, Gabe."

His hand found the edge of the bath, and when he sat on its rounded rim it creaked. The flavours of New Year's Eve rushed back. Sights, sounds, smells. A new organ opened deep within him, a nameless sack that filled his abdomen, became at once full like sea-sickness, wet and sloshing, and empty and hollow and lonely as space.

"And?" he said. A whisper too, useless.

"And what?"

"And when can I see him? Her?"

A long moment. A breath. And then: "You can't. He's gone. Gone away."

A beep killed the static of her breath, then the phone as silent as fog in his hand.

"Hello?" he said into the emptiness. "Did it hurt?"

All through the Cape winter, when the cold Atlantic produces its best waves and surfers struggle into wetsuits to risk the great whites, Gabriel had ridden his own swell, had clung to the face of it to elude dissolution, the threatening void.

At times he had believed that the void was shrinking, retreating, and then he had worked to restore it, battled to bring it back through dark drawings and discordant music and his poetry of misspellings. He'd fed it, restored the vacuum. Because if it went away, so would the absence of the girl, and therefore, finally, the girl herself. Gabriel knew that holes are only defined by what's around them; to maintain a hole you cannot allow it to fill in, and Barbara's absence had become her presence: he only knew how to mourn her disappearance by keeping the hole of her alive.

Gabriel looked at the phone in his hand. He called the number; it beeped once as it went to voicemail, and the recorded greeting was un-ambiguous, madly rational.

"Hi Gabriel. If you're listening to this you need to know that I've thrown this SIM card away. You can call as much as you like, but I'll never answer because the phone will never ring. Well, maybe one day it will when the number gets recycled, but it won't be me answering. Bye, Gabriel."

Gabriel howled, a short, throat-scraping alto howl. It bounced off the hard bathroom surfaces, leaving behind a rawness and the sound of the rain.

Downstairs into the silent tension that was his parents. His mother took two plates from a cupboard, flung them onto the counter and reached into the microwave to retrieve the overheated product of Martha's cooking.

She looked up as Gabriel passed by. "Gabe, it's almost seven and pour-ing. You can't go for a run now."

At the counter, his father did not look up from the newspaper, said, "Jesus, Tracy. He runs all the time, what's the big deal?"

"I truly wish you would stop saying fucking 'Jesus'."

And Gabriel, an automaton, went through the door, stepped into the rain, found himself soaked in seconds. Began to run. What could he tell them, the occasional father, the libidinous mother: what could he tell them, and why? There was no difference to be made; there were no holes to be patched. Only a knowing that could not be undone.

He ran over the forbidden grass, down the driveway, through the gate and out into the yellow-lit street. Old Nirvana in his ears, loud because he wanted it to blow hard against his brains and drive back the thoughts that tried to surface, so loud that the words made no sense, treble wailing, the bass working better once he drilled the earbuds more deeply into his ears.

The first hill, an agony, always – each time he attacked it, he did so harder. Now he attacked it harder than ever because it was raining and cold and difficult, because the more he pushed himself the faster the pain would shift from his head to his legs and from his legs to his feet and from them into the tar of Macquarie Drive.

Chris

Tracy picks at the vegetables on her plate, peels the skin off the chicken and then changes her mind and pushes the lot aside. Skewers a steamed carrot and nibbles at it. Stops, drops it onto her plate. Stands, picks up the plate, takes a step towards the back door before she remembers that the dog is dead. Empties the food into the kitchen bin instead. I'm tempted to do the same: the chicken is dry and still cold on the inside, the carrots spongy and tasteless. Tracy rinses the plate with a cursory squirt of water, puts it in the dishwasher, tops up her wine glass and disappears upstairs with it.

I finish my food and look at the kitchen clock. Its faux-antique face has always irritated me with its raku-crackle and Roman numerals. It's barely seven, and the evening stretches long and colourless before me.

I go to my study to review the Murray project, but I cannot rise to the task. The lines and their numbers remain discrete; I cannot connect them, cannot get them to tell their story; the dismembered bits of them show on my screen as though encrypted, refusing to come together. I give up, yawn, look at my watch. I go online, check my share portfolio, the news sites, but the world has had a slow day.

I Google "Chris Hayes". Barely a year later, and the search turns up more than double the results. Despite the proliferation of Chris Hayeses, I find myself on the second page. The link takes me to a press release about the Murray project. The language is inflated and soaked with PR-worn adjectives – prestigious, unique, unsurpassed. I'm unable to read the article, am defeated by its candyfloss prose. Close the window, pore over the lives of other Chris Hayeses: professors of astronomy, gardening experts, drunk drivers, lawyers, gay activists, criminals. The voyeurism puts me in a trance; when I shake myself out of it I put my hand to my chin to check whether I've been drooling, whether my mouth has been hanging open and my tongue lolling like an imbecile's.

And then I check the time.

It's past eight, and Gabriel hasn't returned yet, or not that I'm aware of. He seldom runs for even half an hour at night, and now. Now it's been almost an hour and a quarter.

I grab my crutches and squeak-thunk out of my study. Call his name; there's no response. I shout for Tracy; she doesn't answer either, though I know she's heard me.

I open the front door and peer through the rain beyond the portico. The lights on the outside walls do not penetrate; they create a close curtain of rain, a falling luminescence, opaque. I crutch out beyond the throw of the lights and into the rain, calling my son's name. Hear nothing. Crutch out over the forbidden lawn, through the gate, which Gabe has once again left unlatched. Up Macquarie Drive, though I have no idea what direction he might have taken. The rainwater runs into my eyes; I keep crutching, do not stop to wipe it away. My arms begin to burn, my lungs too as the cold air tears into them. I speed up: I know he is there, know it so well that when I close my eyes I can see him lying like Schultz on the tarmac of the Silvertree intersection, his warm blood – my blood – blending with the cold rain and running diluted into the gutter while a distraught and useless X5 driver stands by, hand at her mouth, hopping from one foot to the other.

I am nowhere near the intersection when the crushing comes. In a place deeper than the scalding in my lungs – that dim, undersea place where the tugging resides – the crushing starts, grows like a tsunami nearing the coast. There's a compacting, a compressing: I am torn in six, seven, twelve different directions, crushed by a great something that squeezes from all sides and shortens my breath and saps the strength from my arms.

I sink to my stump in the thick wet grass, my crutches splayed like broken wings at my sides. As I slide sideways to the ground I wonder if I'll feel better lying down. But I don't, and the crushing attenuates my breath until I can fetch air only in short goldfish gulps. I lie wet and cold and breathless in the night while the rainwater in my eyes turns the streetlights into a kaleidoscope of disconnection; I am as helpless and almost as dead as my son.

Who finds me drenched and panic-frozen, two crutches and three rainsoaked limbs lying in the grass.

I feel him over me, feel the hot-cold drops of sweat and rain that fall from his face onto mine. He puts a cold hand to my forehead.

"Jesus, Dad," I think I hear him say. Why is Gabriel talking down a tunnel? Teenagers are unpredictable, but really. "I'm going to get Mom. Wait here."

I have no plans to go anywhere, I want to say, but I cannot speak.

Moments – or is it an hour, a day, a week – later, the Range Rover roars up. Its headlights on me as the doors open slowly, impossibly so, as though the occupants consider me an interesting but potentially dangerous kind of road kill. Then Gabriel and Tracy struggling to lift my dead weight into the Range Rover and Tracy driving the endless twisted road through rain and tears to the hospital. My wet head on Gabriel's wet lap; I am panting rapid shallow pants like an exhausted dog: before we get there I have lost all feeling in my hands, my arms, my leg. I try to fight, it, know I need every one of the limbs I still have; but the more I fight, the more leaden the numbness becomes, the further away from me my extremities retreat.

Tracy mounts the curb outside Emergency and stalls the Range Rover. Gabriel flings open the door and pulls me from the car, and Tracy is somehow standing there, teleported from the driver's seat – she is wearing pink slippers and an old grey tracksuit and no make-up, looks like a guest on Jerry Springer. But the yellow lights on the walls of the building give her face a softness, youth: I want to tell her this, but through the gasping no words form. Gabriel disappears into the building and Tracy puts my numb arm around her shoulder, and the three-legged monster of us tries to drag itself after him but I don't know what my leg is doing, don't know if I am holding on to Tracy's shoulder or not, and despite the gym-work she is unable to support the weight of us and together we slide helpless towards the wet tar when the medics appear and pry me from her.

They wrestle me inside, onto a narrow hard bed. Push Tracy and Gabriel beyond the yellow cordon of curtains that they have drawn around me. A nurse with spectacles and grey hair places a paper bag over my nose and mouth and tells me to calm down. She scowls down through her glasses as if I am some kind of unpleasant insect. Her fingers smell of cigarettes – is she perhaps irritated because I have interrupted her smoke break? – and I try to swat her away but she is relentless, and in a high voice I tell her to fuck off because she stinks, but she ignores me, she persists, and while the medics produce syringes from somewhere and with them suck up pale fluids and dark juices that they then empty into my arms, the paper bag begins to take effect and my breathing slows and I can feel my fingers again, can feel the polyester of the sheet, can feel the plastic liner underneath.

Then the medics multiply, and within moments there are twelve, fifteen, maybe twenty or a hundred of them, people in white, fussing about in this small curtained space, and no Gabriel no Tracy nearby.

Some of them leave and those who remain stand around and watch as the bed sucks me down and some great powerful magnet in the sky pulls me towards the ceiling. I cannot ask for help, cannot turn my head to look for my family, so heavy has it become, and yet there is a vestige of sentience still: the fragments of the things I hear – the beeps, the squeaks, the whistles and whines of electronic things – and what I hear tells me I am dying.

I am sad, of course, at having to leave so suddenly. But I cannot manufacture tears; my disappointment is like virga, that rain which falls and evaporates before it hits the hot earth below. Then the pain of the crushing subsides and I wonder whether this is it, whether this moment when my heart stiffens and slows, is *it*.

I try to fight it, this going away, because I'm not finished yet. Try to fight the closing of the eyelids, the rolling of the eyeballs. But the closing is unfightable; the fucking drugs have won and I slide away under the caged bed and gently float towards the floor in lazy zigzags; the photocopy of me flutters and then slips paper-thin under a door that leads to a dark, dark place where nothing matters because there is nothing there.

When I awaken my tongue has swollen to the size of a mattress, is stuck to my palate. Eyelids thick, gluey. I hear a rhythmic beeping, feel a far-away pain in the middle of me. It is dark, or supposed to be, yet cold neon spills into the room through a doorway. Sharp points of green and yellow flicker from machines. A bowed blonde head next to me. "Tracy?" I try, manage only a grunt. The head stays down. I grunt again, don't even try her name.

She looks up, blinks.

Puts a hand on my arm, pats it.

"Sleep," she says. Drops her head again. I breathe in deeply, slowly, and although the oxygen from the pipes in my nostrils is sour and smells of warm dust where I expect a cool, fresh mountain scent, it is good.

Fluorescent daylight, and BarryLynnTracyMichaelSylvia stare down at me. A young man steps forward. Is he me or am I him, I wonder in the rapid sunset, such a rapid sunset that it's barely been light when it's dark again.

In the blackness, Ndumiso "NN" Ndlovu holds a flaming torch above his head. He has the pelt of a dead leopard around his shoulders. He puts his face close to mine, speaks in a low rumble. "I can get you out of here, you know. Just like that," – and he snaps his fingers under my nose and adjusts his yarmulke and smiles and is gone.

Suddenly sunrise and still the me-him boy is in my room, closer now. BarryLynn stand blurrily behind, Tracy's face by mine, her eyes ringed in purple and her hair hanging limp, dull. I imagine I can smell the grease of it. You look like shit, I want to tell her but I don't.

"Dad?" the boy says. "I'm not supposed to do this, but hey." And Gabriel comes to me, leans over, hugs me across the tubes and pipes and wires. Chokes or coughs – and then it's suddenly night again.

Time is like a capricious child – flying off madly and then collapsing in a motionless heap. And the world is kneaded and twisted, a ball of dough that brings to me faces, some real, some not so: Alice, faded and gone before she's even properly arrived; Tracy Bag-Eyes – will Botox be enough this time, or will it take a bigger cheque? – in and out, always in the same grey tracksuit. Barry Greyface with his jokey stories, rehashed and retold with a breath that smells like New Year's Eve. Ivan preachy at the witching hour when nobody else is around, an ugly painting under one arm, a crutch under the other. "We Jews are made to wander, Boss," he tells me, "it's our greatest survival tactic. Legs, no legs, it's immaterial. When we need to, we wander." He is gone before I can ask him why, why the wandering. And then there are the slow underwater creatures who consult papers clipped to boards and from secret pockets take vials of liquid that they inject into my drip. Sometimes the needles they produce take dark blood from a vein in the crook of my arm; it is sucked into a transparent receptacle, and on its white sticker they write small blue words.

When between the moonlight and the jelly-breakfast a pigletty nurse brings her big tits and a cardboard box for me to empty my life into I fear that this is it, they've planned for me to die now; now that I've had a sniff of dusty oxygen and seen my family, they will toss the essence of me into the little Sylvia-box. But I can't, won't allow it; instead, I will my heart to warm up and thaw out and grow strong again, and when I awaken, the nurse and her box have disappeared again.

The men and women gradually reduce their ministrations. Time is trained and disciplined and the world again begins to behave as it should, and above me the television set is filled with people who have orange skin and discuss Eurozone economics.

I have spent over a week in the hospital, Tracy tells me on the day I'm unplugged from the pipes and the cables – one tube and one wire at a time – until shaved patches on my chest and a Band-Aid on the back of my hand and little yellow packets of pills are all I have to show for the whole adventure.

Before I'm served yet another baby-bland breakfast, Doctor Something announces that I may take a shower, get dressed, go home. Reminds me that I am lucky, says had the infarction been any more severe, it may not have been compatible with life. Even though the effects of the drugs have retreated, it takes me a moment to translate.

And then I'm out of that dying place. Begin to crutch off the effects of it all – ten steps, then twenty, fifty. So diminishing, demeaning, the status of the afflicted. The doe-eyes it draws and the sympathetic sounds it evokes, the embarrassment of it right up there with having shat in your trousers in a public place. It was a minor coronary event, I remind everyone, in the hope of deflecting their cocked-head enquiries and their lingering touches – I am a man, after all, not a puppy. It was a wobble, not an implosion. And then they nod and look at each other in secret and knowing ways and their eyes slide to the floor, to the window, to the thoughtful middle-distance, to anything that isn't me.

Tracy drives me to the hospital and waits in the Range Rover while the doctors check and probe, prod and measure, palpate and ponder. The prognosis is good, I tell her afterwards.

She says nothing, drives off.

Then: "Not for us, I don't think."

And brings Jono into the car. Brings Dalia. Brings all those Tracy-things that pave the way to the inevitable.

She stops the car at the side of the road. Puts her hands to her face and begins to cry. I place my hand on her thigh; she doesn't pull away, leans towards me instead, is unable to reach across the great divide of the Range Rover console to put her head on my shoulder. I want to tell her it's okay, because it is – but I can't. Hold her thigh until she stops, until she is able to drive us home.

The lawyers arrive with papers and forms and agreements to be signed. Then the once-feared divisions begin. I feel that Tracy welcomes them as much as I do, that she too finds the reapportioning of the accumulations of nearly twenty years pleasantly purifying.

She is the first to choose. She doesn't want the house, wants the money instead. The house will be mine to keep, to sell, as long as I write her a market-related cheque.

She takes some of her things, comes back that afternoon for the balance of it and for Gabriel and his stuff. Even though they will be back the next day and the next to help me with the rest of my purging, my son has tears in his eyes when he leaves. Gabe, I want to say, it's not the pain of love, it's the weight of it and the pull of it. I will be here for you even when I'm not. But I don't, don't have to say anything because he knows, I know he knows, and so does he.

The fabric of the house dissipates like mist under a rising sun as its parts are silently shared: one for me, three for you.

Then, the extrication of what is mine from Hayes Inc, my last meeting with Ivan and Ndumiso Ndlovu. With Ivan's Mont Blanc, "NN" – smiling and amiable, as ever – co-signs the papers that will make my shares his. I am embarrassed to see him after my leopard skin dreams: the silly awkwardness you feel after having dreamt of sex with a colleague, and then bumping into her at the water cooler next day.

Ivan is strangely diminished, wide-eyed, pale. What you wish for.

I wonder as I stand up whether he will ever call Ndlovu "Boss", whether Ndlovu will ever call him "Ive".

He stands to greet me as I crutch towards the door. We give each other an unaccustomed hug. "Just be an architect, Ivan," I tell him quietly as we clinch. "That's what you do best, so do it."

I throw clothes, CDs, books, appliances, shoes, ties, watches, cufflinks, other disconnected bits into cardboard boxes to be sold, given away, set fire to, I don't care. What nobody wants can go to charity or be left on the pavement.

Lynn helps me fill more boxes, Gabriel comes to carry them out, Barry stands by to give directions and to open beer. Tracy comes to collect the last of her things. There is some of the old softness about her now: she has put on a little weight over the past weeks, is no longer quite so gaunt, stringy. She smiles when she arrives, asks how I am. I tell her I'm doing well and she lightly strokes a hand across my cheek. I want to add that I'd be even better if she'd only just continue being a bitch around me.

But I don't.

Epilogue

He pauses at a cardboard box, kicks at it with a crutch. Marvels at its emptiness as it skitters across the floor and comes to rest against the kitchen counter. He feels that the box should house something, *a* something, *some* something, but it holds only dust and air.

There is nothing of meaning left in the house. No thing, no sound. No primary sound, at least, just a secondary echo, a reverberation of what once was. The residue of bitter words and bitterer silences clings to the walls, the ceilings. What is the half-life of acrimony? he wonders. It will take some time, he is sure, for it to leach from the place.

In the emptiness, unhung nails are centred to the stencils of absent artwork. Smudges above the skirting, the shadows of an old dog that had once rubbed himself along the walls. Furry stuff in the corners, the floor dulled by dust and dotted with scraps of paper, bubble wrap, the brown balls of discarded packing tape. Bare windows admit the late-afternoon sunlight, immodest, indiscreet, motes suspended in its beams: the powdery dead skin of the house.

His ex-architect's eye skims over the ugliness of wall sockets, blinds hanging drunkenly askew, the nakedness of it all, sees nothing, has no urge to judge, to beautify, to improve. He crutches to the kitchen counter where a pile of magazines and newspapers lie amidst the detritus of curled tape and paper. He is about to sit when he changes his mind, crutches to the fridge instead, opens its brushed-steel door. An onion and its gas-leak smell share the shelves with half a jar of marmalade and a third of a bottle of milk: opened and sniffed, the milk is passable, but only just.

Beside the fridge, a kettle, and beside the kettle a Father's Day mug with no handle and a cartoon of two mischievous children on the side, and at the bottom, he knows, a cartoon spider – black, graphically naive, intended to shock the recipient dad.

There is a small jar of Nescafé, almost empty. A paper bag of sugar has spilled crystals of itself onto the counter. He takes the Nescafé, decants the remains into the mug. Adds the milk and with a shake estimates a teaspoon-and-a-half of sugar from the packet. Flicks the switch on the kettle, stares through the window at the boughs of the plane trees, heavy with summer leaves. Waits for the water to come to a boil. The kettle is like a clock, but not, rumbling off the seconds, the minutes, to midnight. New Year's Eve: perhaps Barry will be treating selected friends and Unknowns to a braai again, to another bleated serenade with his broken guitar. He is pleased that the invitation has bypassed him this time. So much in a year, so little, and for once he welcomes the death of it, relishes the new day, the new year.

The kettle boils, turns itself off, hushes. He is mesmerised by the south-east breeze and what it is doing to the leaves. The soft and endless shhh of it. Looks for squirrels in the branches, then shakes his head to free his gaze from the tangle of foliage, pours the water into the mug.

There is no teaspoon. He tries to stir the coffee with a baby finger, but it is too hot. He retracts the scalded digit, sucks the heat from it. Swirls the mixture around in the mug to achieve diffusion. The first sips are sugarless and acrid, sour with the turning milk.

He puts the mug on the counter beside the collapsed pile of magazines and brochures and pamphlets, crutches around the counter to a stool.

Sits.

Opens one of the publications before him, a *Farmer's Weekly*, turns to the back, to the "For Sale" section. Takes up a black marker, removes the cap, hovers the pen over the pages, draws a circle. Then, five issues of *Sailing*: another circle. The others: Icelandic fish-packing promises – no circles. Kibbutz prospectuses. Foreign real estate brochures. Pamphlets about Indian ashrams and Spanish pilgrimages. More literature, more careful circling, unmarked magazines dropped into the box. His ill-stirred coffee becomes sweeter the more he circles, the more he drinks off its bitter beginnings.

And later – the coffee no longer coffee but a sugary paste at the bottom of the mug, the squirrels in the plane trees running one last loop between branches and eaves before dark – he selects a black-circled entry from the depleted pile before him, places a forefinger inside the circle, takes up his BlackBerry to call the number.

Sees that he has missed a text message from Alice. She'll be there soon, it says, will pick up pizza and a bottle or three of bubbly on the way.

He smiles. Thank goodness: half a jar of marmalade and an onion for New Year's Eve, well.

Acknowledgements

The title owes itself to a Wikipedia article entitled "An Exceptionally Simple Theory of Everything", a preprint by Dr Garret Lisi, of which I understood nothing past the opening sentence.

I have quoted Kurt Friedrich Gödel out of context to suit my needs. My apologies to the great mathematician and to mathematicians everywhere.

Then there's the research and advice of my sister-in-law, Lauren Snitcher, whose grandmother Bessie Gezunterman was an Ochberg orphan, and whose work culminated in Jon Blair's documentary *Ochberg's Orphans*. The incident of the blood-soaked feathers was Bessie's own experience, as was her rescue and repatriation to South Africa.

To my parents, Erwin and Liz, who adopted me with no idea of what might transpire: how brave can you be?

To my readers, thank you: Julian Snitcher, Phena Snitcher, Paul Warmeant, Vanessa Sass, Nora Watts Snitcher and Frances Keegan. David Kraft, whose e-mail from Texas came attached with a penny that dropped at a crucial moment.

Thanks also to Robin Stuart-Clark, who provided the kind of advice and guidance I couldn't pay for, and didn't. To Nèlleke de Jager of Kwela, for spotting some merit in the original manuscript, to Ester Levinrad and James Woodhouse of Kwela for their enthusiasm, and to my editor, Lynda Gilfillan, for her eagle eye and good sense.

Thanks to my daughters, who for so very long had to deal with their father telling them to shut up. And of course, to my Michelle, who read every draft and loved each of them in turn, as she would.

MARK WINKLER grew up in what is now Mpumalanga, and was educated at St Alban's College in Pretoria and Rhodes University, Grahamstown. He has spent most of his working life in the advertising industry in Cape Town, where he lives with his wife and two daughters. He is currently creative director at a leading Cape Town advertising agency.